Johnny

Comes

Marching

BROOKE ALBERTSON

ISBN 978-1-64492-123-4 (paperback)
ISBN 978-1-64492-125-8 (hardcover)
ISBN 978-1-64492-124-1 (digital)

Christian Faith Publishing, Inc.
832 Park Avenue
Meadville, PA 16335
www.christianfaithpublishing.com

Printed in the United States of America

Introduction

In 1862, the town of Sharpsburg, Maryland, was far off the beaten track, a stopping-off place to towns far more important and much better known. The abiding concerns of the immigrant farmers who lived there extended to guarding against crop failure, keeping their precious livestock healthy, and making sure that the neighboring gristmill for their harvested grain was not overbooked. In past years, they had hefted rocks, leaving them in piles (one such pile, singular to this story, remains recognizable to this day), so as to open up acreage for grazing and growing more crops; they had cleared out some trees as well for the same purpose and had even made room to construct a tiny, nondescript church barely big enough to hold their small congregation.

All this changed, of course, on September 17 of that year, when Union and Confederate armies came to that town and left their indelible mark on the land, a land where cattle had grazed peacefully, and the locals had lived peaceful, if unremarkable, lives. The soil that had known only the feet of frugal farmers and the hooves of tame animals became known for its monuments, plaques, and paved roadways, all to accommodate the tourists who flocked there to memorialize the scene of the single bloodiest day in American history.

In those pre-battle years, nesting birds found lodgment in predictable places, and predators came in search of easy prey, usually chickens; an obscure, zigzag sunken road, which became "Bloody Lane," was familiarly referred to as the "hog trough ditch." This author found that reality truly enticing: what must it have been like *before* all the blood? Projecting myself back to that pre-battle time, I wondered how a fourteen-year-old boy would have felt, devastated by a family in turmoil, agonized on how to find purpose and vindication for a life course gone wrong. And how, in the midst of that, would he have faced the disruption and devastation thrust upon him by war? The result of that endeavor is *Johnny Comes Marching*.

Many of the characters and events herein set forth were real—as true-to-life as the author could manage. Some are the creation of literary license. A few of the incidents, though not historically factual, were, to some degree, historically plausible. There is, for instance, no evidence that the Antietam ironworks were militarily significant. Special Order No. 191 likely had no bearing on the cavalry breakout from Harper's Ferry (Lee's Order, however, was a vital component as to how his Maryland Campaign of 1862 played out; and Col. Miles, the post commander, did, in fact, resist the cavalry breakout and was known to be tipsy much of the time). Was there really a crawl space under the Dunker Church? This is unknown, as the original structure was destroyed in a storm well after the war. Johnny Shipley's carriage ride with Brother Russell, to bring food to Federal forces fighting at the sunken road, is based on an incident that, some sources say, actually did occur. And if the narrative of this story seems unreasonably skewed against most things "Reb," while favorable to most things "Yank" (excepting an overdrawn portrayal of George McClellan), this is, after all, a fictional indictment of the institution of slavery. And since a novelist's prerogative is to move the story—so long as the "possible" is clearly not "impossible"—history purists, I trust, will cut me some slack.

I have "stolen the identity" of a real-life Jeremiah, who, as a freed slave, actually lived on Henry Piper's Sharpsburg farm, survived the war, and lived well into the next century. Mutilations like those inflicted on the Jeremiah of this story (excepting his lashed back) were not commonplace, and self-mutilations, though known to exist, were not often documented in historical accounts. Some of the military figures, such as Col. Grimes Davis and "Autie" (far better-known as a post-war Indian fighter) are historical and portrayed as such to the best of my ability. As for Johnny Shipley, he is an introspective concoction of myself at that impressionable age—with a bit of "Beaver Cleaver" thrown in.

4

Hopefully, this novel will draw you back to the poignancy of that long-ago time and draw you forward into further savoring the American soul.

I believe the very best way to overthrow slavery in this country is to occupy the highest possible anti-slavery ground. [There is] a story of a Dutchman, who wanted to jump over a ditch, and he went back three miles in order to get a good start, and when he got up to the-ditch, he had to sit down on the wrong side to get his breath. So it is with these political parties; they are compelled, they say, when they get up to the ditch of slavery, to stop and take breath. (H. Ford Douglas, runaway slave, summer 1860)

"Do they provoke Me to anger?" says the Lord. "Do they not provoke themselves, to the shame of their own faces?"

Therefore thus says the Lord God:

"Behold, My anger and My fury will be poured out on this place—on man and on beast, on the trees of the field and on the fruit of the ground. And it will bum and not be quenched." (Jeremiah 7:19, 20, New King James Version)

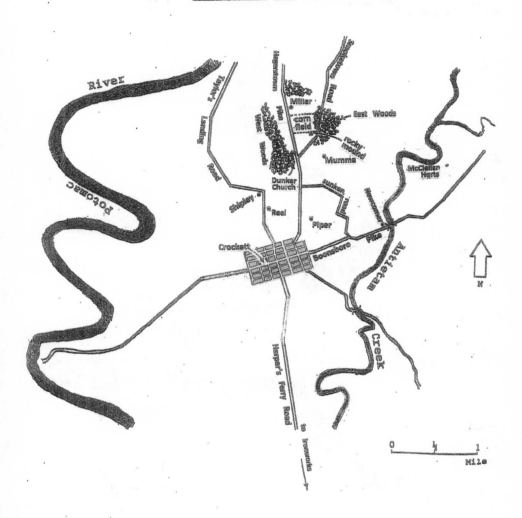

SHARPSBURG and vicinity

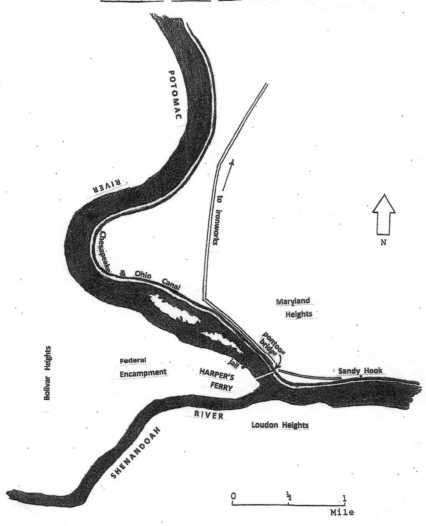

HARPER'S FERRY and vicinity

Chapter 1

Sharpsburg, Maryland (August, 1862)

When times were good, I most always called him "G'Pa." But the world has been turned on its head. On top of that, he seems to think he has answers for everything. Everything! So sometimes it's just "grandfather" now. He had no answers at all, though, for what happened to my father at Kernstown, fighting with Stonewall four months back, so I bloody well gave him a piece of my mind!

"Pa was no coward! No matter what anyone says about him being shot in the back."

"Rumors, if such they are, will be taken at face value by most folks," he replied in that lawyer-like way I'd come to despise. But did he believe the rumors himself? It wasn't long before he threw over his law practice in Baltimore and shied the both of us off to his isolated summer retreat in Sharpsburg, way the other side of the state. Maybe he reckoned that cooler creek bottom air, remote as it was, might take off some of the heat?

His shabby white-boarded cottage was tucked away a mile north of town, where it hid behind a sharp left turn on Taylors Landing Road, not far from the Potomac River. It looked discouraged up there amid all the tangles and the mushy apples fallen from a neglected orchard of ancient trees. Fixing up the place was as hard for him as a cold hard truth: he had a mighty hard time fixing his eyes on me, because I so strongly resembled his dead soldier son—my pa?

No relief from the heat, either. The high corn summer sun kept trying to fry my brains in the rolling hills backwater town where most of the folks were stodgy farmers who sometimes spoke in broken English, or broken German, or maybe both if they got excited, which was hardly ever.

I held to the hope that Grandfather would come to his senses soon and take us back home to Baltimore. After all, he had brought along the gold-lettered sign that for years had hung above his office door: "Charles Shipley & Son, Attorneys at Law." He even made sure it was never far from his eyes.

I had brought along some things myself, the only items sent back to us from the battlefield: a small silver locket with my late mother's likeness, a gold pocket watch, and an almost-new pair of calfskin boots. Course, that was before boots and shoes became leaner pickings for Southern soldiers than decent grub.

The boots were monogrammed with his name, "John Shipley," and my name too! And though a little large for me, wadded-up paper gave my toes some of the comfort they would otherwise lack. Besides, wearing pa's boots seemed to keep his memory alive.

Wouldn't that help me walk in his footsteps, too?

His pistol came back as well. But that is another story. Grandfather kept it locked in our trunk out in the shed. He refused to let me touch it, to even feast my eyes on the splendid thing. Instead, he had preachifying words for me. "Be still and know" was one of his favorites. That meant that I was "rampageous," unwilling to wait on the Lord to guide my steps, which was nonsensically unfair, it seemed to me. I had no need to wait. My pa had run off after Stonewall, and that was good enough for me!

"He should not have gone South! Slavery is wrong!" Grandfather threw that at me shortly after we'd heard about Pa. "Regrettably, I know this firsthand," he gloomed. "Someday, perhaps, I will be able to tell you the whole heartrending story. But you're not yet ready to hear it."

"But this war isn't about slavery. Pa told me it's about states' rights. That's why he and his friends jumped at the chance to fight for the Confederacy, with Stonewall. Me, too!"

Grandfather didn't seem to want to talk about that. After a long sigh, he said, "This nation is suffering from growing pains. Like you. We all must have the courage of our convictions. But which convictions are noble and right? Coming to grips with that can be terribly painful, even deadly."

I must have looked puzzled, because he stopped talking, sighed again, and ran his fingers over the Bible he kept closer company with than he did with me.

He was right about convictions, though. And I already had them! To fight with Stonewall—fourteen years of age was not too young! And I had more than enough courage for that! But first I had to shake Sharpsburg's dust from my boots, with Pa's revolver stuck in my belt!

Shortly after we arrived, I snuck up behind the old man as he peered through cobwebs obscuring the only window we had. He gave a quick little wave to a smallish man, toting a staff or something, before disappearing into cornrows across the road.

When I asked who it was, he nervously shook his head. "You must not concern yourself with him. And as I have warned you before, always stay within range of my voice!"

I was pretty certain the man had been limping and almost positive the man was black. I was cocksure, though, of one other thing: Grandfather reached for his pocket a lot, where he kept the key to the trunk where that pistol was hidden.

After several more attempts at pleading my fitness to go for a soldier, I stared him down, declaring that, from then on in, I would sleep in the shed, right next to the trunk, an arm's length away from Pa's revolver!

And that very night, I could swear I heard cannon. The rumble bumped the edge of a dream, a dream of a pistol firm in my fist, a glorious vision of Yankee Shipley-killers dropping like pintail ducks shot from the sky.

Another rumble. The floor of the shed shuddered against my backbone; the lock on the trunk shivered and buzzed. I reared up and shot a look at the door I'd left cracked against the night heat. A small breeze found me. River air, blown up from the Potomac not far off. Was that booming coming from down that way?

Bouncing to my feet, I blindly slid into my pants and groped for my boots, but I couldn't find them. Never mind, I had to act fast. The last piece of my plan to escape had just clicked into place.

That low rumble again. Now I was sure. It came from the south. Blue Ridge timber, Stonewall's stomping ground!

Giving no further thought to my boots, I made for the door, stopped, and grimaced over my shoulder at the empty flour sacks Grandfather had thrown over the trunk like a shroud. That trunk was home to a near wagonload of family treasures but only one treasure I itched to get my fingers on. One last try.

Thrusting a hand under the burlap, I yanked at the lock. No give at all. The old man had no right to treat me this way! I lashed a foot at the trunk, remembered too late that my boots were off, cursed my luck, and jerked myself back to the mission at hand. I needed darkness more than I needed boots. Stealing away on the balls of my feet, I felt something squish up between my toes, a hard-cider smell: apples, souping the grass that reached to my knees.

I firmed my mouth, certain my plan would soon bear fruit, and waited for cannon to thud again. At length, the sky flickered above the mountains that humped darkly and endlessly away beyond the Potomac. Blast! Only lightning and thunder and ragged clouds scudding through, a first hint of rain.

Barely could I make out the steeples that poked above the uncaring town but had better luck detecting David Reel's big barn a long stone's throw down Taylors Landing Road. I knew those high stone walls and stout oak beams all too well. The job of looking after the ungrateful mule we boarded there had fallen to me. My grandfather's job seemed to be guarding a spider-crowded windowpane.

Roadbed grit bit into my feet, still without socks. I squinted, pondering, just to be sure. What I was hell-bent on doing, was it a leap in the dark? I had already decided the thing was right. How could avenging a father be wrong? But why had I been so stupid so long? Even if Pa's pistol was out of reach, for now, all along there had been another way. Just inside that barn. No, not a leap in the dark at all.

A couple weeks past, I'd made the stirring discovery. Small wonder I'd almost missed it, half-hidden as it was in a jumble of bridles. From now on—because I was a Stonewall man, almost—I would have to keep a sharper eye.

The dim bulk of the barn loomed up. No noise. Any animals making a racket, my mission would come a cropper. Ty, especially, David Reel's big black farm dog, had better be steered clear of. The old boy had practically adopted me, sprawling at times by our cottage door. His insistent nose had better not be too took up with smelling me out.

Near the entrance, I caught my foot on an empty grain bag, went down hard, leaped up, tugged open the big hinged door, and thrust myself into the pungent aroma of livestock and hay.

The mule stomped at my approach and started banging the sides of the stall. But being a nimble-witted Johnny Reb, just about, I hoisted myself on the slats, stroked him some, and blew warm air in his ear, and we both settled ourselves. If I was even a trifle sharper than a stubborn mule, I was head and shoulders above any mule-headed Yankee, like as not.

I couldn't see where to place my feet but knew exactly where to go, my fingertips tingling as I stumbled to the wall, steered my hand over splinters, hit leather, then the very thing itself. My breath coming fast, I clutched the elegant grip, lifted slowly, lowered my arm so I could run my fingers over the cool length of barrel, explored the fluted cylinder, and caressed the clean-cut pattern of loops and swirls I couldn't see but knew was there. Finally, I sniffed the barrel's end. It seemed like the weapon hadn't been fired in a very long time. Would anyone care, even know, if it went missing, just for a while?

I started to leave, abruptly stopped, and swiped hair from my eyes to clear my mind.

Chuckling at my uncommon good sense, I went back, plucked a soft leather pouch from a peg on the wall, and jammed it in my pocket. The clinking cartridges reassured me. Now, properly armed with such a corker of a weapon (just borrowing, just borrowing), I was rigged up to prove that Shipley gumption wasn't dead on the field at Kernstown.

Holding the revolver tight to my chest, I eased myself outside, turned my face up to spatters of rain, opened my mouth, and vainly tried to catch the drops. Stonewall's stirrups! If the rest of my plan fell into place, what was still a boy's dream would become a man's truth!

And what was to stop me? At least once a day, horsemen from that Yankee garrison, Harper's Ferry, twenty miles or so to the south, came slinking through town, up this very road, skinning their eyes for any Rebels that might threaten the bridges, the railroad line, and the barge canal, down where the Potomac and Shenandoah Rivers rushed into each other. Most times they skulked past in twos or threes. And when that happened, I would be more than ready, now that I packed me a pistol!

Oh, but rocks and ruts can put a terrible torment on bare feet! Even though I was no mooncalf tenderfoot, the softer margin along the fence line seemed the easier way.

Where better to put my mind to what I would do the next time any bluebellies dared show their faces? By then, by jiggers, I would have an even better feel for the powerful thing I now possessed. Yes, I would lay in wait, right about here, hunkered down behind that old worm fence, flimsy though it was. A steady aim, a knowing squeeze of the trigger.

Those raindrops were pelting down now like pebbles on a drum, maybe confusing my ears. Or maybe I was just bewitched by the lovely feel of the revolver I clutched in my hands. Anyhow, I was flat-out taken by surprise.

I had never known Yankees on horses to appear so early, the sun not even properly up. But there they were, two sudden ghost shapes—not even from town, from the other direction—swinging around the bend in Taylors Landing Road.

Strangely, my legs became rooted stumps. I knew they'd spied me, looking as feeble as a drowned cat, goggling at a long-barreled pistol the darkness and rain could hardly hide. Nowhere near as fancy as my pa's, certainly, but one any gunman, even a Yankee, would have a hankering for.

My heart bubbling up in my chest, I knew at once what had to be done. I hoisted the weapon with both hands, manfully pointed it at the rider in front, and took a quick breath. "Both you men, you, you've had it!" I waited for their faces to register horror, shock, something.

The troopers merely grinned, their teeth showing white through the gloom. Unconcernedly, they eased their mounts to hedge me in, backing me up to the shaky fence.

My trigger finger went as stiff as my legs. Fast as a hangman's trap, one of the troopers lunged. Before I knew it, he was inspecting the revolver, holding it up to catch what little light there was.

After a chilling pause, he crowed, "Pretty, ain't it! But would you believe it, Artie, it ain't even loaded!" They both hooted loudly.

The trooper threw a look at Artie, made a show of dropping one of his own bullets into the cylinder, then, grinning hugely, aimed the weapon straight at my head.

"Way I'm seein' it," he said, "we bagged us a small fry that fancies his self a Johnny Reb. Ain't it our duty to bring 'im to justice?"

The nervous horses snuffled and stamped, their nostrils steaming. Artie moved in for a closer look. "This puppy don't hardly seem man enough to be a soldier. Maybe a spy, though. Better hang 'im, I reckon."

"Needs to be taught a lesson an' that's a fact," said the grinning Yank, now taken up with spinning the cylinder with his thumb. He leaned down close to my face. "See the perdic'ment you got us into, tadpole?"

By now, I could tell they only wanted to taunt me, so my mind wasn't addled too awfully much. Still, I'd forgotten to load the bloody thing! I'd actually drawn a bead on them, and they'd captured my prize fast as prunes through a goose!

Artie came closer. "Maybe this whippersnapper got confused in the dark an' mistook us for Rebel scum. If he's a loyal Union man, why he'd be plumb proud to fork over that—there peashooter. For puttin' down unlawful rebellion don't you know!"

I tried to swallow the lump in my throat. What had happened to Shipley gumption and sizzling lead? Shouldn't curses be crackling on the tip of my tongue? The trooper tittered a little. All the same he drew the hammer back, I heard the *click*.

"I—I'm not a soldier or a spy. That pistol, it's—it's not even mine!"

Those bluebellies, they glanced at each other, leered down at me, then filled the dawn with brassy guffaws. Without so much as a backward glance, they nudged their horses into a casual, leather-creaking gait and began to rag one another as to which of them had the better right to clap that pistol into their holster.

Gradually, the sound of their palaver faded as they ghosted off down the road. I heard one last bellow of laughter before it was drowned by the rain.

I bit my lips till they bled. That revolver had been my soldier's credentials, my ticket out of this no-account edge of the world. No longer would I have had to chase the chance to prove myself. Not just anybody could bag a Yank or two. Only a man. How G'Pa would have shined up to there being two less Shipley killers left alive. Why, he'd have thrown open that trunk, practically forced Pa's pistol into my hands, would have come to his senses about Southern valor, and a pat on the back when I hightailed it off for the Stonewall Brigade! And I'd let it all get away.

Still backed up to the fence, I stifled a scream when something brushed me. I nearly bolted but caught myself. The easy panting, the rich, comfortable smell – my very best friend.

I kneeled on the soaked earth and opened my arms. Ty greeted me as he always did, raising his paw. Just the two of us, no one could see. For a minute or two, I wouldn't have to prove a thing, not to Ty I wouldn't. Sensing the look in his autumn eyes, I buried my face in his fur, finally got my sensibleness back, and made a promise. Next time I wouldn't fail! Next time I got my hands on a gun I would prove myself. Nothing could bring back a father the Yankees had butchered. But nothing could stop a son who meant to settle the score!

As I started to tum in the direction that Stonewall, even now, must be poised to strike, my attention was yanked the other way.

A fitful sound shrilled from the sky to the north. Through the rain, I saw what it was. A dark arrow of geese, furiously winging south. My eyes followed them, till they were soundless specks far down the shallow valley of farms. South. The way I had to go. How and when, I didn't know. But I would find a way.

Chapter 2

Six trembling notes. As the last of the chimes from Judge Hiram Crockett's hallway clock lingered in the feverish evening air, the buzzing grew louder. Flies hummed in every corner of the dining room, and more kept flitting in through the wideopen window. I kept hoping that even one might find its way out. Oh, to get away!

Grandfather and I were late. We had footed the mile into town under a sun that had scorched the puddles of morning into afternoon chalk. Earlier, once the rain had blown through, Judge Crockett had come spanking up to the cottage, his plump pink hands firmly in control of his carriage and pair; his blond-haired little granddaughter Betsy was perched on the seat beside him.

At once the carriage became his courtroom: "It's the girl's twelfth birthday, Charles. Her parents are stuck down in Richmond, despite the fact that food is becoming in short-supply down there."

Grandfather went sort of rigid but gave in pretty quickly. Not because of the Judge's ornery insistence, it seemed to me, but because of the pleading look in Betsy Crockett's sky-blue eyes.

As flyblown and humdrum as the evening had turned out so far, it was nowhere near as bad as what had befallen me before the Judge and Betsy had come bowling up to our place.

In my hurry-scurry that rainy morning, I'd been careless—as if being bamboozled out of the pistol wasn't enough—and so had gone slapdash back to the barn. I had cleverly covered over the empty holster, but the cartridge pouch—what had caught my eye in the first place—was flat-out conspicuous by its absence. I had to get that prominent pouch back on that plainly visible peg, lightning fast!

I'd made lively tracks down the Landing Road, was almost through the door, pouch in hand, when I heard people talking inside. Whoever was there, they would nab me with the goods!

I dove behind a pile of hay still steamy from the rain. For long seconds, all I could hear was the hammer in my chest, then, a voice, shockingly familiar. Now, what was my grandfather doing there? And why was his voice so hushed, so strained?

"Concerned for my grandson's safety, taken to sleeping out in the shed, much too dangerous." That was all I caught.

Another voice, a little stronger. It was Barbara Reel, the farmer's dark-haired daughter. "And what if that bloodthirsty man does come back, Mr. Shipley, lashing out with those enormous steel-toed boots of his, like before? Or maybe worse, trying to make good those deadly threats? He swore he would get back at you, at all of you, if he had the chance. And if the Rebels ever come this way—"

Get back at all of you? If the Rebels ever come this way? I strained my ears, but the voices had gone low again.

Judge Hiram Crockett's wife, plumply efficient in a starched plaid apron, and nearly as pink as the Judge himself, fluttered in from the kitchen, stirring up gravy with a big wooden spoon. I squirmed in my chair, looked sideways at my grandfather, and frowned my renewed bafflement at his oddish behavior back at the barn. He only stared at his plate; he was frowning too.

The Judge was in an expansive mood, beaming, waving one hand at the ravenous flies, shoveling out helpings of roast pheasant with the other.

"We been friends too long, Charles, for me not to put it plain," he said, as he began to attack his plate. "Your son, de facto, was a patriotic and honorable man. But he's gone, and you got to be accepting of it. Barricading yourself up there north of town simply won't do!"

"Hiram's right," said Joshua Newcomer, Betsy's uncle, who still wore his farmer's overalls and brought the smell of his fields with him. "Gotta be hard on your grandson, too, you reining him in like a skittish colt." I grinned my agreement. G'Pa didn't see; he kept his eyes on his plate, his food untouched.

Judge Crockett continued to preside over the gathering with breezy cheerfulness, accentuating his remarks with thrusts of chin whiskers the color of milk, gesturing grandly with a fork full of food.

"So you up and dump your law practice and plop yourself way out here, you and Johnny-me-lad. Losing you wife year before last, and now your son, is lamentable in the extreme, I confess, and the boy being without a mother at all." The Judge cut himself short. Grandfather had lowered his head, blinking as if something bothered his eyes.

"Well, Charles, you're always welcome here, of course," the Judge resumed, "but Baltimore is still your real home. Keep your digs out here for a sometime summer sanctum, as it were, mountain air and all, though God knows we've had precious little of that."

"Baltimore is nothing but a hotbed of Copperhead agitators and proslavery talk these days, Hiram," Grandfather said, rigidly in control again. "Not a healthy situation for my grandson or any right-minded person."

I knew there was another reason. That vicious rumor about my pa. At least that lie hadn't made its way to Sharpsburg yet.

The Judge was waving his fork again. "You wouldn't even accept my offer of a ride down here. Seems you're still embarrassed I used my judicial discretion to extricate you from that legal scrape you had last spring, while you were settling in out here and Johnny-me-lad was packing things up in Baltimore. Accept the decision I rendered without remorse or further ado. As for that big-booted devil and his saber-rattling death threats—empty words!"

Judge Crockett paused, as if reconsidering. "Still, you can't be too careful. That monster knows he can find you here, doesn't even know about Baltimore. Yes, Baltimore's the place for the both of you!"

"Best think of the boy, Charles." Joshua Newcomer rubbed his squarish jaw before cocking his head at me. "It's safer away from here, no mistakin' that. In Baltimore, you can concern yourself with sequestering juries, not with sequestering the two of you way out here."

"I was real sorry to hear about your father, Johnny," said Betsy Crockett, all prinked up in a snowy frock and a hair ribbon that matched her eyes, "even if he did fight for the South," she continued, blind to the fact that her dimpling smile and sky-blue eyes gave her no standing with me.

I nearly choked on my pheasant. Slapping down my fork, I looked daggers at the girl. She met my gaze, all innocence, adding, "Don't you think slavery is wrong?"

"Now, now, m'dear, you know nothing about it!" The Judge began to talk and chew at the same time. "Thing is, we are a people of laws, and the South, quite apart from the slavery issue, had a legal right to secede from the Union. Let 'em go, I say!"

"But, Grampa, the war is because of slavery, not because of laws. And slavery is wrong!"

"Not about slavery a'tall. Indeed, there shouldn't be war among civilized men. Peace! Both sides reasonable. Discussing their differences. Like a court of law. Not killing each other. No use talkin' 'bout slavery bein' wrong in any case." The Judge began to swing his arm up and down, as if the fork had become his gavel. "Why, Congress has legislated the thing, the Fugitive Slave Law. The Supreme Court has ruled on the matter, the Dred Scott decision, *res judicata*. The thing has been adjudicated.

"Uh-huh! Nigras are a subordinate people, subjugated by a dominant people, ordinary articles of merchandise. It's a stigma they bear because—"

"Stigma!" Betsy chimed in. "S-t-i-g-m-a. 'A slur or false accusation' or 'a mark impressed upon the body resembling the wounds of Christ.' I learned that in school."

"Not another word, m'dear. Be a good girl and eat your goose, it's—"

"It's pheasant, Grampa. Don't you remember? Uncle Josh brought it and—"

"Quite right," Joshua Newcomer broke in, "and uncommon lucky to bag any a'tall, what with that confounded varmint prowling around my place. Managed to shoot the last of these birds just hours ago. Whipped 'em up here lickety-split, without getting myself gussied up. A bird in the hand beats a bird in the bush, so they say!"

Varmints. Pheasants. Tame stuff—compared to gunning for Yankees! Judge Crockett, like me, had more important things in mind: "Now then, I'm sure we can all agree that the unfortunate

African race has been excluded from civilized governments, from the family of nations because—"

"But didn't you tell me," Betsy broke in, her yellow curls dancing, "that all men are created equal, that life, liberty, and the pur—"

Judge Hiram Crockett, his face gone a shade of brick, held up a hand for silence. He grabbed his wineglass, splashed it full, and drained it all in two quick gulps. "Too clear for disputation that nigras was never intended within the broad scope of the Declaration of Independence."

For me, it was all clear enough. "My pa would never have fought for the wrong side. And what was good enough for him is plenty good enough for me!"

"Good or bad, right or wrong, ain't at the nub of it," the Judge declared, his refilled glass a little shaky in his hand. "It's all 'nunciated in the law, you see. Dred Scott 'stablished that slaves ain't got legal rights, they's never free. Less'n, of course, you set 'em loose. Ain't to say they don't hanker to escape the sorry mess they're in. Heard tell one sable gent so desperate he had his self stuffed in a crate an' mailed to Philadelphia!"

For a few seconds, I found it hard to catch my breath.

"Ain't the point," the Judge continued. "On account of stickin' to the law is the price we pay for bein' civilized!"

Betsy, her· eyes glistening, was wringing her hands. "It doesn't make any sense at all! How can we be civilized, if slavery isn't fair?" Her voice was quavering; then it got a little stronger. "And I didn't say the war was *about* slavery at all. I said it was *because* of slavery. So there!"

I blinked a few times, lifted my chin. "About? Because? What's the difference?"

My grandfather's eyes came up; there were sparks in them I hadn't seen in a long while. "And a little child shall lead them," I thought he said under his breath. "Betsy is wiser than any of us," he said more forcibly. "She intuitively understands that our Country's ills—our Constitutional pros and cons, our agrarian–industrial confrontations—are grafted, root and branch, to the institution of slavery. We have split apart and gone to war because of that."

We all looked at Betsy, as if she were the one who had hit upon some great truth. "But they aren't fighting about slavery," she declared, "about whether everybody should be free. At least not yet, they aren't." She darted her eyes around the table, then turned them on me and kept them there. "But just you wait. Pretty soon, everybody will understand what is really going on!"

The room seemed stuffier, warmer. "What makes you think you know so much?" I demanded with what I thought was suitable heat.

"I know good from evil," she said, meeting me stare for stare. "And maybe that's worth fighting for." And then she did something strange. She dropped her eyes, touched a tiny gold cross suspended from her throat, smiled a secret smile, and didn't say another word. It was plain. She had no idea why I was on fire to get a gun and drill Yankees.

"Betsy has the right idea, of course," G'Pa said, looking mostly in my direction.

"It has been said by some that this war is a penance for the sin of slavery, a sin that can be purged only with blood. Can we not agree that the 'peculiar institution' is not just a peculiar conglomeration of nameless black faces? That they are individual, hurting human beings? Such as the one who mailed himself to Philadelphia?"

For a minute or so, the sound of knives and forks on china plates competed with the buzzing flies.

Mrs. Crockett, her face a little more pink, broke the silence, "Betsy, dear, your cake and presents are waiting. And thank your Uncle Josh again for bringing these delicious birds we had tonight."

Judge Crockett, nodding vigorously, dragged a sleeve across his mouth. "And we must thank you too, m'dear, for preparin' such an excellent meal. Best wild duck I ever ate!"

*****

The Judge's big brick house trapped heat so well its timbers creaked in protest.

Huge maples in front tried to fend off the sun, while elms out back gave whispery thanks whenever a breeze puffed through.

There was hardly any breeze tonight, just enough to fetch the scent of corn pollen, mixed with fresh-cut hay, from the farm fields that fell away to the winding creek east of town. Everything seemed lifeless, drooping in the heat. Snatching some of Betsy's cake, I tried to force my mind away from slavery talk and to do the same with Betsy's giggles as she dove into her presents.

The girl fell to her knees, her eyes misting with enchantment at her grandparents' gift, a small white dog with a wildly wagging tail. On the spot, she named him "Wags." He must have had retriever in him; he chased anything that moved.

"Johnny, you haven't heard a word I've been saying!" Betsy challenged, when the old folks left us to ourselves. She didn't seem to notice the eager paws whisking at her dress. "Did you believe everything Grampa said? About the slaves, I mean?"

"I've never known any slaves. Besides, you heard what he said about the law."

Betsy sighed and looked out at the garden. When she caught my eye, she had that disturbing secret smile again. "Grampa jabbers a lot about the law, about slavery, too. But he reads the Bible a lot. In fact, he had slaves once that he inherited. But he set them free, way before the war. In spite of what he jabbers about, he really thinks slavery's wrong. What do you think, Johnny?"

The girl kept trying to turn the talk in a direction that made me curl my toes. I decided to stiffen my back and fold my arms. I told her, "Well, at least he sees nothing wrong about the Southern states forming their own Country."

"Oh, that. I've heard him say the very opposite thing when he jabbers with Union folks, which the folks around here mainly are." She hesitated, frowned briefly. "Grampa knows your father was a Rebel, and well, I think he didn't want to say anything that might make you feel bad."

"You were quick enough to let me know my pa fought for the wrong side!"

"Oh, do you maybe think he did?"

I made fist and made to shake it. I patted Wags instead.

Josh Newcomer was still going on like a butter churn, about a varmint: "That fox don't allow me a night's rest!" he moaned as he waved his arms. "And now that pheasants are scarcer than swearing in church, the bloodthirsty creature's snitching my laying hens! Other farmers are getting hit, too. That varmint's as vexatious as the plagues of Egypt!"

I would have stalked away from such blather, if it hadn't been for what the agitated farmer spouted next.

"A hundred dollars! That's the bounty I'm offering. Anybody interested, they can even have the use of my gun, and a fine gun it is!"

If my eyes went as large as china plates, no one seemed to notice. I almost missed it when he added, "No mistakin' the creature, either. The beast is lame."

Then and there to my own surprise, I made a decision that forever after would change my life. Avenging my father would have to wait. Somehow, I wasn't sure why, it had become terribly necessary to secure my grandfather's approval, his confidence. Killing Yankees, yes that would be honorable, what they deserved for shooting my pa—a tooth for a tooth! But the name "Shipley" still counted for something. How better to let everyone know it—especially G'Pa—than for me to bring down this pheasant-killing, chicken-snitching scourge of the Antietam Valley?

It was a good thing I had my wits about me; it wouldn't do to appear overanxious. They might take me for a greenhorn, if I jumped on this terrific stroke of luck too fast.

But what would G'Pa think? Stay within range of his voice? Wouldn't he be down on me hard as hogs on slops? Maybe not. Once I proved my mettle his belief in me would bubble up as fast as water on boil!

My grandfather turned down the Judge, again. No ride home. At least the man ran true to form. And even though he kept his eyes on the road and didn't speak, there was something I simply could not put off any longer: "What were you and Barbara Reel talking about in the barn this morning?"

Maybe he didn't hear. He merely moved a hand under his coat where, I knew full well, he had concealed Pa's revolver. I kept looking sideways at him. Silence. Darkness was closing down on us. From faraway across the fields, an animal's piercing cry.

No, G'Pa must not have heard. He plodded on, his eyes away from mine, his mind on things beyond my reckoning, I suppose.

Chapter 3

Halfway across the stone bridge below Josh Newcomer's farm, I leaned out over the creek and studied my reflection in the copper-colored water. I was way beyond the range of my grandfather's voice. But where was the harm if things worked out? And hadn't he said, or was it Betsy, that life should be fair?

With a start, I felt my slouch hat go off and grabbed it back. I could almost feel myself gliding south, like the creek, as it washed on through the three stone arches beneath the bridge. Fingering the foxtail pinned to my hat, I exulted in my reflection one more time, a mirror image of a Johnny Reb!

I caressed the stock of the .52-caliber Sharps rifle and felt my heart expand.

Quivery with the effort it took to raise the heavy weapon, I sighted down the barrel at an imaginary Yank. At the imaginary explosion, my heart expanded a little more.

Betsy Crockett's Uncle Josh had been hard to convince. After a sleepless night, I'd bestirred myself before the early-rising Mr. Newcomer and had been waiting nearly an hour to plead my case.

"A man growed," he grumbled, knuckling sleep from his eyes. "That's what I figgered when I promised the rifle."

Slowly, I drew myself up a little taller and told him, "I'm a real good shot!" And I was—at least with a cutoff shotgun, when ducks were floating on a pond.

"What makes a sprig of a lad like you so sure he can bag an elusive fox? Every man-jack who's tried so far has come up short." Rubbing his jaw, he looked down at me from a great height, his eyes doubtful.

I used my tiptoes, cunningly, to raise myself the slightest bit. "I'll knock myself out, hunt all day, all night if I have to, and I'll polish that off with target practice, I'll—"

"You'll waste all my bullets with nothing to show. How long you figger all this is gonna take?"

I smelled victory and snatched at an answer. "I'll have your rifle back in a week, Mr. Newcomer. And I'll have that fox's tail with me!"

"Mighty sure of yourself, aren't you? And what if you can't live up to your brag? What will you give me for mooching my rifle and squandering my ammunition?"

Betsy's ornery uncle had the closest thing to a gun I was likely to see. Not for shooting Yankees, but for dropping that fox, proving to G'Pa that fourteen years were within an ace of being a man, a man ready for war!

"Pheasants!" I told him. "You said the fox is after pheasants. Wouldn't they rightly nest in those thickets next to the creek?" Yes, surely that's just where they would nest, out of harm's way. "If I don't bring down that varmint in a week's time, Mr. Newcomer, I'll bag you a couple pheasants. No, make that three of 'em!"

"Only three? Well, that's three more than I'm likely to bag myself." He paused, grinned at me. "Course, you'd be needing a shotgun for that."

Letting my tiptoes slowly bring me down, I quickly shook my head. A fox, elusive or not, was no match for a Shipley armed to the teeth and pheasants if it ever came to that would be mere child's play.

Mr. Newcomer went into the house. I followed, figuring that unless he had eyes in the back of his head he couldn't see the size of my grin. All of a sudden, he whipped around, sporting a grin as big as mine, before exclaiming, "A fox is mostly noctivagous, you know!"

I made sure I didn't look perplexed. I couldn't allow him to size me up all wrong.

As the man sauntered after the rifle, I spied something I couldn't take my eyes off of. I decided to press my luck. "That hat," I prompted, pointing, as he came back through.

"Huh? First you snooker me out of my rifle, and now you want my hat?"

The rifle was all I truly needed, but Stonewall's stirrups! I would cut a mighty fair figure wearing that hat! "For, uh, keeping the sun out of my eyes, while drawing a bead on the varmint!"

Josh Newcomer's mouth seemed fighting to keep itself straight. "So first my rifle, now my hat. Well then, you might as well have something else, too."

He went to a closet, grabbed hold of something, and held it out in his big calloused hand. I stared. A bushy red tail. It looked for all the world as if the tip had been dipped in cream.

"Compliments of my son William. There used to be three of those varmints. Now there's just the one. William got real lucky. He's a mighty poor shot. Maybe his luck will rub off on you."

Josh Newcomer paused, looked me up and down. He wasn't grinning much now. "Luck. Yes, you'll be needin' plenty of that…from here on out."

*****

Getting a grip on the bridge coping, I took a last quick look at my wavering image and pushed myself away from the water. Ty came to nuzzle my hand. Though gray-muzzled and stiff in the joints, farmer Reel's big black dog had taken to lumbering after me down the rutted roads and across the stubbled fields, a mighty good sniffer, too.

Could be he had a nose for varmint. Course, so did I.

One week, time enough. After all, someone who had the look of an honest-to-god slayer of Yankees was someone to be reckoned with. I felt the Rebel yell bubbling up in my throat but fought the holler down. All the farmers within earshot would come unhinged, probably. Well they'd be heaping thanks on me soon enough!

I looked back up the road I'd come down. Heat waves already were bouncing off the Boonsboro Pike. Uh-uh. Steeper than a barn roof and hotter than brimstone. Even a hard-knock foot soldier would fight shy of going that way.

Gripping the rifle possessively, I wheeled around, my eyes watering from the glare off the creek; like a burnished sickle, it curved out of sight to the north, unknown ground. I squinted and tugged at my hat. Scout the lay of the land up there? Yes. Because somewhere in those boundless humps and folds of ground an elusive fox was living on borrowed time.

*****

After more than an hour of poking around corn patches high as my head, of stumping up and down endless hummocks and gullies, I stumbled to a halt on the spine of a ridge. A noctivagous varmint? I might as well be searching for frogs' hair. My poor feet. I slumped down in a white sea of clover and pulled off my boots. Where was Ty? Seemed the old boy had the good sense to know when enough was enough. Struggling back into my boots, I creaked myself to a standing position. Without warning, my feet tangled. I went pitching down the clover slope—like a soldier who'd been shot or something—plowing into a worm fence, knocking some of the rails into the roadway below.

After ridding myself of the wobbles, I finally got my bearings. Having chanced on this sunken roadway before from a different direction, and well beyond the range of my grandfather's voice, I thought that the surest way home was a straight shot across this trench-like lane, then through the cornfield and the orchard behind it.

I'd moved a few paces down into the road, when up piped a warbling voice, shrill with irritation. "Naw! Naw! Mist' Piper don't allow no guns onna place. Y'all be gettin' off Mist' Piper's prop'ty. Off! Off!"

The strangest creature I'd ever beheld came bobbing between the cornrows. Not much taller than me, his black face was shiny as any catfish's belly, and he was sort of hunched over, as a cripple might be. His straw hat had been got the better of, and his coarse linen shirt was several sizes too big. He brandished a garden hoe in one claw-like hand and flapped the other, as if waving me good-bye and good riddance. It was only after he stumbled closer that I detected the black patch over his eye.

Out came the hoe as he jabbed at my rifle. "No truck with such as that," he warbled as he jabbed. "No truck a'tall, sure as my name's Jeremiah. Who're you?"

"None of your blasted business! But if you must know, my name is Shipley. Johnny Shipley."

The man, looking like some grounded prehistoric bird, stopped flapping and tilted his head. "Shipley, you say," he muttered in a halfway normal tone as he peered at me with his one good eye. "Shipley. Yes, I do guess it shows."

Seconds ago, he'd appeared demented, ready to swipe his hoe at my private parts.

Now, he was as unruffled as an eagle in a tree. "How come you know my name?" I demanded.

He wagged his hoe as he wagged his head. "Can't be tellin' you that. Someday, maybe." Then I noticed the hand clutching the hoe. The tips of two fingers were gone.

Something told me he might have been waltzing me around the mulberry bushes.

I tried to catch his eye. "Why did you pretend to be loony just now?"

"Maybe, if I blow enough smoke, folks won't see the fire inside." Yes, that eye, it smoldered some, though there appeared to be a hint of humor as well.

Hearing familiar barking, I searched down the length of the slope-shouldered road. Ty, his tail a-wagging, looked to be smiling as he padded up and deposited a large dead rat in front of my boots. I blinked my bewilderment. "I didn't reckon that dogs this old went chasing after rats."

"I do believe you're right. Even so, in this-here world chasin' after weaker things is reg'lar business."

"What do you mean?"

As he arched his brows, his single eye seemed to glitter a secret knowledge, amusement maybe. "Could be I'll be tellin' you that, 'fore all's said an' done. Ifn your granddaddy don't beat me to it." He must have figured he'd told me enough, for he turned on his heel, shouldered his hoe, and strutted back into the head-high corn.

It dawned on me, finally: an elusive figure, toting a staff, dodging into cornrow shadow, G'Pa watching, waving...

As I dragged up to the cottage, still pondering Jeremiah's bewildering talk, I idly wondered whose swayback white horse was hitched to the fence. Didn't matter. Too dead on my feet to even yank my boots off, I turned to the shed.

From inside the cottage, a keening voice, all undone. I recognized it. Samuel Mumma, whose sprawling farm sat downslope from Reel's, next to the Smoketown Road. "*Ach*! This war, how I hates it!" the man wailed. "I can bears it no more! It destroys our *kirche, korper, und seele*! That is why I convenes a special meeting of the elders. But we is needing someone *unparteialisch* to preside, or we goes all to pieces. You, Charles! *Ja*! Our church peoples, they all respects you, your calm Christian charity, they—"

"No, Sam! It does not involve me. Me and mine, we are staying out of the whole sorry mess, uninvolved, like my son should have been, like we all should be, at least until we meet, head-on, the true reason we are fighting this war."

Familiar talk. No need to listen. I took two or three steps, pulled up, and turned back, because—

"That fox! It comes again. *Letzte nacht*. It is wanting my chickens! I shoots at the creature, but it gets away *leicht*. *Und* now, Henry Piper's hired man, he is back in my fields. Crazy, that is what! Snooping about with that hoe of his!"

My heart began racing. The fox got away, a thumping good thing, that varmint was mine! Best get in there, double-quick, so they'd know, right off, that Captain Shipley's boy was about to turn up in unlikely places at unlikely times. And he wouldn't be toting a hoe!

Making sure not to catch my grandfather's eye, I gushed out what I aimed to do. He was too polite to raise the roof, what with company present. Still, he blanched. Oh, I would catch it later! But I could deal with that. I had a bone in my teeth, and I wasn't about to spit it out! Besides, wouldn't he be showering me with praise pretty soon?

"*Ungeheuer* piece of ground!" After hearing me out, Sam Mumma pointed accusing chin whiskers at me. "Four square miles, it is, from Poffenberger's farm up north, all the way down to Newcomer's *platz*. I hope you gots yourself *gut* pair of legs, *jung mann*!"

Since I'd come this far, it wouldn't hurt to get one other thing straight. "What, uh, does noctivagous mean?"

Mr. Mumma hooked thumbs in his galluses. "It means you must *sehen* very good at *nacht*! A fox, he sees better than you, in day-times, too. Even if he does not *sehen* you, his nose and ears will tell him where you are. It is too much sad. You are in the dark when it comes to matching *witz* with a fox."

Something dawned on me then. If I could get myself nearly lost in broad daylight, what about when there was only the moon?

Chapter 4

Moonshine glancing off ridgetops. Dark. Silent. Tripping over bushes. Dropping the rifle. Rock outcroppings playing tag with my boots. Fighting to keep my eyelids propped up.

Briefly, as a haphazard breeze found its way down my neck, I heard sharp screeching and squawking, on the far side of the Smoketown Road. Minutes later, Ty went stock-still, raised his nose, and sniffed the air. I went flat to the grass. Nothing.

Finally, I hauled myself back where I'd started, perched on a rock near Sam Mumma's henhouse. It seemed like all a body should have to do was have his rifle at the ready and keep from forever nodding off. I'd been halfway successful. So where was the fox?

Slowly, the sky stained red behind the hills to the east. I took a long, weary breath, smelled smoke, found it coming from Mumma's farmhouse chimney, the smoke taking on the hue of the sky.

Enough was enough! I needed more than hit and miss roaming to root out the varmint. I needed to know the ins and outs of every misshapen field, all the way to the creek.

*****

Jeremiah, his elbows braced on the fence, stood gazing down the sunken road.

Had he been waiting for me?

He wagged his head, pursed his lips, and lifted his brows, as I explained the pickle I was in. And he had a few questions.

"So you're takin' after this fox 'cause it's eatin' your chickens?"

"Oh, no. We don't have any chickens."

"Umm, then you're afraid it might eat your cabbages or your mule or some such?"

"Course not!"

"Could be you want to eat the fox?"

"That's crazy!"

"That fox must be doin' you some serious mischief, hmm?"

Short on answers, I glared at the black scarecrow for treating me poorly. But he wasn't finished: "Like I tol' you before, Young John, some things in this-here world is hunted down reg'lar. Now that ol' fox you're pigstickin' after, it has nothin' to prove, outside of how to survive. Survive! That's what I been tryin' to do my very whole life!"

With that, he threw down his hoe and peeled off his shirt. Ye gods, the flesh of his back! It was crisscrossed by fissures and ridges and knobs! My insides started to prickle.

I cut my eyes to the sky.

"Some of what you're findin' there," he said, "it arrived at the end of a cowskin lash, well laid on from time to time. On other occasions, it was the smart of a rope, a hickory switch, or a cart whip, whatever was closest to hand. Each one was leavin' its own special mark, though each one was doin' the very same work."

I caught him looking at me closely over his shoulder as I tried to focus my eyes on clouds. His lips were pulled back—it wasn't a grin.

"I'm able to feel the differences," he resumed, "the differences 'tween the ups an' ins of my hide. My own flesh an' blood, they doctored me as bes' they could. So their fingers learned me what thing it was that did me that way."

"Meaning you can feel here and now which of those things left every one of those scars?"

"Fact is, so can you. Jus' be placin' your fingers, gentle like, on what you're findin' back there an' I'll tell you what it was that left behind what your fingers is touchin' as you move 'em round."

Immediately, I went around to the front of him. "You're just trying to make me feel bad. Like Betsy, a certain little girl I know."

"So I ain't the only one that makes you feel bad?"

My fingertips were still tingling. But hadn't the Judge made things pretty plain—Dred Scott and such? I didn't have to accept the dare of placing my fingers anywhere, if it rubbed me wrong!

"How long were you a slave?" I asked, since there was no real harm in talking about the subject.

"I' se still a slave, in the eyes of some."

"You mean you ran away?"

"Glad you asked. Oh, I be puttin' my duds back on, bein' as your fingers ain't eager to go explorin'."

I hoped he didn't see my sigh of relief.

"As for runnin', it has somethin' to do with this," he continued, holding up a finger that lacked a nib above the joint. "Had me a wife. Oh, I did! An' a beautiful li'l daughter too. The onliest joy of my days."

Jeremiah's chest began to work; he opened his mouth a few times but only licked his lips. At last, he said, "The man what owned us, down in the Valley of Virginia it was, he up an' sold his place, every stick an' every soul. We thanked the good Lord us three wasn't split up. But shortly, that new man, needin' some cash for his gamblin' debts, he done sold my wife. To a wifeless dirt farmer, seven miles up the road. Seven, I say! 'Cause I knew every inch of them long, weary miles."

"So, right then, why didn't you run?"

"Oh, but I did! Leastwise at night, when I had me the chance. Seven miles up, an' seven miles back. They cotched me up a few times, though. Now, one of my legs is a trifle less steady. Care to see what them chase dogs done to me there?"

He eyed me for an uncomfortable second or two as he lowered a hand to rub his leg. "But that ain't the all of it. That hogjaw feller at the far end of my seven-mile scoot, he grabbed hold of me once when he found me an' my wife abidin' together. He up an' stuck a lash in my hand an' bid me use it on her. When I froze up, he done it hisself. Now, if you could have a look-see at her poor back! An' I knows what else he done to my darlin' girl!"

"Stop it! Just stop." He'd gone too far. It wasn't fair. I had to shift the talk. "What does all this have to do with—?" I pointed at one of his tipless fingers. At once, I knew I'd gone too far.

He held out the finger. "Go ahead, Young John. Touchin' what's left of it won't be near as hurtful to you as it was to me."

I quickly stuck my hands in my pockets. "They cut it off? Just because you went to visit your wife because she'd been sold?"

"That ain't it. They was set on my back, you see, not on these meat hooks of mine. Cripplin' a field hand's hands might cripple his work. Backs heal up. After a fashion."

"But your finger. Why?"

"'Cause she was sold one more time! Way, way south. For grubbin' sugar or cotton, from first light of mornin' to last light of day. An' likely for other things too. Things that pretty li'l black gals is laid open to sometimes. An' I couldn't run that far."

"So, then and there, why didn't you run away your own self?"

"Still had me my daughter, Lord be blessed. The onliest thing that kept me from runnin' or endin' it all." He made fists of his hands. For a moment, I didn't have to look at his fingers.

But then he flexed his fingers and held them out. "Part of me was gone, you see. Surely gone." His voice was reduced to a whisper. "Somehow I had to truly show till my dyin' time how deep my heart was cut—the hurt she had, as much as me." He stroked, lightly, what remained of his finger, as if he might bring the rest of it back to life.

Uncomprehending, I struggled to remember what the Judge had said and sort out something to armor me from this black man's ghastly words. I couldn't think too well or remember much. But I did remember the look in Betsy Crockett's imploring blue eyes, when she'd spoken of slavery.

Suddenly, I recalled that Jeremiah had another finger partly gone. Uh-uh. Not now. Enough was enough.

*****

"What are you trying to do to me?" I flung the question at Jeremiah's back. He was getting too far ahead as we stumped along a meandering swale.

"You come a-fetchin' me, I recollect," he threw back at me over the hoe on his shoulder. "Wasn't it 'cause you're needin' to learn a thing or two, 'bout foxes an' such?"

I refused to answer. He'd whipped me up one side of his slavery talk and down the other. Now he was bossing me over the same ground I'd covered the night before. Still, if I was to nab that varmint, to find favor in my grandfather's eyes...

Ty lumbered off after Jeremiah. I couldn't let a runaway slave leave me eating his dust, so I hotfooted after him and when I caught up found no harm in trying to solve a puzzlement: "Why are you helping me? I'm the son of a Confederate soldier. Pretty soon I'll be one too!"

Jeremiah gave me a guarded look. "I'm payin' a debt. You bein' a Shipley an' all."

Too much nonsense: a vicious rumor about my pa; a dangerous man with steeltoed boots, who'd been in some kind of legal scrape with G'Pa; and a curious debt, because my name was Shipley.

Too much of the rifle: nothing but hefting and toting, my arm was used up, my shoulder was done. I had more questions but couldn't stifle a huge yawn. Jeremiah saw it. "We got us a lotta ground to cover. Course, ifn you ain't up to it..."

I clapped my hat more firmly on my head. "Where are we going?" He pointed off to the left. So why were we going right?

He seemed to sense my bewilderment: "You'll learn better this way. Meanin' you gotta think like a fox. So stick to the low ground, wherever it goes. Harder to see you and smell you down here. Not like last night, plain as day up on that rock."

My heart skipped a beat. I slowed to a stop. What did this pokery creature know about last night?

As I stood scratching my head, the black man crested a ridgetop and looked back down, a small dark shape nearly lost against the vast morning sky. Because I'd gotten behind, I couldn't see whose voice it was that rose above the cricket chirp: "So it's you again! You're trespassin'! Haul your black arse off my property!"

Jeremiah froze. I swiveled my head and desperately searched for a tree, a bush, a rock, or something large enough to hide behind.

Ty had gone up the slope. The black man and the black dog stood together, watching me, waiting.

Did I really have to go up there? What would my grandfather do… or my pa? I forced myself to shoulder the rifle and trudged on up to where they were.

A man I'd never seen before came bristling toward us, brandishing a pitchfork as if he wanted to use it. When he saw my white face, his manner changed abruptly. "Well now, young man. Good morning to you! Is this here darky in your charge?"

The man kept looking at me. And me, I kept looking at a pair of shimmering dragonflies.

Jeremiah refused to wait. "Yassuh, dat's right, I'se in his charge. Ifn we's trespassin', we'll jus' mosey ourselves on over to Mr. Mumma's place." He paused a moment before adding: "The air's a mite better over there anyways, the light too. That Mr. Mumma sees things better'n some folks do." He caught my eye, shot his eyebrows up, shoved the hoe to his shoulder, and stomped off. As I marched after him, he seemed to want to catch my eye again but his eye patch made it hard to do.

We struck off north, Jeremiah back in front. Since he couldn't see me, I gave into another yawn. I couldn't put the glint of the pitchfork's prongs out of my mind. But… nothing—no, not a thing— I could do or say.

After plodding for twenty minutes, we scrabbled over fence rails by the Smoketown Road. I fell farther behind. Jeremiah, supporting himself with his hoe, waited atop a long mound of earth where a few young trees poked up through the rocks. He pointed at an angular slab. "Be careful there, Young John. When it comes to choosin' 'tween white an' black meat, them ground hornets don't see no difference." I dodged as one of the hornets buzzed past my head.

"Anything here strikin' your eye?" he asked, aiming his hoe here and there. I shook my head.

The man walked off, beckoning, using his hoe as a pointer. I followed him some fifty paces to a well-weathered fence. Behind it were countless rows of ripening corn smacked up to a big patch of woods.

"What're you makin' of this?" he asked, his hoe tapping one of the low-slung rails. My eyes sped to a clutch of rusty red hair hung up on a splinter; the wood around it was shiny–smooth, the grass below it worn almost bare. Could it be?

Jeremiah stood bobbing his head. "In the corn that fox feller's sheltered from the storm. Out here, though, he's guardin' his flanks. Enemies is always waitin' to pounce. Sound familiar, Young John? Survivin', that's what his life's all about!" Again, he was trying to catch my eye. "Somethin' else you should be knowin' 'bout this-here place."

A few months past, he went on, he'd come by this very spot, at night, on what he called his "wanders." He'd spied some feathery wisps, some gobs of blood-spattered fur. "Brownish fur, not reddish like this-here. From a little fox cub, I knowed right off. An' them feathers—from a great horny owl, I take me an oath. Any need to tell you which one survived? Goes to show what can happen when a youngster strays too far from home."

"Mr. Newcomer said there's only one varmint prowling after his chickens. And that it limps. Why do you reckon that is?"

Jeremiah scrunched up his eye. "That'd be the feller you're gun-nin' for. But there's more to the tale. Over there."

He went back to the rocky mound, his hoe pointing again. I peered, more closely this time. "Animal dung, huh? Scratch marks too, real deep, on the trunk of that tree."

"See them beetle shells an' seedy things all mixed together? Fox scat. Not like a dog's a'tall. Your nose workin' yet?"

I sniffed something, sharp and strange. I looked to Jeremiah for an answer.

"Fox pee. Don't smell so bad, does it? A fox, you see, claims his turf by markin' it, time an' again. Now, what about them scratch marks?"

"The fox did that, I bet. Claiming its turf."

"Not on your life, Young John. Remember what I said 'bout enemies lurkin'? Listen hard of an evenin'. Maybe you'll hear loud screechin', from this self-same rocky place. Bobcat. Uh-huh. At odds with my long-sufferin' brother the fox. Look hard at them scratches, an' feature the claws what left 'em there. Yes, sir, a bob's claimin' this turf too. There's a war goin' on. Right here."

39

A war? Here? Hardly! I guessed I'd better humor him, though. "The fox will win, won't it?"

Jeremiah made a slow inspection of a finger that was an inch or so too short, then dug it under his eye patch, as if to scrub away a botheration. "Maybe my brother the fox will win," he said, casting a mournful look at my rifle. "But only ifn he's usin' his wits, 'stead of relyin' on his claws. He knows his possibles, an' knows his limitations, too. Course, a fox can come up short. Even when tryin' to use his wits." His stubbed finger went to the eye patch again.

"You don't make any sense!"

Unperturbed, Jeremiah waved off my remark. "That family of fox critters I was speakin' of? Well, the momma of the brood, I knew 'er by 'er size, she went down right about where you're standin' now. That bobcat got 'er. Look at the grass there under your feet."

Yes, the grass was different. Faded, crinkled, sickly looking. "Spilt blood, it leaves a sign. Even the grass can tell a tale."

I took off my hat, let my fingers riffle the foxtail. "How come you know all this?"

"Out on my wanders, I was. Trespassin', some folks calls it. Which is one of the reasons I go at night. Heard the commotion before seein' the result of the thing. Found that ol' momma fox exactly there. Gave up 'er life to save 'er cubs, I do believe. She looked at me defiant-like, then she jus' closed up 'er eyes. Even usin' 'er wits, she'd done all she could do in this-here world tryin' to keep 'er family alive. She's still here, though. Under them rocks."

He hesitated, his breath coming fast. "I ain't likely to get me close-up to that bob. But ifn I do." The hoe was a lethal-looking weapon as he held it up and shook it.

"So that's why you carry that thing around all the time!"

"Never go wanderin' without it. But not because of the bob. The stakes is way higher than that. A life an' death thing. For me. For your granddaddy. An' maybe for someone close to his heart."

More puzzle. Best pry things out of him bit by bit. "You still haven't told me why that fox has a limp. Or why you wander around at night."

"Limp? Why, that bobcat broke up that fox feller's family. An' broke up some of the youngster hisself. Now he survives by his wits. Specially after the last of his family was shot dead by that Newcomer boy. He's all alone now." Jeremiah took a hard look at the tail pinned to my hat.

"Why are you so noctivagous?" I put to him smugly.

"Gotta keep you in the dark about that. Started out mostly in daytime, though. That's when I seen what was happenin' to them-there rats in that-there road under God's own sun."

Jeremiah recounted how he'd caught sight of a fox in that trench-like sunken road—surprisingly, in the bright light of day—the creature not moving an inch, its muzzle thrust forward, as clods of earth shifted where the bank pitched up.

Jeremiah himself assumed the pose. I might have laughed but for the utter seriousness that etched his face. "A pointy nose come out of the dirt," he whispered, "then the beady eyes." He pounced, his fingers gnarled like claws. "There! One less rat to chew Mr. Henry Piper's corn! But that-there road is riddled with rats. An easy meal for a critter knowin' his possibles."

Something clicked in my mind. It was Ty that had come with a rat in his jaws. There had been nary a fox, unless—

"Do you reckon it's possible Ty could've snitched that rat from under the varmint's nose?"

With the help of his hoe, the black man pulled himself up off the ground. "You an' that dog could've caught the critter off-guard. Him down in the road, you comin' on from back of the ridge. He ain't gonna let that happen again. No, sir! He's sorta like you. Still learnin' his possibles."

"You keep saying *he*."

"Didn't I show you?"

I shook my head.

Jeremiah got down on all fours again. "A fox, you see, wets the same ol' spot time an' again, leavin' its mark in the same ol' place. See that tall grass, all pale-like up at the tip? Now, a female wouldn't be peein' that high. But a boy fox..."

Jeremiah actually cocked up a jiggly leg and hissed through his teeth. He looked back, pointing to where seed heads had withered from repeated dousing. "See there, this li'l feller's come out on top. So far." He took a pointed look at my Sharps.

Before I could get to the meat of his wandering talk, I spied something, something peculiar. I scrambled forward and reached behind a slab of limestone. "What's this?" I asked, holding up a mess of feathers and a ragged length of cord.

"That? Why, uh…"

"You gotta tell me everything! How else am I supposed to learn? And by the way, how did you know I was out here last night, up on that rock? And why were you waiting—yes, you were! Waiting for me when I came by this morning? And that debt you're paying and that man with big boots and that hoe you carry around like a battle ax…"

Jeremiah took off his battered straw hat, drew a sleeve across his forehead, and fiddled with his hoe. "I can tell you a handful of things, Young John. The rest you'd best be learnin' yourself. Yes, I knowed you was out here, 'cause I was out here my own self. Even followed you some."

"Followed me! Now that rips it! What gives you the right to spy on me when I'm out all alone in the dark?"

"Me an' the fox, we're the all-alone ones. You had your dog. Growled at me, he did."

Yes, Ty had heard something, but nothing had been there. And those bonechilling squawks, near to these rocks? Too much blather! Too many unanswered questions!

The Judge was right. Slaves were subordinate creatures. It was time to set things straight. "Where do you get off sneaking after me? Making fun of what I don't know? Throwing 'possibles' in my face? Well, whatever needs doing, I can do by myself!"

Jeremiah sighed and stared at the ground. "Didn't mean you no harm, Young John. Fact is, I was out on my wanders before you was even out an' about. I apologize jus' the same. Maybe the both of us got somethin' to learn. But that fox, he's already learned more'n you. He knows what he's fightin' for."

Chapter 5

Alone. Day and night. No rest. No varmint. No Jeremiah, either—
not hide nor hair nor hoe.

The fox refused to creep out of moon shadow to cock up his leg
and refused to pounce after rats in the sunken road. A phantom. But
at night, those same bone-chilling squawks. Now, the morning was
gone. And so was the week. Joshua Newcomer would be wanting his
rifle. Yes, and three pheasants.

But the brambly patch that hugged the creek refused to yield
any pheasants. Chips of limestone heaved into the tangles brought
no movement, no sound. Neither did poking my head into thickets
and thorns, tearing my flesh. Only one thing to do.

"You don't say!" Josh Newcomer seemed hardly surprised as, hat
in hand, I recounted my story. "Nary a pheasant? But you still want
the use of my gun? How much you figger the rent of it's worth? Not
counting pheasants, that is."

"I don't have any cash money," I told him, hoping he was just
conducting business with me, despite his silly grin. "But I can do
chores for you around your place!"

"Got me a hired feller already. But yonder up the valley, I hear
that David Miller could use a hand. Something about that mighty
big cornfield of his. It's a man's job, though. Which maybe rules you
out."

I made a grab for the man's arm as he started to turn away. "No,
uh-uh, a man's job is what I want!"

"Well then. At the end of a week, you'll pay me how much?"

I leaped at a figure the bounty on the fox would cover many
times over. "Seven dollars! A dollar a day. And I won't squander your
bullets, either. I fired your rifle only three times, at a fencepost, and
I almost hit it!"

Mr. Newcomer grinned some more. "Splendid! A fair figure for the rifle and cartridges." I beamed my approval. "Now," he went on, "how much for the hat?"

I felt my face fall, but Josh Newcomer's grin only got wider. "Just kidding, son, just kidding." And then he added, "Course, you'll be getting your granddaddy's approval first. My, but you surely do take after him. Same gray eyes, same set of the jaw, the way you carry yourself. Same, same! Anybody tell you that a-fore?"

"I take after my pa, you mean!"

"Maybe so, maybe so, I didn't know your daddy all that well. I say again, you're a chip off the older block." And still the man grinned.

I guessed that I should grin too. But I was afraid that somehow my face might break.

*****

It was out of the question, totally. It had been donkey's years since I'd seen my grandfather so upheaved. I argued every-which-way that Miller's farm was no more than a whoop and a holler away, that I was the man for the job, whatever it was.

He stared at Pa's photograph on the bookshelf, then at me, then out through the cobwebs. "There is grave danger," he began, "because—"

"Because of a man who wears enormous steel-toed boots!" His reaction made me quick to add, "I heard you talking to Barbara Reel."

G'Pa refused to go into it much, only to tell me that no Shipley could rest easy, that the man was a cold-blooded killer and could show up at any time. "Slavery breeds evil you cannot even imagine," he said, actually sweating. "Evil that brought that monster here. He may be gone for the moment but—" He reached for his pocket: the key, the trunk, the revolver...

He remained quiet. I don't know how long. He kept no clocks, as if time didn't matter. I couldn't afford to wait or to get his permission. Snatching what food I could, I hurried outside. A man-sized job was waiting for me, just a few pegs up the Hagerstown road.

*****

I had never set eyes on David Miller before. Maybe, if a kindly sort, he listened more than talked? Could fathom the pickle I was in? Offer a sliver of support? After all, my grandfather was standoffish and carping; Jeremiah song-and-danced me with firmness and spoofery; Betsy thought me up a wrong tree; and her Uncle Josh painted me greener than grass. Could Mr. Miller be different?

The hearty, round-faced man hired me straight-off and immediately steered me to the far side of his sprawling farm. I attempted to sneak in crumbs of my predicament along the way, but he seemed not to hear, talking full-tilt about his livestock and crops and how woefully hot the weather was.

Hitching up his overalls, he went tromping over tufts of grass and heaps of dung, beating his way along the snake-rail fence that closed off his thirty-acre cornfield. I spied a familiar rocky mound in the distance, forced my attention back to the chattering farmer, and went on his heels into the large patch of woods just back of the corn.

The man had a positive passion for wood: "This woodlot here provides me with multitudinous necessities!" He gestured at a near-dead oak, at a woodpile, at thinned-out places, and at neighboring stumps. "Firewood, timbers, shingles, barrel staves, even ashes for soap!"

He stopped and thrust a finger at one of the many rotting fence rails. "Sacrilegious! The man in my hire who did that job used unseasoned wood. After a couple years' work, the fence gave up, like some other good-for-nothings who've crossed my path!"

The man went rattling on, explaining that he took no further chances. He girdled his trees and stripped away bark, so that they lost their sap, seasoning as they stood dying. "When it's dry, wood cuts easier, burns better, lasts longer, and doesn't weigh as much. I give trees the respect I'd give a man. Let 'em stand upright on their own ground till the sap of life runs out. Barrel staves? Why, they come together like newlyweds, when properly seasoned!"

He paused, regarding me narrowly. "Are you properly seasoned, Jimmy Shipley?"

I didn't correct him, just gave my head an emphatic nod. "So, you're up to it then?" he added, examining me from hat to boots.

Just what I was supposed to be up to wasn't clear. I figured it must have something to do with repairing the fence with seasoned wood from a girdled tree. I wanted a better fix on that, but he beat me to the punch, prattling on about tools and how to employ them with respect.

He went through the motions of wielding the beetle hammer and striking maul, the metal wedge and wooden glut, how to work an ornery grain. At last, he shut his mouth. When he started to leave, I figured he must be done. Not so.

"That hired man I told you about? He ran off. Ran off to the war of all things! Like that schoolmaster fella down in town, who should be teaching you right now. Oh, yes, he took leave of his senses, then he took leave of me! You wouldn't do something crazy like that?"

Vigorously shaking my head, I crossed my fingers. I hoped he didn't see.

*****

I could feel my back beginning to blister. Stripped to my waist, flinging sweat from my eyes, I had no doubt that I could drag the massive limbs and chop them to size and trim them clean and split them into rails and snake them together crisscross fashion as well as any grown man could have done.

Clawing at welts raised by flurries of insects, I stood back to admire my work, sucking the finger of one blistered hand and the thumb of the other where I'd slashed myself a time or two. My stomach rumbled; my throat cried out for something wet. It hit me then. I'd failed to mention a single thing about getting paid.

I dug into my lunch sack: chunks of dry beef, crumbly corn bread, warm buttermilk, and a tiny pot of honey a bee-keeping farmer sold to neighboring folks.

I immediately went for the honey. At once, buzzing things came out of the corn, flitting around my hands, my ears, my eyes. Flailing my arms and cursing my luck, I backed away to the nearest shade. Some young leafy trees, and the rocky mound made a decent seat.

More honey was practically in my mouth. I stopped my fingers. The scatter of feathers and the ragged cord that had spooked Jeremiah so much, they'd vanished!

Way too hot to ponder that. Jeremiah was beyond reckoning anyhow, so my mouth got serious again with the honey. Soon my fingers were dripping and sticky. And the shadows were such an agreeable, lulling diversion from straining, from sweating.

The weeds behind me went *swishh*. I whirled. Somehow, incredibly, Ty had found me. I wanted to scold him. Instead, I opened my arms, and he raised his paw. It was way too far for the old boy to come and near miraculous that his nose could sniff out my scent—a good country mile of roads, pastures, fences, and rocks. I gave him most of my beef and held out my syrupy hands. As he was lapping my fingers, he stopped, raised his head, worked his nose, and pricked up his ears.

Lumbering faster than I'd ever seen him, he went to the fence, stopped, and stared past it. I went after him, my eyes following his: nothing but row upon row of head-high stalks crisping in the sun, ears unshucked, and some way off... leaves a-flutter.

Ty lowered his nose, went along the fence line, sniffing, then into a crowd of Queen Anne's Lace next to the woods. He froze in his tracks, his eyes never leaving the corn. I was curious, but something even more curious caught my attention. Another fur-rubbed rail! And something more: blood-stained feathers and a snippet of cord.

All morning I'd had a suspicion nibbling the hook of my mind. Now, I reeled it in: the woods, the fence, the corn, an elusive varmint prowling for chickens, and Jeremiah so took up with chickens that the palms of his hands often were white from the mess they made. And his nocturnal wanderings—was he somehow getting close-up to that fox? Because if he was doing what I thought he was doing—I had to know. Which meant turning the tables. Me following him! It would be easy. If I was careful, and it wasn't too dark.

*****

I leaned back, gave the oak tree my weight, let the bark rub my achy shoulder blades. Deep woods behind me, leafy scents lingering as the sun slid away. A choice spot for staying hid, on the alert. A clear field too for ranging my eyes. Soon, Jeremiah would be out on his wanders, shuffling up the road from Piper's, my eyes following his every move, him slinking by me, me dogging his steps. He would come, all right. When it got sneaky dark.

The shadows grew longer, more chilly. A last scolding of crows, some crickets, a frog. A shiver of anticipation coursed through me.

I looked behind me. Across the clearing a last ray of sunshine struck the side of a tiny white building, the glare off the bricks blinding me briefly. A church, I'd heard someone say. Plain-looking, boxy. Funny, no steeple.

Drawn to the splotch of warmth, I went over, sank down on a swelling of earth, yawned, and shook my head: stooping, dragging, whacking, lifting–all day long the fireball in the sky a throbbing, scorching foe...

Jerked from prickly musings, I knew right-off. Bugs had found me! I slapped at my neck, my arms, my—yee gods, I was parked square on top of an anthill! I jumped up, squirming, swiping. They were all over me. And now I saw why.

Large black ants were pouring out of the hill, spilling over whatever got in their way, and scuttling to meet them head-on, a long line that went clear to the trees, an army of smaller red ants, the reds sweeping into and over the blacks, driving them every which way, spurting on in a frenzy, some of them up the inside of my britches, my shirt.

I jigged and batted and slapped. To put a stop to the madness, I stomped my boots in their midst, but the ants scattered, reformed, stormed over the flesh of my legs, surged upward, and stippled my crotch. I leapt away, threw myself to the ground, rolled over and over, writhing, sputtering.

My plan had gone terribly wrong. The next moment it went all to pieces.

The figure, near-clothed in shadow, was hard to see. But the hoe jutted up like a spear, the metal blade catching a fleeting slash of the sun.

"Gettin' yourself primed up for church, Young John?"

"Ch-church?" I managed, tumbling, spanking myself.

"I'm takin' you for one of them holy rollers, though I never seen such goin's-on before with them Dunkers."

"Drunkards?"

Jeremiah put down his hoe and a boxy contrivance he had, leaned down, and pulled me to my feet. "Dunkers," he repeated. "This-here's a Dunker church. When baptizin' with water they dunk their people all the way under. Course, there ain't no water to be dunkin' you under here an' now. Too bad. Now strip!" I protested, backed away, still batting myself.

"Off with them clothes! Off! Off!"

Fast as a fly down a frog, I shucked off my clothes. At once, the man was slamming my shirt, then my pants, against the bricks, so forcibly you'd think he aimed to batter down the building.

"See there," he said proudly, holding up my togs like a pair of putrid alley cats, "no more ants in your pants. Leastwise, not for a while."

The commotion appeared to have rid my clothes, my unclothed anatomy too, of insects. But another presence revealed itself. Though Jeremiah had covered over his box with a cloth, he couldn't fool me. "*Cuck, cuck*," said the box.

Though mostly naked and hugging myself for warmth, I was jubilant. "I know exactly what's in there, and I'll bet I know why, and—"

"Found them feathers an' cord, did you? Well, I ain't all that surprised. Ifn you got half the sense your granddaddy's got, you—"

"There you go again! Rattling on about my grandfather. I have to know why. Out with it now! Out! Out!"

"Trouble is, Young John, you don't know what it is you're truly needin'. Or why."

"Ain't so! Just because you think I'm discombobulated…"

"A few nights back, I'm followin' you. Now, I'm takin' bets, you're layin' up for followin' me. Are you comin' or goin'?" He cast a look at his box. "Bein' as you're so took up with that-there box, an' with comin's an' goin's, maybe, this time, you'd best be comin'."

He reached for the box; it still was emitting some testy cackles. "Better to lose jus' one ol' chicken," he said, "than a whole henhouse full of 'em."

He lifted the cloth and peeked beneath it. "Tendin' Mr. Piper's leghorns, you see, gives me a leg up on snitchin' a few, now an' then. Thing is, it gets a mite messy." He rubbed his palms together and held them up. I could plainly see the pale chicken mess begriming his hands.

"Stakin' out jus' one of them birds," he resumed, "appears to satisfy my brother the fox, so's he don't go after more of a night. Good thing, too. Folks with guns is also out of a night. They're fightin' their war. He's fightin' his. Why're you so keen on fightin', Young John?"

Fully clothed again, I was ready for him. "Same reason Stonewall fights for the South. Their homes have been invaded. They just want to be left alone. Their whole way of life is… is the South is just trying to survive!"

"Your mem'ry's slippery. You appear to be speakin' of the fox. I'm askin' 'bout you."

The black old cuss, he just didn't get it.

As we stood eyeing one another through the gloom, the silence was broken by a piercing shriek that went straight to my teeth.

Ignoring the box, Jeremiah snatched up his hoe. "Bobcat!" He snarled the word. "Come or go as you like, Young John, it's up to you."

He didn't look back as he made for the road but seemed to know I was right behind. "Jus' short of that corn we'll take to the fields," he tossed over his shoulder.

I struggled to keep up, kept falling behind, my legs as stiff as his bobbing hoe.

With painstaking effort, I followed his awkward shadow over the posts and rails alongside the pike. Way up past the cornfield, a pair of windows in Miller's farmhouse glimmered like two watching eyes. Jeremiah halted, thrust up a hand.

I staggered to a stop, tried to focus my eyes. Aside from the crickets and our own labored breathing, there was utter silence. Piles of fresh-cut limbs, waiting for splitting, littered the ground a couple dozen paces nearer the woods. Just to the right were a rocky mound and a huddle of trees. There were more rocks to the front of us. Ducking behind one, we dropped to the ground.

"That's where we found that fox dung." I tried to point. Jeremiah stopped my hand. "The bob's took off," he whispered, "but don't make a move or a sound."

A finger went into his mouth, then, very slowly, up in the air. "Jus' testin' the breeze." His voice was no more than a sigh. "We're downwind. Ifn we ain't twitchin' too much or flappin' our tongues, we may see somethin' of a war goin' on. Right here."

Jeremiah had talked of war in these fields before, all because of some shrieking, some running around? A tom-foolish notion!

A good half hour since that unearthly yowl. I fidgeted, cautiously peered over the rock. A farm dog yapped down by Mumma's. Stillness again.

Heaving a sigh, I told him, softly, "You're barking up the wrong tree. Ain't nothin' goin' on here." He rushed a finger of warning at me. "We wait," he murmured. After a few minutes, he said, "Peculiar goin's on. That fox feller has always answered the bob. A yelpy bark, a trip to his little hill yonder, so's to stake it out as his own again." Then he added, glancing at me, "Used to stake somethin' out there myself."

"Then you went to another place. A place you hope I wouldn't find!" I looked sideways at him. Surely, he must see how sharp I was!

Jeremiah let silence lay between us. Just when I thought he had missed my remark, he said, "Oh, I figgered you'd find it. Hoped you would, anyways."

I cocked my head. Hoped I'd find it? Hoped I'd uncover his devious stashing of chickens? I was ready to challenge him, but he got his own words out first: "Somethin's different. Somethin's got between him an' his habits."

My memory flashed. Course! "That fence up there, I fixed it, part of it. The broken part, with the fur on it, I got rid of that lickety-cut. He can't scooch through there like he used to."

"Why, bless my soul! Appears you're learnin' how fox fellers think. Could be there's hope for you after all. So we wait some more."

Maybe ten seconds passed, and the wait was over.

Fifty paces away, a flicker of movement. A shadow appeared on the fence. A full minute went by. No movement. No sound but insect thrum. Nothing but moonshine glancing off trees, brushing the corn. All at once the shadow was gone.

Jeremiah touched my shoulder, pointed to a ghostly shape stirring the grass, moving slowly toward the rocky mound.

Atop the knoll, in a splash of moonbeam, the shadow took form: pricked-up ears, a bushy tail, even fuller than the one pinned to my hat. I waited for a yip of defiance, a leg cocking up. The fox, unmoving, could have been part of the countryside.

More minutes. Utter stillness. A puff at my ear: "Never seen the like. Up to strange business, he is."

Very strange business. The sharp nose went up in the air, down to the rocks; after a pause, the same routine, a half-dozen times.

Again, the soft voice: "That nose full o' bobcat put a burr in his tail. He ain't gonna take it standin' still, neither!"

Jeremiah was dead-on, for once. With delicate steps, nose to the earth, the fox took a circuitous path out into the meadow.

"I'd have me a perfect shot!" I fumed in silence, just before the shank of night shut down my view. But Josh Newcomer was right. The creature was lame.

Without turning my head, I felt the black man's eyes and sensed a question about to come.

"Figgered it yet, Young John?"

"Figured it?"

"You been wonderin' why me an' that fox is brothers. 'Cause we're the same. Enemies always chasin' us down—us both gotta live by our wits. Stakin' a place an' aimin' to stay—him an' me both. Purely on our own with no one to care. Brothers, you see."

I knew hocus-pocus when I heard it! But now was not the time for chopping this queer potato down to size. He would bloody well know who had the whip hand, once I'd dispatched his four-footed brother!

At length, the fox came back to the mound, lowered his head, shook it furiously, then on very stiff legs went back to the fields. For nearly an hour, he did it again and again and again. Brothers? They both must be crazy!

"He's done." Jeremiah's voice was back to a whisper.

The animal backed away from his mysterious doings, turned, and padded back toward the fence. He stopped once on the way and—about time!—cocked his leg over unfamiliar cuttings of wood that lay in his path. In the next hushed instant, he melted into the darkness.

The black man retreated into silence. From the corner of my eye, I watched the battered straw hat bob thoughtfully, my own mind flying off in all directions. I could stand it no longer. "What was all that about?"

"I been tryin' to get inside his head. An' maybe I done it. You got a notion?"

"A notion? Me?"

"Well, sure as sunrise, he won't be rompin' back here again this night. Not even for chickens. I'm thinkin' his taster don't want no more work for a time."

"Tell me!"

"Show you instead."

We hoisted ourselves. The moon was a bright yellow disk; the clouds were gone; the rocky mound stood out in bold relief. I went and inspected the rocks and the poking-up trees and looked for something amiss. Nothing but clawed-up bark, bone-white grass where the varmint had sprayed, a few scattered piles of animal droppings.

Jeremiah waggled his head. "Seems like you're still blind to the truth, Young John. Even when you got two good eyes to see it with." Pursing his lips, he pointed his hoe. I looked more closely and pondered some more. "You're at it again!" I told him at last. "Playing gabbling games, poking at droppings that—"

It was hard to see. I pushed my head closer. "Wait. It's different! No seeds or bones or beetle shells, like you showed me before." Pleased with my powers of observation, I looked up in triumph. "The fox didn't do this. The bobcat did!"

Jeremiah stamped his foot, yanked off his hat, clamped it back on. "The bobcat's been here, an' scratched up that tree. Any fool can see that much. A bob marks his turf too, an' that fox feller, he knows it. But that-there scat..." He sounded too vexed to go on.

"Well, if the bobcat didn't do it, and the fox didn't do it—"

"Get inside that fox feller's head, Young John! What would you be doin' when facin' off with somethin' stronger an' quicker an' with a long streak of mean? Wits! Wouldn't you try usin' your noggin?"

My failure to respond brought a sigh of annoyance. "Them two," Jeremiah went on, still sounding vexed, "the fox an' the bob, they're both of 'em timid as toads when it comes to menfolks an' their—" He jabbed his hoe at the scat. "This time I ain't about to demonstrate what the critter done did!"

"Dogs! You mean that fox went out and... and actually carried that stuff all the way back in his mouth? So that the bobcat would sniff it? And reckon that dogs had staked out this place?"

"Like I tol' you before, he's smarter than you! He don't nose after things that ain't his necessentials. An' when he smells out the truth, he uses his wits."

"You're saying I haven't smelled out the truth?"

"I'm sayin' you're jumpin' at things harum-scarum. Ifn you bite off too big a chunk of your wants, you'll choke to death, before even knowin' your necessentials."

I must have looked blank.

"You can be learnin' a thing or two from that fox, Young John. He's already smelled out his truth. Freedom! That's his real business. Maybe the real business of this war too, hmm?"

Hadn't I already smelled out the truth about my own business? I couldn't let him get the better of me on that, so I said, "Speaking of smelling, what's to stop that bobcat from smelling those chickens you're so keen on stringing up?"

The black man's gap-toothed grin was a visible thing, even in the dark. "Mos' times I get me up close, so's the bob takes off when he gets a good whiff of my stink."

"But then the fox would get a good whiff of your... of you, too," I offered wisely.

"Don't seem to bother 'im, not no more. Took the longest while. But now that fox knows he's smellin' not only chickens, he's smellin' his brother."

"You're crazier than a june bug! You keep repeating yourself, about the fox being your brother."

"Course I repeat it. You need to hold onto the thought! But there's more. On account of I learned my necessentials, how to survive, from a wise ol' fox, a fox Virginia folks was tryin' to hunt down for the sport of the thing. That critter got away time after time. I set about learnin' how he accomplished the job."

"What did you learn?"

"That-there critter turned them huntin'-down folks ever which way! They took to cryin' an' cursin' 'bout him settin' false trails, doublin' back on hisself, throwin' them an' their dogs clean off the scent."

"So that's how you got away? You learned from a fox?"

"It's the onliest reason that big-booted feller an' his loud-barkin' catch dog didn't grab me up through all them Blue Ridges. Oh, I snookered them two for a time! But had me only roots an' berries to put off starvin', an' many a day an' night never closin' my eyes. An' so, they cotched me at last. Snugged up to a mule. In a barn hereabouts."

Jeremiah's yarn, was it starting to untangle? "Your granddaddy, he saved my life. Miss Barbara Reel an' Judge Crockett too. 'Specially your granddaddy, though. 'Cause as things turned out, it was him put his life on the line—for me! I owes him. All that I got. Which ain't much. Jus' me in the flesh."

"But that has nothing to do with me!"

"But it does, Young John. That's part of what you need to be learnin' your own self. Maybe me an' the fox is part of that. Together, we might be showin' you, like brothers do, what's necessential to your own life now. To your granddaddy, too."

"My grandfather told me it's just the two of us now."

"Your granddaddy's got somethin' to learn his own self, maybe?"

When I only twisted my hat, Jeremiah said, "We're all of us brothers. That's right! An' that's a truth worth layin' your life on the line for. Like your granddaddy done for me!"

I merely moved my head up and down. Why rile the man up? Let him settle down some. Jeremiah was wrong about one thing, though. That fox was no brother of mine!

I grabbed a rock and hurled it in the direction the fox had disappeared. Jeremiah had turned away and failed to see how hard I could throw. Course, with only one good eye, he didn't see much.

*****

I still had the rifle. Soon, I would have the lure for springing the crashing good trap of the sneaking good plan I'd contrived. I would use my wits, all right! If only I could keep the varmint's brother out of the way.

Though I still had a ways to go on the fence, by noon the following day, I was ready to dicker.

"About my pay, Mr. Miller. Could I take some of it out in one of your chickens? And a box of some kind? And, uh, some cord."

David Miller blinked a few times and pulled at his nose. "Why not just wring its neck, truss it up right here, and be done with it?" he said, using his hands to demonstrate how to do it. "Maybe two birds. One for each hand. A balanced diet!"

I tried to match the man's delighted expression but couldn't bring it off. I was still achy—that fence was a man's job and more—and in a quandary from the previous night: brothers, false trails, and such, and this was serious business besides. But I just about had me a chicken.

Jeremiah had learned me more than he knew. He'd put me on to getting the varmint within a few short yards of my rifle site. Blast! I'd bamboozle them both!

I needed a place to stash the bird till dark. And I thought I knew the perfect hiding spot. I'd caught a glimpse of a little latticework door—before armies of ants had done me in—an opening to the underside of the place, a crawl space of some kind. Yes, no safer place than the Dunker Church, a place to tuck away my cackling bait.

A small fly in the ointment, though. How to keep Jeremiah at bay after the sun went down, when that mischief maker would be out on his wanders?

My legs still felt like logs. To steady myself, I picked up a straight-shafted limb from a wind-blown tree. As I inspected the thing, something like a firefly sparked in my brain.

Why, Jeremiah was as good as out of the way! The old fool wouldn't be prowling around in the dark. Not if he couldn't lay hands on his confounded hoe!

*****

Making off with the hoe took nothing more than rested legs and a mad dash to the henhouse wall while Jeremiah fussed with all the cackles inside. Besides, wouldn't I have the thing back before dawn?

Best keep G'Pa in the dark. At least till the varmint was riddled with lead, that great-looking bushy tail firm in my grasp. As for snitching the hoe (no, borrowing, borrowing), that was just cracking good Shipley brains!

"I deserve me a pat on the back," I told myself as I peered through the uncertain late-evening light, because the spot I'd selected was prime, precisely where we'd hid ourselves the previous night. I'd roamed the whole area. It was good to be sure. Yes, the choicest spot from which to squeeze off the fatal shot. The rest would be easy. I knew precisely where to glue my eyes and knew exactly where that creature of habit would spring to the fence.

Propping the Sharps against the top of the rock, I let the night air brush the flesh of my arms. Downwind of the varmint. Foolproof plan. It wouldn't be long.

The mid-September days still were scorchers, but the nights weren't, which probably explained why I couldn't rid myself of the shivers.

"Gotta keep my eyes skinned all the time," I reminded myself. One shot was all I would get. Course, that was all I would need.

I riveted my attention on the rocky mound where I'd staked out the hen from the selfsame rock Jeremiah had used. Maybe he was right, a war going on in these fields.

Darker now. Hen in a dither, jerking at the end of its ten-foot cord. Veiled movement above me, a sudden *swish* past my head. Blast! Other varmints were out here tonight.

The quick discovery of human presence must have driven off the plummeting owl. The chicken, though, was still flapping and squawking. If that fox wasn't deaf, he'd bloody well know it was time!

One thing kept pricking my steadiness. Prowling the pasture, I must have left the grass and rocks tinged with scent. That varmint wouldn't be smelling his brother this time. But wasn't his nose over-eager for chicken?

Minutes dragged to an hour. "Bound to come from the corn," I assured myself for at least the tenth time. I waggled the rifle, sighted at shadows, my eyes hankering, roaming.

I began drumming my fingers on the stock of the gun. Nothing but moonshine was drenching the meadow. The hen strutted and poked, strutted and poked.

We're all brothers.

Too bad the man who rambled hither and yon with his hoe rambled so much with his mouth. His jabber kept flitting around only morsels of meaning. Bothers? Freedom? The fox taught him that?

A jitter of motion. The chicken at it again. I let my finger caress the trigger, took a deep breath, and fixed my eyes on the fence. In the moonlight, the rails were cadaverous bones. But no varmint.

Wait! What if the bobcat comes?

The hen started jigging an idiot dance. Wasn't that a flicker of something out there, behind that frantic ol' bird? A bushy tail? Same as last night? Even if he didn't come from the corn this time, wouldn't he have his mouth just itching for feathers!

Everything depended on a steady aim. Squeeze the trigger, don't yank the bloody thing, just aim and squeeze, like picking off pintails on placid blue water, easier even.

No, this was different. Everything was at stake. My reputation, my Shipley worthiness, my acceptance by G'Pa.

The trigger wasn't hair but didn't need much pull. No, don't pull—squeeze 'er nice'n easy like.

The yawp of the chicken was nearly lost in the *Poom* that slammed the night air. The rifle butt walloped my shoulder, but my heart pumped out a trip-hammer message that spoke to my feet, so I reared up, unable to restrain the whoop that announced to the world that I'd done it! An absolute killing, when every other man-jack around had come short of the mark!

Cut off the rascal's tail. Course! I'd planned to all along, had the knife for it in my hand already, because this brush was even bushier than the one pinned to my hat and would look lots better than—

Abruptly, at the edge of the rocky mound, my boots wouldn't move. Even the hen had stopped hopping and squawking. And I stopped breathing. My fingers, my arms, and my legs turned to water. The Sharps and the knife went clumping onto the rocks.

I tried to tear my eyes away but could not. My bowels began quivering, a tingling that shuddered up to my chest and quickly back down, and I felt something leave me.

The powder flash flared again, this time deep within my head, behind my eyes. My mind cried *No!*

I should have had a haunting suspicion I might be followed. I only knew that my well-aimed, lightly squeezed rifle shot had torn into the black head of the best friend I had in the world.

Incapable of normal weeping, I gurgled. My vision began to blur as the bushy black tail flopped one time. Ty tried to raise his paw, but--

I would have to do something quickly but didn't know what. The world had gone crazy. It didn't seem to bother the crickets. They went on and on as if nothing were wrong.

Chapter 6

I needed something to prop me up, to crutch me along. The Sharps was wicked support. I got no steadiness from it and kept going down. Ty's blood had congealed on my hands, on my face, had clotted on my clothes, in my hair; the soles of my boots were greasy-slick with Ty's blood. I kept going down, onto my knees, onto my back, onto my belly, clawing the grass, thumping my head on the grass, sobbing salt tears, spoiling the grass. I buried my face in his fur, hugging poor Ty, breathing his blood, rocking atop the stiffening body, pleading his forgiveness, choking on his name. I tried to lift him into my arms. I hadn't the strength. I was forced to drag him. A quarter hour to pile the rocks. A special place for my friend, a place he'd come once before, to share a meal, to lick my sticky fingers clean. And now my fingers were sticky again.

No going home, not now, maybe not ever. What could I say? How to explain away my stupidity, my worthlessness? I needed a place to hide myself, an all-alone place. Maybe lay there a while. Maybe lay there forever.

I knew such a place, within hobbling distance. A place that could maybe bring comfort, and it must have known death. In a slash of moonbeam, the place looked as pale and lifeless as a tomb. Yes, the Dunker Church. It surely knew death.

As I crutched past the anthill, I booted it hard, to remind the creatures inside that the world outside was a cruel and dangerous place. The kick sent pain blazing up my leg, which I deserved. Best make plain my utter disgust with myself. I flung down the Sharps.

With one hand, I attacked the stinging in my eyes, with the other fiddled with the latch on the latticework door. With a whine of its hinges, the thing worked open. As I squirmed into the desolate darkness, something slithered or scurried away from my head.

I probed for the hoe, yes, right where I'd left it. Too bad about that jittery chicken. But hadn't it squawked its annoyance, just trying to scold me? Who could blame me for pasting it with the butt of the Sharps? But wasn't I the one who deserved a kick in the teeth? My eyes had betrayed me, my ears wouldn't work even now, throbbing, ringing, imagining things that—

No, my ears did hear something—horses, out on the pike, clopping closer, wheels spattering gravel, bits and bridles a-jingle, stopping right next to the church.

For the next several minutes, by fits and starts, others came on, from the north, the south, maybe down the slice of the Smoketown Road.

The front door to the building squeaked open above me. A scuffling of feet, voices murmuring, flustering. No business of mine. Still, it was uncommon curious…

The voices grew heated. I couldn't make out the words. I reached out a hand, felt the flooring two feet up, cocked up an ear; my hat fell off, and still I couldn't make out the words.

Scuffing along on my elbows, I inched forward, found metal, a crusty pipe of some sort; it went up through the floor, leading to the base of a stove or some such, and now those voices came down to my lightless world plain as a preacher on Sunday.

David Miller, I picked him out, though his voice was pitched up. I could picture him, gesturing furiously, fisting his nose, his fingernails black with the soil of his farm.

"Hard lines for all of us soon," he was bleating. "There is fighting, not far away, up on the mountain, I hear. My brother-in-law, just back from Williamsport, he is. He saw them, he did. Crossing the river, they were. Heading for Harpers Ferry, he says. And not just any Rebels, neither. It's Stonewall Jackson! What of our valuables, our women and children, our very lives?"

Another familiar voice, almost a wail—Mumma's: "I say we must *stehen* by the moral believes of this *kirche*! No war for us! Not to be *helfen einer seite*! We stands apart! Like Maryland herself! If those armies comes this way, *himmel verbieten, mich und mein*, we are getting out. Fast!"

"We recognize trouble, yes, but answer to need," a calm voice put in. "Water, succor for the wounded, if worse goes to worst. The needs of all, both sides, without espousing either. Christian charity. I mean to stay."

"But if we are recognizes this war, we are approves of the sin of it! We becomes *verantwortlich, korpe und sehel*," Sam Mumma was getting more excited, stamping his boots or pounding on something. "We must, all the times, holds to our believes! We are *verantwortlich* to them as surely as we are *zu Gott!*"

"And may God have mercy on us," someone gloomed softly.

I squeezed my eyes shut, dug my fingers into the dirt. There was no hope for me. These God-fearing people were at each other's throats. Where did that leave a clubhead like me? My latest feat was shooting my friend.

Nowhere to go. No one to turn to. My grandfather? Would he disown me?

Jeremiah? Not him by any stretch, he'd be pining away for his hoe by now, and pretty soon—he never missed a trick—he'd figure out the hideous truth.

I lost track of how long I lay there. My heart had squeezed to the size of a seed. It had grown deathly quiet. Tenseness seemed to hang in the air. At last, cheerless feet dragged across the floor and outside. The door sounded snappish when at last it clicked closed.

One of the wagons groaned out on the turnpike. Or was that sound coming from me? I had never felt so alone in my life.

I wormed back to the opening. Black and forbidding outside. Inside, a smothering prison. A bonehead throbbing beat at the back of my eyes. I had to get going, somewhere, to make up for the foul thing I'd done. I had even more to prove than before.

I scraped through the latticework door, cuffed it shut, remembered something, creaked it back open. Yes, the hoe. I owed Jeremiah that much.

I looked up the pike: too dark to see much of the road. Once again, Miller's farmhouse had two yellow eyes, watching me, judging me. Never mind that I hadn't finished that feisty farmer's falling-down fence. It was, after all, his voice that had quavered the remarkable news. Stonewall was marching! On Harpers Ferry! And now, at last, I knew where to go.

*****

If the Dunker Church was a tomb, the shed was a coffin. It pressed in on me, down on me, like Ty's heap of rocks.

I was mortified by the gore I had on me, no longer wet or sticky, but a persistent, rasping crust. I couldn't stop shaking. I tried to lay quiet. I couldn't stop squirming. I craved sleep but craved something else even more.

I got up, struggled into my clothes, fumble-fingered with the trunk, tried to pry open the lock with the ramrod of the Sharps.

I should have waited: for first-morning light or should have got my hands on a match or should have just clamped my eyes shut till nothingness took me. But Pa's revolver, it was inches away—never mind the darkness or the racket I made. But I should have waited.

The door to the shed scraped open. Cool breeze crept in, then my grandfather, holding a lantern. I'd failed to clean myself up. Stupid again! If only I'd waited.

G'Pa stood silent, not breathing too well; the lantern seemed having the jitters; the air had stilled; I could hardly breathe.

Needing both hands, he set the lantern atop the trunk. He must have seen how gory I was; he backed away; he seemed to have lost the power of speech; the robe he had on drooped around him like a windless flag around a pole; night air whiffed in, moving his robe, the lantern light aquiver on his ivory face; his fingers shook as they went to the ramrod hanging bent in the hasp of the trunk.

I refused to meet my grandfather's eyes. He must fancy I'd gunned down a varmint. He didn't even know about Ty.

He raised his hand, as you would to brush away a troublesome bug. I hoped it was no more than a despairing, broken gesture—but the hand came down on the trunk spank-hard, unsettling the lantern, the sound of metal and glass striking the floor with the clap of a musket shot; the flame wicked out.

I backed away from the smoke-gray eyes. I couldn't see them, didn't want to now. I knew they'd be filled with hurt, or contempt, best left in the dark. It was an opening. I had to take it. I dodged away, snatched up the Sharps, edged to the door, slipped out into the uncaring world. I kept my face to the shed, hoping that maybe—

(I loved this man who repeatedly opposed me. And because the war had pierced holes in my heart, turned it into a leaky boat, I needed firm ground on the shore. Hadn't G'Pa tried mighty hard, in his way, to be the safe harbor I needed? And I was like him, in a way. Oh, I was mostly like my pa, no mistake, but a chip off the older block, too? My pa was gone from me. But my grandfather was not, at least didn't have to be, if I chose not to go. But hadn't I already made up my mind about that?)

He did not come out. And me, I couldn't go back. I waited a few seconds longer, just in case, then backed up some more, squishing an apple with the heel of my boot. And still he didn't come.

There seemed to be no life in the shed—at least not much—only what my ears could barely pick up: a convulsive working that must have come from G'Pa, a thin, racking, faraway sound.

Finally, I turned my back on the shuddering near silence in there and tried to blink away whatever was burning my eyes. I reached for the hoe, remembered something, the ramrod. I'd left it back in the shed, just dangling.

Chapter 7

Taylors Landing Road can be nasty on your feet; it needed repairing: pointy little rocks, hard-rutted dirt, and holes the size of chamber pots. And worse, the dew made it slippery, which wouldn't go away till the sun had been up an hour or so. Now, two weeks into September, it didn't rise so early; it seemed almost reluctant to come over the rim of South Mountain, looming to the east.

There was hardly any light to see me off. My boots kept stubbing into things as I scuffed away from Reel's barn. I was sodden from head to foot; my clothes were clammy against my flesh. Letting loose of the rifle and the hoe, I hugged myself, found no warmth at all. I was free of Ty's gore, at least my skin, not so lucky with my clothes. The nightmare itself, it wouldn't scour.

No soap, just plenty of scrub, and numbing well water from the wobbly lift pump outside the barn. All night long, the unforgiving hay kept prickling me away from the sleep I craved. Ol' Poke, our mule, had grumped at my intrusion into his stall but had banged the slats only two or three times and kicked me only once. My only company now was a half-awake rooster and hazy kitchen smoke. Best not get comfortable with normal things.

Get rid of the gun. The hoe, too. Jeremiah, first-off, get that nuisance off my plate. Then dump off Josh Newcomer's Sharps—the Judge's house, on the quiet, slant the gun against the door. So now, across those lifeless stubble fields, an unavoidable quarter mile, quickest way down to Piper's farm, sun trying to flush up, more crimson now, glinting across the cutoff grain, still brittle beneath my boots.

Naw! Naw! Blasted crows! Always flighty and riled about things, forever agitated, never satisfied.

Why the collywobbles? The closer I got to Piper's, the more my belly resisted my steps. Because I'd not had a decent meal?

Toss the hoe over the fence? Uh-uh. Make a proper job of it. Set it back. As if I'd never filched the useless thing. Useless! The way Jeremiah worried his shoulder with it you'd think he needed it to stay alive!

(Is he what he appears to be? A walkabout ninny? Spit on a skillet? At least on the surface. But underneath? What he lets you see, is he just pulling wool over your eyes? Yet beneath all the flummery, he appears unflappable, which is odd, in a world where white folks have the whip hand. A runaway slave, who'd stopped running, because of G'Pa, who I'd left all alone in an empty shed.)

Good to know that Jeremiah hadn't the power to stop me, even if he snared me before I really got going. Course, all he could do was toss around words in his roundabout way (and fix you with a sizing-up eye that went clear to your soul).

I stashed the rife in a patch of weeds, slipped over the fence, and crossed a meager cow path that came down off the pike. Moving on the balls of my feet to the backside of the henhouse, I stopped and bent my ears.

No telltale noises, no human stirrings, only lazy chicken sounds. I moved around to the front, froze for a moment, holding my breath. Nobody. A good sign. Jeremiah wasn't the only one could slink around like a fox.

Less queasy by the second, I leaned the hoe, gently, in the exact same—

"Much obliged!" The voice came piping from apple trees a dozen paces away. I flinched, wanted to draw into myself like a turtle.

"Must've mislaid the thing," warbled the voice. "A bad habit, it is, lettin' things that are good slip through your fingers. Folks might take a notion that I ain't so loony, after all, ifn they find me without my hoe. Ifn I'm loony, I must be harmless, hmm? But that ain't the onliest reason I haul it around. How can I be hoin' the dirt empty-handed? Can't be turnin' the garden over in my mind, can I now? Not to mention pokin' after Mr. Henry Piper's pigs when they go to rootin' his vegetable patch."

"And always toting that blasted thing around like it's the difference between life and death! What about that? And what about my grandfather laying his life on the line? Because of you! Nobody will tell me! And now that I'm going—"

I squatted in the dirt and waited for answers. It didn't matter how long it took, since I was going.

Jeremiah came and hunkered down beside me. He stared at his hoe, finally reached for it, as if to an old friend. "Take this-here piece of business. 'Mongst other things, it allows me to earn my keep round here."

I took a long breath, let it back out. As usual, he wasn't going to tell me a blessed thing.

"I don't jus' tend chickens, you see," he wandered on. "Take them vegetables yonder. Turnips an' carrots an' beans. Better tendin' the beans than spillin' the beans. Which is to say, there's things I gotta keep to myself. Your granddaddy, he's the one to be tellin' you 'bout layin' his life on the line."

Best keep the talk off G'Pa. It would unsettle me further and no telling when I would see him again. Challenge Jeremiah instead. "All you ever do is bamboozle me!"

"Maybe you bamboozle yourself, Young John. Appears you ain't gonna learn your necessentials till you go through the fire an' out t' other side."

"Through the fire?"

"I'm takin' bets it'll be that way, flamin' up an' smokin' off the way you do. A life an' death way of doin' things." He patted the hoe, lovingly ran his fingers over the toil-worn shaft. "Now, my long-handled friend here is a life an' death thing. It's the onliest weapon I got, 'specially when I go to warrin' with weeds. Ain't life the same? Bad things always gangin' up on the good, an' usually stayin' one step ahead? Which is to say, the good has to cut on through," he made a little slicing motion, "or cut an' run," and now he made running motions with his fingers. "Do you follow me?"

"I, uh, don't get what you mean."

"In some folk's eyes, slaves is unworthy. Weeds, you might say. But what if we ain't weeds? What if we's crops?"

"What do weeds and crops have to do with me? Or with my grandfather? Or with that man who chased you here? Or with life and death things? Or with anything?"

"Young John, I can't chew but one pickle at a time. Follow me now! Crops is good! Weeds is bad! Your granddaddy, now he's a good man. A crop an' a half. An' that big-booted chasin' down feller, he ain't but a weed. Slavery too. Slavery is weeds! Everyone's lookin' so hard at their turnips an' carrots—their Unions and Confed'racies—they ain't seein' that weeds is killin' their crops."

"My grandfather doesn't have any crops, just apple trees."

"But he's got his necessentials. He's fightin' 'gainst weeds!"

My head was spinning; the birds in the henhouse were nervous now, nothing but cackle. But wasn't there more to find out, before I took to the road? "What about the Confederates, like my pa? They believe they're fighting for their rights, their independence, their—"

"Oh, they be fightin' an' hurrahin' for sure! Union folks, too! But they ain't none of 'em lookin' 'neath the skin of their crops. Weeds is growin' under there!"

"So how can you tell a crop from a weed, tell good from evil?"

Jeremiah, in what appeared to be a deliberate motion, ran a stubbed finger up under his eye patch and worked it gingerly. "Some folks is keepin' turnips an' carrots, while tryin' to keep slaves at the very same time. Now turnips an' carrots, they grow together in fine fettle. But slaves, they don't grow healthy with nothin'! When one thing purely ruins t'other, it's easy to see what's a weed. Choose yourself a good crop. But ifn weeds is always messin' things up, bes' be cuttin' 'em out!" And again the little slicing motion.

I lowered my hat to keep the now-brilliant sunshine from plaguing my eyes.

Jeremiah jabbed a gnarled finger under his eye patch again. The movement brought an itch to my curiosity. There was something I had to know, had been afraid to ask, was still a little afraid to ask. Last chance.

"You, uh, never told me about that patch, your eye."

Jeremiah's face lit up, like he was relieved I had put the question to him; then his mouth went stiff. "Through the fire, an' out t'other side. Didn't I say somethin' of the sort?"

I nodded and waited. As I waited, he reached down for an apple which at some time had rolled from the orchard, fetching up to the henhouse wall. It was dusty, a little bruised. He picked it up, carefully wiped it on his sleeve, and placed it in his pocket.

"Through the fire?" I prompted.

"Some things is worth savin'. Other things is worth givin' up." He had a dreamy look, if a single eye could mirror such. He made another move to his eye patch, the finger stopping this time, dropping, fragile as ash, to the dirt at his feet. Slowly, he began to scratch in the soil.

"What are you doing?"

"Writin', I am." And he was, now that I studied the frail impressions in the earth. Carefully, unwaveringly, he spelled it out: S-H-I-P-L-E-Y. I looked at his eye, searched more deeply into it, and beheld agony but undeniable pride as well.

All because he could write a little? I looked again. The eye was filling, tears welling up, spilling down his grizzled cheek, a solitary blot damping the unsettled earth near his hand. I had to turn my face, to study the apple trees.

"My wife, she could read an' write a bit," he resumed. "But she couldn't let on, you see. I surprised her one time. Readin' at her Bible, she was."

"So? Why was that so almighty earth-shaking? And why couldn't she let on?"

The man's shoulders sagged; his fingers quivered like the wings of a resting butterfly. "Readin', it ain't allowed, nor writin' neither. Ifn a slave could write, why, he might hornswoggle a white man, maybe scribble out a safe-conduct pass. An' ifn he could read, he might improve his mind or cheer his soul. Ifn a dog could read an' write, it might look for somethin' besides a bone to chew. Breakin' them readin' an' writin' rules can bring down a flame of hatefulness, on anyone bein' in the middle of that!"

"What about going through the fire?"

Jeremiah appeared not to hear me. "My wife, I made her teach me to read an' write. On fire, I was, to improve myself. Bad mistake." He began to rapidly blink his eye, then clamped it shut, and finally scrubbed at it. "One time, before she was sold off far away, she was Bible readin' to me." His voice caught, grew heated again. "We was prayin' together, reachin out to the Lord, to cheer ourselves. The overseein' man done found us out. Bein' a slave makes you a good cash crop. But this time, you see, money weren't the reason my wife was sold!"

I thought he was done; his eye was still closed tight, his lips forming silent words, his face turned toward the risen sun.

I started to ask a question but stopped myself. Good time to be off, on my way finally, why wait? I began to hoist myself. He reached out an arm and held me back. "You gotta hear the all of it. Bein' as you fancy the fire so much."

I sank back down. A white chicken jittered past us, jerking its head as if dodging a blade.

"Searchin' for truth puts a man on the road to bein' free, Young John. 'Cause when you know the truth, you know what good an' evil's about. That's why we started our Bible readin', needin' to be on that freedom road. When my wife was sold, she hushed her Bible into my hands. Made me take it. Made me promise to keep on readin' an' prayin' with our little girl, that daughter she'd never see in this life no more. I done it too! Even knowin' what hellfire might come my way. For her, I done it. Bye an' bye, they found me out an' took that Bible. I stole it back, so then they took—"

This time, he didn't stay his finger. Without warning, he reached and pulled the eye patch up. *Ohhh!* All at once I was unable to swallow, a horseshoe seemed to have clamped onto my throat. In spite of that, I ordered my eyes to not look away.

He held the eye patch up no longer than you'd take to cut off a chicken's head, and in that instant, I lost control of my eyes. I blinked up at the sun, cut to the ground, and found a spot of wetness on the grimed leather of my boot. I hadn't felt it fall.

For several seconds, we sat in silence. The other tipless finger? No. Not now. Not yet.

Switch the talk to something else, anything else: "So you think my going off to the war isn't right?"

"Your war ain't gonna prove who's right, only who's left, when the fightin's done."

"You're always making me put my foot in my mouth!"

"Ifn the shoe don't fit, Young John, only you is knowin' the pain." Somewhere in the apple orchard, a chorus of crows jeered at my clumsy words. "Reckon I heard me a gun poppin' off last night," Jeremiah offered, letting his eye wander over my blood-stained clothes, looking away from me then, searching pretty hard for crows.

I felt a flush blaze up from my breast, felt my cheeks ignite, managed to bob my head, then senseless words flooding out, a bursting dam of words of how I'd shot my friend.

The knarred hand hovered a moment, then found my shoulder, the fingers weightless as falling leaves. "So now you're goin'," he said softly. "I understand. Maybe it's best. Maybe I'd be goin' my own self, to oppose you, ifn black flesh was allowed inside a blue uniform, an' black hands was allowed to hold a gun. Course, that won't happen till white folks is able to tell crops an' weeds apart."

As I groped for words, a sudden snorting and scrabbling erupted out behind the henhouse. We jumped to our feet, ran to the noise. We were confronted by two spotted pigs, their eager snouts dripping with muck. The vegetable patch was rooted up, the earth savaged.

"Don't that beat all," said Jeremiah, lifting his arms in mock surrender. "Reckon someone's in over his head this time." I don't think he meant that he'd forgotten his hoe, he wasn't even looking at the pigs. He was looking at me. He stuck out his hand. "Can't be offerin' much. Only luck. An' prayers, bright as fire."

When his gnarled fingers let loose of mine, I knuckled my nose and my eyes, then wheeled away. I trudged back to the fence, reached for the Sharps. The pigs still were making a stubborn racket. But so was Jeremiah, grumbling and stomping through the vegetable patch. It sounded like he'd got his hands on the hoe again and was poking at pigs as best he could.

*****

The day had turned steamy. My boots were so hot I could have baked beans in them, which might have been messy without fresh paper up front of my toes. I grimly thought of Harper's Ferry: long, foot-weary miles away.

Back in town, folks strolled beneath the shade trees; horses plodded down dusty streets; dragonflies hovered, idling. Just another lazy day.

I cradled the rifle in both my arms, pushed my boots through clinging dirt, and headed for Main Street, Judge Crockett's house.

I hid myself in shadow, behind an enormous maple tree. For several minutes, I studied the windows and watched the door. Time flew by. Unable to keep my boots from dragging and scuffing the gravel, I made for the steps, tiptoed up to the door, and propped the gun.

I was halfway back down the steps when a white bundle of fur came tearing out from the back. Wags took one look and began to bark. I searched for a ball to throw, a stick. The door flew open; the rifle went thudding. Betsy stepped outside.

She stood looking down at me, her arms folded. She had on an oversize apron, and her sunbonnet was all frilly around the edge. Neither matched the color of her eyes. She stooped, took the rifle in tow, and looked pointedly at me, then at the Sharps.

I swung my eyes back at her, found her frowning. "Johnny Shipley, I have to talk to you!" She made an even more sour face, let the Sharps go clumping onto the porch, gently gathered up the dog, cooed him into the house, and slammed the door. Prickly as a hedgehog, gentle as a swan! For the first time that day, I think, I smiled.

"This isn't funny!" she declared, grabbing my hand. I pulled it away, but she grabbed it back. I allowed her to drag me out to the street. Turning right, she began to walk briskly, hauling me with her. "It's no more than a block," she announced, pointing to a white building with a boxy tower. "We attend services there at St. Paul's. It's the very best place I know for getting things straight."

Settled into a pew, I made a point of squaring my shoulders. My mind was already made up, wasn't it? Nothing she could do or say? Besides which a slip of a girl would have no notion of why I was going. Funny she knew I was going at all.

A stained-glass window was cracked open. Sound drifted in with the stifling heat, low, worshipful tones from the graveyard next to the church: "*The Lord gave, and the Lord hath taken away—*"

"Hurry up and have your say!" I told the girl.

For two or three minutes, Betsy didn't open her mouth. She could at least stamp her foot, flounce her curls, or prattle some girlish poppycock. She only stared at her hands, clasped in her lap. Course, I could keep my mouth shut too and didn't have to tell her a blasted thing about what I meant to do or why.

I turned my head away and waited and waited. Finally, I stole a look. Her head was lowered; her eyes were closed. First Jeremiah, now Betsy. Too much praying going on! I shuffled my boots. It must have brought her back.

"I guess I won't even try talking you out of it," she said as she twisted her apron. "Your grandfather already tried that, I suppose?"

I only nodded, taken aback that she wasn't exploding with tears or some other predictable nonsense. There was no challenge in her eyes as she looked straight at me. And then she said, "The way you were talking the other night, about slavery and fighting, your words sounded kind of toplofty."

"Top what?"

"Now don't get mad, but your words seem to march out like soldiers and then just sort of fall down flat. High and mighty words that don't stand up real well. Toplofty, if you see what I mean. Because, deep down, you know the war should be about something more than you say it is. Isn't that so?"

I didn't need to answer, of course. Weren't her words as toplofty as mine? With no warning, she took hold of a slender gold chain at her throat, drew it up over her head, and held it out.

I frowned at the tiny gold cross. "Wh-what's this for?"

"You don't have to wear it right now. It might not even fit. But maybe it will help you, where you're going."

I attempted to give it back. She simply raised herself up and sat on her hands. She was smiling, not what you'd call a happy smile.

"I'll keep it then, not that it'll do me any good." Clearing my throat, I changed the subject: "I figured you'd go hysterical or preachy when you brought me here. But you were mainly calm and reasonable."

"Oh, that," she giggled. "Well, I know the right words will come out if'l just think of what Grampa would say."

My eyebrows must have shot up a foot. She smiled again, glowing now. "Then I just say the very opposite thing!"

The unexpected whimsy was a sparkle between us, but it flickered out quickly. I squeezed what she'd placed in my hand.

Will help you, where you're going.

Uh-uh. Betsy knew precious little about my going, about what was waiting for me. And the help I needed? I would find it at the business end of a gun.

Outside, the respectful voices droned on and on. Inside, a breeze flew in through the open window—a cool, sudden, summer-dying breeze that whiffled the foxtail pinned to the hat that kept wanting to slide off my knee.

I rose without speaking and made for the door, Betsy's soft footsteps right behind.

The solemn next-door voices were still grimly intent on the business of death. I looked to the south, the way I'd be going. I gave the tiny gold cross another squeeze—but it didn't seem to do any good.

Chapter 8

The Harpers Ferry Road stretched endlessly southward. Deserted. Lifeless as sun-bleached bone. My boots kicked up dust that tasted like chalk but felt like sand when it went for my eyes. It seemed like the road wanted to tug me forward and tease me back.

But back to what? An empty shed? And the frightful news about Ty, it must have spread by now, like foul smoke.

I ordered my boots to get more lively, every step farther away from G'Pa. And yet couldn't I sneak a look back, see how far I'd brought myself? No. Not if I had to slam the door on the past. Still, the quickest look…

I turned and squinted through the afternoon glare. I could spy only the faintest tip of St. Paul's, almost lost to me now, the town itself more remote with every tread of my boots, and me, a shucked ear of corn, stripped of respect, powerless, lacking a gun to show I ready to fight, too dull-witted to fetch along a few swallows of water, a mouthful of food, leaving me hollow and dry as a rain barrel out under the sun too long.

Maybe a near-starved belly brings zest to your nose. Blackberries! I smelled the tang of them before the stickery bush grabbed hold of my sleeve. Not enough grub to crowd a man's insides, but enough to take the grumble from his guts and more than enough to fill his slouch hat to the brim. It didn't take long before my fingers were stained red; and the smudges on my clothes: I was the only one knowing the difference between blackberry juice and—

My boots seemed to move with a will of their own. But soon they became wooden, wanting to stop and take root, so I had to move them by the force of my mind, and my mind was living down in my boots, with their ceaseless tromping, and I felt some inner part of me vanishing, drifting away, like thistledown.

The pulse of my thoughts and the heft of my boots—besides, I refused to look back anymore—played tricks on my ears. The sluggish tread of hooves on gravel was near on top of me. I whirled at the sound.

"Good day to you." The figure on the mule sounded friendly enough. And the lack of expressiveness sounded vaguely familiar, like my grandfather—on one of his better days.

The man wore dust-covered black; dust, too, covered his hat, pulled way down, nearly hiding his eyes, eyes that seemed to flicker amusement as they went from my mouth, to my hands, to my upturned hat stuffed with purplish mush.

I worked my tongue around the slurp of my mouth and put some trim in my backbone. "I'm for Harpers Ferry," I said in a voice that came out higher than I figured it should. "Stonewall's headed there. My pa, he was in the Stonewall Brigade!"

"You are a soldier?" The stranger's voice had a dubious ring.

Couldn't I at least look like a soldier? With a sweaty sleeve, I worked at my mouth, then dumped out the contents of my hat. "I aim to be a soldier," I told him, my hat slanted back where it belonged. "Just like my pa was. The Yankees killed him!"

"I see." The black-garbed man seemed to slump in the saddle. I waited for him to say something more. Only the sound of gravel clopped up by his mule filled the silence. Too much quiet going on! I had talked to no one since Betsy. Friendly words, words of encouragement—any kind of words—that would be heartening, so I told him who I was, where I was from, even threw a thumb in that direction.

"I am sorry if I appear preoccupied, Mr. Shipley, but I was struck by the insistence of your filial devotion."

"My, uh, fil—"

"Filial devotion. In other words, your pertinacious veneration of pa-pah. Something I am able to speak of firsthand. I am headed for Harpers Ferry myself, at least somewhere in that general direction. Only God in his wisdom knows for sure. I am Brother Russell, by the way, from Keedysville, across the creek and up the hill from where you live."

"You kind of look like a preacher." Searching under the shadowy hat, I detected a tight smile, a well-trimmed beard, and a round reddish face.

"A preacher, indeed," Brother Russell replied, tapping a large cross suspended from his neck. His chin had been down so low I hadn't seen it at first. "In truth, a circuit rider," he continued. "Like yourself, I am attempting to follow in the celebrated footsteps of my father. An illustrious man. A bishop, in fact. Preeminent among notables of the United Brethren Church. Resourceful and witty as well. Oh, yes!"

I nodded my understanding. "Sounds like my own pa, in a way. He was the jimdandiest trial lawyer you ever did see! You must be pretty proud of your father, huh?"

I pulled up with a start. Brother Russell had begun to laugh with an energy that made even his mule stop and look back. "Lord, yes!" he declared. "I am in awe of the man! He started out as a circuit rider himself. Swimming swollen rivers, blazing trees so as not to get lost, making his own shoes, repairing clocks for his neighbors, doing menial service in the fields, bounding off to pray and sermonize among the unsaved. Now, he has a three-hundred acre farm and a fourteen-room house. I mean to say the man is a temporal and spiritual success! I ask you, how can I, his son, be anything less? Filial devotion, you understand."

Where were my words of encouragement? I ran a finger under my hat, alarmed when it came back besmeared with blackberry pulp. Jamming my hat down on my ears, I wondered how this gloomy circuit rider could have urgings and uncertainties much like my own. I thirsted to know.

"You look somewhat peaked, Mr. Shipley," Brother Russell remarked as he reached for a canteen hanging from the saddle horn. "A bit on the dry side as well."

He held out the canteen, and I snatched it and sucked it greedily and immediately was coughing and spluttering. "Lordy, what is this stuff?"

Brother Russell laughed softly. "Not branch water, I assure you. My father the bishop is, as you might imagine, an inveterate temperance man. He finds all the fortification he needs in Holy Writ. 'Unthwart yourself!' he tells me. 'Seek redemption!' says he." He paused, his smile fading. "I, on the other hand, find myself taking more crooked steps at times." He hoisted the canteen to his mouth and took a protracted pull. "You see before you, Mr. Shipley, evidence of what can befall a man determined, at all cost, to emulate his father."

My boots kept moving; the mule kept plodding; gritty little plumes kept trying to get in our way. Brother Russell once more had gone quiet, eyeing me from under his lowered black hat. I had to say something: "So, who are you going to preach to? Yanks or Rebs? Must be tons of both down where we're going."

"It does not matter. My father says, 'Preach!' So I preach. Even though, at times, his unceasing directives go against my grain. In any case, the good bishop and I agree that the message is the same for all men, blue or gray, black or white. The message is that enslavement of one human soul to another is abomination in the eyes of our Creator!"

"Sounds like a message for Rebs."

"Not necessarily. President Lincoln insists that this war is only for putting down secession. Are any blue soldiers truly fighting to set men free? And how many of your gray compatriots own any slaves or have a particle of interest in slavery at all?"

I let that bump around in my head. "I guess I sort of thought that the Rebs are fighting for their independence, which is maybe good, and that their slaves are part of that, which is maybe probably bad. It's too confusing. Because the war is not really about slavery, is it?"

"Not yet, Mr. Shipley, not yet. And there is the rub. Most Southerners profess to beat the drum for political separation, while a plurality of Northerners beat plowshares to swords for political union. Most of those patriot souls, however, become quite mute when it comes to slavery. Do you know why?"

I shook my head.

"Because to their politic minds, a slave is nothing more than a bothersome skunk. Refuse to mess with it, and if you are lucky, the creature will not set off a damnable stink. Yet unlike a skunk, a slave is not immune to the stink he is in. God-fearing souls like me—and my father—are not immune either."

"Which means?"

"Which means, most people want to keep the skunk locked up, out of the way. Then you may fight over the protocols of government, not over what writhes and reeks beneath the statecraft and flags and marching bands. A skunk, once out of its cage, you see, can reach you where you live and breathe. And that is unforgivable."

"You're going to preach about skunks?"

"I must at least try! Northerners and Southerners both have had to make hard choices in choosing up sides and in deciding why they must fight. Eventually, however, they must comprehend what is at the heart of it all. The freedom of enslaved human beings! Otherwise, they will continue to tilt at political windmills. Do you know why?"

I blinked my confusion.

"The line of least resistance, Mr. Shipley! Chunks of theory are easier to swallow than morsels of conscience. Men will fight for beliefs they deem to be worthy. But if elements of discomfort stick in their throats, they will cough them up. So, you see, it does not matter to whom I preach. Because, sooner or later, the collective coughing drowns me out."

We plodded on in silence again. Despite the choking dust, I took pains not to cough. But a grumbling belly is hard to hide.

Brother Russell reached into the saddlebag and lifted out the choicest loaf of bread I'd ever seen. He broke off half, handed it to me, then shoved the canteen in my direction. "Pray have another go, Mr. Shipley. Something to wash down my fatuous prattle. After all, who am I to moralize? Notwithstanding my illustrious ancestry, I feel myself not to be cut from ministerial cloth."

I refused the canteen. While chewing, I said, "First you tell me I don't have a good reason to fight. Now, you tell me you don't have a good reason to preach. Your words are toplofty. You go around in circles."

"Going in circles. Yes, that is what I do, mainly. With my mule, if not with my mouth."

"So go on in a different direction!"

Between swallows, Brother Russell appeared to think about that. At length, he said, "I believe in the message I preach. It is the messenger I have misgivings about. If I had had the courage to break away from paterfamilias at your young age, perhaps now I would be marching to my own drum, such as teaching school, lecturing youngsters like yourself, where imparting knowledge does not always precipitate fits of coughing. Perhaps you need a different drum yourself, Mr. Shipley. Do you know why?" Going in circles was still on my mind. I blew out my breath, waiting. "Because nowhere in Scripture does it say, 'Do unto others as they have done unto you.'"

He smiled wistfully and gave his mule a friendly chuck. "I myself, however, remain as stiff-necked as Old Pharaoh here when it comes to seizing the main chance. Still, I have a few ounces of faith to draw upon. And if, as I believe, faith without works is a dove without wings—Hello, what is going on up ahead there?"

I peered through shimmery waves of heat. Yes, a flap of some sort. Giving ear to my droll companion, I'd been more intent on my boots, on the barren brown fields off to the right, on the green mountain wall off to the left, than on the yellow dust cloud lifting over the roadway ahead.

People afoot, riders slouched in their saddles and hunched in their wagons, came dragging toward us. As they drew closer, the travelers looked to be excited, some waving their arms.

One of the less agitated tried to explain: "They closed down the ironworks! The whole Rebel army is on the loose! East of us, coming through the mountain passes. Up north as far as Hagerstown. Up there, too." He swung an arm toward the lofty timbered flank of Elk Ridge Mountain, which, I knew, ran all the way down to Harpers Ferry, where it came to an abrupt and craggy end high above the white-water gorge that compassed the town.

"You left out west," I put in, pleased with the reaction it brought. "Stonewall crossed the river yesterday, at Williamsport."

"If that's so," the stranger replied, "the grease is truly out of the pan. The two of you had best turn around and come with us." He paused, studied the man in dust-covered black. "Unless," he added, "unless, of course, your business is to deal with the dead."

*****

I had been by the busy ironworks before, from the other direction, my trip out from Baltimore in the spring. Now the place was plainly deserted. Three huge waterwheels that provided power for the plant, and for the gristmill and sawmill sharing the site, stood lifeless, the stilled paddles undripping in the lowering sun.

At the edge of the barge canal that hugged the nearby riverbank, a flatboat appeared ready to float away from its moorings. An over-turned casket of nails, lacking most of its contents, rolled a faltering half-circle on the deck, the freed nails imitating the motion, leaning and bumping in the slow drift.

Flopping down, I gulped a mouthful of rust-colored water and gagged. Still, I had the presence of mind to plunge my head and scrub my face, my hair, and the inside of my hat.

Hobbling some—I simply could go no further, not without a long breathing spell—I moved toward the hushed cluster of buildings. Abruptly, I pulled up and tilted my head. "Listen!" I called out, turning my eyes to the south, to the east.

Brother Russell shrugged his shoulders. "Your young ears are far more impressionable than mine. You will partake of your sanguine illusions soon enough, I fear. But partake of something more life-giving first. Here, try another loaf." I took the bread but kept testing my ears: a shudder of something, bumping, jarring.

The shadows grew longer, trembling as a freshening breeze found the leaves. I sniffed the air, smelled sawdust, grain, charred wood, and something more, like smoke almost, a long way off.

With a start, I saw that Brother Russell had climbed back on his mule. For a long moment, he gazed out across a stonework bridge, then farther on down the Harpers Ferry Road. The man was going, leaving me here, in this desolate place, with night coming on.

"A one-day journey, that is what my father instructed," Brother Russell explained. "I would offer you a ride, Mr. Shipley, but Pharaoh here would have none of that. If his burden is too heavy, he has the good sense to throw it off or to dig in until reason prevails. There is a moral there, I believe. Regrettably, I am too stubborn to listen."

The man waved, gave Pharaoh a nudge. After riding off a little distance, he turned back and cupped a hand to his mouth. "Honor thy father, Mr. Shipley. But vengeance is mine, saith the Lord!" And then he made Pharaoh take him away.

*****

The sun ducked behind the darkening trees. I sat hugging myself, looking up at maple leaves—not quite red, but you could tell they were getting ready to fall.

My stomach began its protest again. I picked up the bread, put it back down, and studied my monogrammed boots; the name was getting harder to read. My mind drifted to thoughts of my father. Kernstown. A nameless grave. Shot in the back? Again, I picked up the bread and worked on a mouthful for nearly a minute. It had dried up some and was harder to chew. I spit most of it out.

More wind sighed through the trees. An owl spoke from the pine grove behind me. Other wild voices, my sole company now, began to—

"*Hey, boy.*"

Funny how the wind in the trees can trick your ears, sounding almost like—

"*You, boy.*"

My neck hair prickled. That wasn't the wind and wasn't the owl in the pine grove that came brushing the bushes, scuffing the ground, close-up to where I pressed myself to the unforgiving bark of the maple. Best slow my breathing, show no alarm. I forced myself away from the tree.

"Who... who's there?" I sang out, a little disgusted that my hooting was a near match of the owl.

"Needin' somethin' to eat," the voice came back, nearer now.

"Got me nothin' but crusty ol' bread, sawdusty tastin'."

A sound then that sent an icy shaft through my intestines—a hammer going on cock.

"I... I ain't got me a weapon. Don't mean you no harm." Reflexively, I sucked in my breath, got a good whiff of him, sensed the gun pointing. He sidled closer, finally in front, a scarecrow, in tatters, a forage cap lodged on top. Not much older than me. I tried not to look too hard at the long-barreled musket, at where it was pointing.

"I'll be havin' that bread," said the youth, dropping a hand from the rifle to claw at himself through a rip in his shirt.

"Best be puttin' that rifle aside." I wanted to sound conversational, like someone who'd shared soldier fare before.

"This-here bread ain't so easy to get outside of. Maybe I'll have to hold that-there gun on you, 'fore you'll swaller it down!"

The youth reached out but drew back. "Certain sure you ain't packin' a weapon?" he asked, his eyes never leaving the bread.

Unclenching my fists, I showed him hands that were empty—not even shaky—and told him that I bloody well would have a weapon, just as soon as I got– I stopped mid-sentence, mulled a question, and finally asked it: "You're a Reb, ain't you?"

The youth gave a scornful laugh. "Couldn't you tell straight off? No uniform worth speakin' of. Belly so pinched it don't throw a shadow." He paused, looked me up and down, and let his eyes rest for a moment on my foxtail hat. "Course, wouldn't you be knowin' that your own self?" he resumed, licking his lips, eyes again on the bread.

Why, he mistook me for an honest to god man in the ranks! I adjusted my hat, a little more rakish.

The youth lay down his musket, grabbed the loaf with both hands, and began gnawing and swallowing, his breath a series of grunts and gasps. He sank down next to me and sighed contentedly. "When you ain't et in over two days, bread like this-here puts you in high cotton!" He burped, made an attempt to retrieve crumbs from a wispy beard, darted a look at me, as if trying to make up his mind about something.

He sat swiveling his head like an owl, peering anxiously through the uncertain light. "I, uh, made up my mind when we hightailed it out of Virginia an' took north across the river. Couldn't muster it, though, till we got clean of Frederick Town. Been dodgin' chasers ever since. When, uh, when did you decide?"

"Decide?"

"To skedaddle, of course!"

"You... you mean you're a deserter!"

"Mean to tell me you ain't?" Again, he had both hands on his musket.

My throat constricted. Mistook for a hard-knock foot soldier one minute, for a deserter the next.

"I'm for joining up with Stonewall!" I fired at him. "Same as my pa. He... he wouldn't never turn tail. Me neither!"

"Sounds like you ain't never seen the elephant, bub. I'm for get- tin' as far away from Ol' Jack as my pore bare feet will carry me. If he thought any Yankees was hidin' in hell, he'd foller em there, my brigade in the lead! An' talk about grim. Why, even when there's somethin' to tickle your funny bone, he glums up an' takes to suckin' on lemons! I take me an oath, he's stark-ravin' mad!"

Mad? Couldn't hardly be. Didn't Stonewall turn the Yankees inside out and upside down? It was this deserter who must be mad!

Mad or not, he charged right on: "I was all fired up for bein' a foot-cav'ry man when Ol' Jack come through our town, ever'body hurrahin', 'specially the gals, so me an' my buddies joined up fast as we could. My pa got so eagersome, he joined up, too!"

Joined up with his pa. Maybe not totally mad. Then I sniffed him again, watched him squiggle his toes in the dirt, and heard him force air through the tail of his britches. But even if a little bit mad, why'd he desert? And why wouldn't he stop scratching himself?

The youth wouldn't stop wagging his tongue, either, insist- ing on telling me that "the dysentery didn't do me like it did some, though it was after me fierce an' taught me I'd best wear my trousers half-mast. Prancin' the green apple quickstep, we calls it."

"What did you mean by 'seeing the elephant'?"

"Goin' into battle the very first time, an' it's worser than your worsest nightmare." He started shaking his head, as if to shake away his worsest nightmare. "Can't be knowin' what it's like, till you see it, an' hear it, an' taste it, an'—"

"Taste it?"

"I mean to say! Didn't seem to bother my pa none. But me, that gunpowder, it got in my mouth, an' up my nose, an' in my eyes, an' burned my throat, an' the smell of blood, an' all them mangled bodies, an' the screamin' an' moanin' they set up, all that jus' jumbles together an' gets square inside you, an' the taste of all that is some-thin' you won't never forget, or want to remember, neither!"

"You, don't, uh, have to tell me all about—"

"No, no, I ain't done! It stuffs up your memory too, even when tryin' to sleep it away. Lookee here what I got me down at Frayser's Farm." He jerked off his cap and poked a finger through a circular hole. "I dream about that-there, every single night!"

I looked at the hole but not very long.

"Why, I can still feel that minnie partin' the hair on my noggin! Ain't no glory in soldierin, an' I ain't never goin' back to it! They'll cart me away in a pine box 'fore I do. I ain't like my pa. He's still out there soldierin' somewheres."

"So, you don't want to be with, I mean be like your pa?" There was little thought behind the question. But as soon as I asked it, it seemed terribly important.

"Best you be knowin' nothin' 'bout me, or 'bout my pa neither, in case chasers throw down on you, askin' questions."

"Throw down, on me?"

"They're ever'where. Provost guards. Yeller ribbons round their arms. Course, deserters is ever'where too."

I seemed to lose my eagerness to hear what he and his pa had been through, yet, at the same time, wanted to catch every word.

"Real lucky to slip the noose back there at Frederick, but they come right along too, chasin' after me an' some other fellers what was plumb sick of tastin' war. Almost jiggered me at Burkittsville an' again at Solomon's Gap 'fore they took to the mountain yonder. Now, if I can jus' get me past them bluebellies down Harpers Ferry way, I can swim the river at Shepherdstown an' get back home, to Winchester."

Even in darkness I could make out the dreamy smile that lit up the youth's face when he spoke the name of his town. And this was from someone who'd paraded away to war proudly, along with his pa, who'd shared Stonewall's fame on the glory road.

The Reb from Winchester wouldn't stop: "I jus' gotta make it back there, see. Yanks get me, they'll lock me in some stinkin' prison where I'll rot to death. Rebs get me, they'll shoot me sure, for slippin' the collar an' goin' home. Both ways I'm a deader. All stiffed up in a pine box."

The youth's head began to loll. Worn out from talking? From running? Even running away from his pa?

No longer able to fit my back to the shape of the maple, I went flat to the ground, hands under my head, my hat sloped down to cover my eyes. Everything black, the only sounds the uneven breathing of the Winchester Reb, the wind, the creek.

I found it hard to keep my mind off the way the youth had spoken the name of his town, and the way "pine box" had stumbled off his tongue. And I couldn't get comfortable with an uncommon notion: he didn't want to be like his pa.

Propping my hat back up, I studied the figure beside me. His chin had dropped to his chest, one hand still clutched the rifle, too dark to see the hole in his cap.

The owl hooted again. The wind picked up, discovering leaves right over my head, blowing in grim, persistent, fuzzed-up thoughts: a corded-up chicken, strutting and poking, a black tail flopping, ever so feebly, a church full of Dunkers, excited and moaning. Jeremiah, lifting his eyepatch, poking at pigs.

The poke in my ribs jerked me fully awake. The Reb, too, shook himself, thrust the cap from his eyes, jumped to his feet, scampered for the pine trees, clutching his musket, gaping over his shoulder.

"Halt! I'll fire!"

The Reb from Winchester kept running, stumbling, his voice stuck on a single word. "No! No! *No!*"

The sharp *crack* that followed echoed off timbered rock across the creek. It was followed by the sound of something thumping the ground.

I refused to look. For several seconds, I stared at the dull gray sky and at last brought my eyes back down, to men on horses, three of them, and one more, dismounted, holding something that still showed smoke.

I stared and stared. The horses, stamping and blowing in the cool dawn air, had a gray look about them, and so did the troopers. But I knew they weren't wearing gray.

Finally, I dared myself and stole a look at the youth who'd spoken the word "Winchester" in almost reverent tones. It was only a peek—too quick to see any blood, he looked asleep—yet I could see that he'd let loose of his rifle and lost his cap.

The troopers kept throwing words at me, demanding answers to questions that made no sense; my innards thrummed like piano wires.

"Your brigade, whose is it? What regiment? How many in it? Where is it now? Where is it headed?"

It must be a dream, a horrid dream. My head seemed to belong to somebody else; thoughts and words wouldn't fit in it.

The dismounted trooper threw himself back in the saddle. He reached down, hauled me up behind him, turned, and said, "Reb, some of your grayback friends are no more than a mile behind us, and they'll come on like buzzards at hearing that shot. Grab hold of me now, and don't let go! Reb prisoners who try to escape don't get very far!"

I heard the warning, but the meaning was lost, because I was struck by just one of his words.

Then my backside was bouncing, my legs were flopping, as the horse broke from a trot to a run, and the swing of the horse, the unfaltering hooves, pummeled my brain with the sound of that one word I couldn't escape. Reb. Reb. *Reb*.

Turning my head as I bounced, I tried for one last glimpse of the Winchester Reb.

All I could see was billowing dust and a gray dawn lifting. Now, only one thing struck me as certain. The youth from Winchester would never see home. A pine box? Only if he was blasted lucky.

Chapter 9

Riding full tilt, the riders kept searching behind us. I turned and looked. Where were the Rebs? Had they heard the shot? Were they closing the gap? All I could make out was the tip of a smokestack sticking up from behind a quickly receding screen of trees.

On and on, mile after mile, slowing just a few times, we pelted along the narrow road, the wind playing havoc with the brim of my hat.

Up ahead the sun pushed up from the mountain spine. The morning crackled, louder than the hoofbeats drumming the road. I smelled smoke—it was close! The tiring horses, they must have smelled it, tossing their heads, flinging froth from their bits.

Suddenly, the horses were plunging downhill, and the river was there and the barge canal.

I found it harder to breathe; sulfur-charged air skewered my throat. Now all the riders were coughing. One more time, I tried to make myself heard: "I'm not a soldier!" I called out in a voice made unsteady, I think, by the jaw-jarring ride. Why did they pay no attention? I was only telling the truth.

We careened around a bend in the road, spattering gravel, picking up speed, hugging the bank of the barge canal. In front of us foggy white streamers floated near the crest of a high green scarp, the tops of trees barely visible where they jutted up through the smoke.

Popping peppered the air; the horses shuddered and flicked their ears. I dug my fingers into the trooper and felt wetness trickle down my knees. And I hadn't even seen the elephant yet. My teeth chattered as the horse broke stride.

Barely could I hear the river's rush to our right, on the far side of the placid canal.

Someone seemed to be shaking a giant rattle high up in the dirty, drifting haze.

The horsemen reined in their mounts so suddenly I grabbed more of the trooper to keep from toppling. We turned onto a narrow bridge-like contraption supported by a long line of flat-topped boats. Other blue soldiers were riding or running or dragging across, going both ways, the bridge swaying like a clothesline bumped by mistake.

Downstream, just beyond the bare-boned remains of a railroad trestle, the Potomac and Shenandoah Rivers surged together, thrumming through a gap in the towering Blue Ridge rock. Ahead, bunches of buildings huddled together on the flats next to where the water ran. I had been here before. But the only smoke then had come from a train.

We clattered up off the bridge. The town seemed drained of life. Dignified stone and brick buildings were tucked across the street from the river; tiny clapboard houses were perched on terraces that slanted up sharply.

The troop broke right, pounded along a cobbled street that followed the river; vacant buildings, echoing hollow, discharged the biting smell of a candle just snuffed.

The horses clacked to a stop outside an enormously long brick structure that fronted the river. Heaps of bricks underfoot kept company with the remains of a roof and there in the midst of the rubble, a cluster of scarecrows.

The trooper thrust back a hand and gave me a shove, as if I were no more than a sack of spuds. "In there!" He didn't point, just aimed his chin. I ground my teeth and stepped away from the horse. "Remember what happens to prisoners who try to escape!" he fired at my back.

I turned on him. "How can I be a prisoner? I ain't even a soldier!"

"Course not!" The man gave me a wicked grin, then grinned at the guard posted in front of the makeshift jail. He touched his horse with his spurs and appeared to forget that I was there.

Searching out a solitary corner mostly free of bricks, I eased myself down. My legs had a watery feel; my belly juices were acting up; my mouth was dry as sand.

One of the scarecrows stumbled over and plopped down beside me. Only remnants of cloth covered his feet; he stank worse than the Winchester Reb. I turned away, ran my eyes over the other prisoners, a half-dozen in all. A sour taste came to my mouth. Ragamuffins. Except for one.

The clean-shaven man wore the gray uniform of a Confederate officer; gold loops and coils glinted as he tugged at a crisp, cream-colored hat. He stood apart, sizing me up with eyes as gray as the uniform coat he'd gathered in with a bright yellow sash.

"I'm thinkin' the Cap'n there believes you was planted among us'ns to spy out our plans fer bustin' loose," the unspeakably dirty thing next to me mumbled through a hand partly concealing his mouth. "On account of you don't look like no sojer a'tall."

Folding my arms, I glared at the scarecrow. "My pa was a soldier, an officer, in the 27th Virginia Infantry! Maybe I ain't a soldier yet. But what do you mean, I don't look like one?" I grabbed for my hat to prove that I did. The hat was gone. Somewhere—along the Harpers Ferry Road, I suppose—I'd lost a part of myself.

*****

Sometime past noon, another blue soldier showed up and tossed a wooden box onto the cratered stone floor. The scarecrow beside me jumped up, scrambled forward, his fingers clawing. The other prisoners leaped for the box, shoving, groveling. These brutes were no better than ants! And ants could attack you, a witless mob, out of control.

The scarecrow thrust a hand in the box, grabbed some wafer-like objects, shambled back, and pitched a couple of them at my feet. In disbelief, I watched as he snatched a brick and began to hammer away at his own tiny hoard with the intensity of a cobbler at his bench.

"Hardtack needs a bit of help!" he exclaimed. "But it can stop a minnie at fifty yards," he managed while cramming a wad of the stuff into his mouth. "Now this-here's prime! Ain't fared this decent since gorgin' myself at Manassas Junction nigh-on two weeks past. Been chewin' straws so's my teeth don't fergit their job!"

Could my officer father ever have served with a brute like this? I looked over at the unsullied Captain. Surely, he must be scornful too? The officer, however, reached down and scavenged among the leavings. After wielding a brick of his own, he began to mechanically work his jaws.

I stared at the wafers next to my boot, finally reached for one, and carefully tested it with my teeth. "This is decent grub?" I asked, now testing my teeth.

The man nodded and chewed and swallowed in blissful silence. He picked at his beard, popped a few last crumbs into his mouth. Finally, "Fergit about the worms, them wiggly fellers ain't so bad til we get us some decent meat!"

With a sleepy smile, he leaned back and rested his head on a brick. For a minute or two, I studied his comrades. They were grinning foolishly, smacking their lips; the Captain was dragging an immaculate sleeve across his mouth. Heaving a sigh, I reached for a brick.

Across the river, high up the hill, it sounded like hailstones hitting a barn. The ground began jerking from the deeper thunder of heavier guns. Unaccountably, every fiber in my body insisted on doing the same.

The scarecrow, not flinching at all, was primed for more talk: "Cap'n, he tol' us we gotta kill us some Yankees, not sit around on our tails. There's but one guard, says he, makin' it toler'ble fer slippin' across the river. Lots of our boys t' other side. Onliest thing is, I can't swim a lick. How's about you?"

"I can swim like a fish! But why should I even get wet? I ain't a soldier!"

"So's why's they puttin' you in with us? Ifn you ain't no sojer, yore a spy, maybe. Spyin' fer us, the Yanks'll hang you sure. Spyin' fer them, the Cap'n, he'll snuff you his own self. He's keen fer breakin' out, so's to commence killin' Yankees again."

Something in the man's nonchalant manner riled me. Killing Yankees harum-scarum, coldly, randomly? For me, it was different. Avenging a father. Shipley honor. Brother Russell, though, had knocked some of the props from under that notion. And the Winchester Reb had scraped some of the shine off the glory of being in the Stonewall Brigade. Course, I still had a mission. I'd pledged myself.

My appetite was gone. I tossed the hardtack among the bricks.

"Why tell me your confounded plans about killing Yankees?" I threw at the man.

"Cap'n, he says I got me a overfondness fer talkin' too much, which I 'spose is kind'a possibly so sometimes, maybe, I guess. See, war scrambles a man's brains. Talkin' lets me know I'm still upside a hole in the ground. Cap'n, though, he puts up with me all the same, 'cause I'm sort'a historical-like. Been marchin' with the Gen'l an' croakin' Yankees m'self since even before Ol' Jack got that-there 'Stonewall' moniker at First Manassas, way back at the beginnin' of things."

A Stonewall man? This sorry creature? First, the Winchester Reb and his gloomy tales about tasting war. Now, this smelly, cold-blooded killer. Men who'd fought side-by-side with my pa?

"Up an' down the Valley," the man was running on, "wastin' Yankees, marchin' circles round 'em, whippin' 'em fer fair every time, 'ceptin' at Kernstown, an' that was only because—"

"*Kernstown!*" My outcry caused everyone, including the guard, to turn and look.

The Rebel Captain sprang to his feet, his eyes boring in. The scarecrow appeared as unaware of my flare-up as he was of the relentless racket across the river.

"An' we would've smoked their bacon at Kernstown too," he plunged ahead, "ifn it hadn't been fer that-there-lawyer-type feller a-ridin' up an' a-hollerin' fer ever'body to skedaddle fast. 'We've lost the day, boys!' cries he, a-wavin' that-there gingerbread pistol of his, leadin' the retreat hisself, before he got shot. Why, he—"

"What's going on here?" the Captain demanded, shoving between us.

My heart began dancing a crazy jig; wadding seemed to have got in my ears. Lawyer type? Gingerbread pistol? What could a shreds-and-patches cutthroat know of such things? Besides which, my father's pistol wasn't gingerbread by any stretch. The slightest bit fancy, maybe…

"I said, what the devil is going on?" The officer grabbed me by the shoulders and shook me, as if clearing grist from a gunnysack. "What has Alvin here been telling you? More to the point, who are you, and why are here?"

"I… they just threw down on me, at the ironworks, and hauled me away, when they saw my hat."

"Your hat? What hat?" Tugging at his own, his gray eyes narrowed. "Listen up now," he said, his lowered voice gone icy-cold. "No matter what Alvin here has been babbling about, you had better know that—"

"I won't say a blessed thing, Captain!" I felt a tingle of pride. I was a Shipley, would always be a Shipley, would always be rock-solid dependable! I told him, "My father, he was a Confederate Captain too! He was killed at Kernstown! See, you can trust me!"

For long seconds, the officer glared at me; then his eyes lost some of their glitter. "Yes, I take you to be a gentleman of discretion. However, I would not hesitate to enforce your silence, concerning our plans for getting out of here."

"You Rebs!" A Yank with shoulder straps stood regarding us from out in the street. "Knock off that jawing! And get rid of any fancy notions. We'll gun down the first mother's son even thinking about escape!" The Confederate Captain turned his back, squared his shoulders, and stalked away.

"Now then," the Yank went on, "which of you Rebs is the one they brought in from the ironworks this morning?"

I adjusted my shoulders in a fair imitation of the Confederate officer. The time had come to set things straight. "That would be me. But I'm not—"

"Graybacks! Vermin! That's what you are! And you, you're from the ironworks? Come with me!"

I attempted a look at the gray-eyed Captain, but he was staring out at the river. "I really did have me a hat," I called over my shoulder. Wasn't that more than enough to display my good faith? He turned a hard gaze on me. For a moment, our eyes locked.

Suddenly, my lips went stiff. This Stonewall man, could he have been at Kernstown? Could those judging gray eyes have seen the retreat?

The bluebelly officer gave off jawing with the guard, drew his revolver, let it point the way. It was only fair that I should have questions: "Where are you taking me? Why are you taking me? What did I do?"

The officer slowly shook his head. "Colonel Davis wants to interrogate you himself. Why he wants to parley with small change like you beats the bejabbers out of me. For some reason, he's singled you out. Said it's almighty important and not to keep him waiting. Move now!"

We went back past rows of empty offices and shops, the stone and brickwork fractured in places, our steps echoing off interior walls, a dull undertone to the thunder and rattle across the river.

Turning uphill, we continued past houses that showed no life. A droop-tailed dog lifted his leg and scurried away, my own legs like matchsticks the higher we climbed.

In not much more than a half hour of leaving the jail, we came within range of a vast village of tents, on higher ground up behind the town. I put on as grim a face as I could. I was square in the camp of heartless devils—the enemy that had snuffed the life from my pa!

As I swung my eyes to the smoke-veiled bluff on the other side of the river, I was nearly mowed down by a raucous jumble of bluebellies; most were out of uniform, and several wore nothing above the waist. Armed with nothing but sticks, they converged on a bush, whooping and hollering, and at once, a terrified rabbit ran out, the whooping and hollering in hot pursuit.

The Yank officer grunted his disgust. He holstered his revolver and pushed me toward the tents, pitched neatly in rows, spotlessly white in the afternoon sun.

Another ragtag soldier came lumbering up. Ignoring the officer, he shoved a dog-eared volume under my nose. "The Further Adventures of Dick Turpin!" he sang out. "Only a dime!"

The officer shouldered the man aside. Undeterred, the man—no, no more than a boy—was hawking his book to the nearest person within his reach.

Looking as if he'd swallowed a turnip, the officer said, "The Colonel is in that big Sibley over there, the tall pointed tent. Now, if we can just get past these—"

"Hey, rook," a soldier called out to me over his playing cards, "make sure the quartermaster issues you a cane. It's standard gear for sore foots!" His fellow players hooted as if the remark was the most uproarious thing they'd ever heard.

Silently cursing my faltering legs, I cut my eyes away. I wanted to find something choice to fire back at the bumpkins, who surely were ignorant of pine boxes and circular holes in forage caps. I brought daggers to my eyes, looked for someone to feel my wrath. But the whole wolfish crowd appeared to consist of boys with cards; boys with sticks still chasing a rabbit; and somewhere down a long row of tents, the name Dick Turpin was nearly as loud as the frightful popping slapping back across the water.

The shoulder strap announced himself at the entrance to the Sibley before he rudely shoved me through. The hot canvas smell made me want to fend it off with my hands.

"You sure this is the one, Lieutenant?" The goateed man looked a bit like Shakespeare come to life. He sat with elbows propped on a paper-strewn table, looking me up and down with a doubtful expression. "If this lad is a Confederate soldier, I feel certain the Union is secure," he added, dismissing the officer with a half-hearted salute. I felt my face grow hot. Like all the others, this Colonel took me for a tenderfoot.

The man introduced himself: "Colonel Grimes Davis, 8th New York Cavalry, at your service." In conversational fashion, he tossed questions at me: Who was I? How old? Where from? Why had I been at the ironworks?

I lied only about my age and kept mum about the ironworks. Maybe he wouldn't notice.

"My men tell me you claim not to be of the military persuasion." The Colonel appeared amused as he clasped his hands behind his head. "And I'm forced to admit that seeing is believing. But fess up now. When they put the grab on you at the ironworks, you were close company with a Rebel soldier. How do you own up to that?"

"That Reb, your men shot him for no good reason!" I brought up the palm of my hand, tried to cool my face.

The Colonel let out a sigh, pointed to a campstool. "Sit down, Shipley, sit down." Ashamed of my outburst, I sat.

"I'm asking all these questions for a reason," Colonel Davis continued, "and a very good reason it is. But before I tell you the reason, I have to know what manner of man you are."

I shifted on the stool. Maybe, after all, he thought me a man?

"The point is, I must know if you can be trusted." The Colonel's gaze was calculating, seeming to test me for shifty eyes. "You say you're not a soldier. All right then, let me ask you something else, and not just in passing. In what direction is your political wind blowing?"

"I…I'm not passing, uh, blowing any wind."

The Colonel's mouth seemed to quiver some. "Figure of speech, Shipley. I mean, what are your convictions? Even a broth of a boy—that is to say, a young man like yourself—must have convictions about why we are fighting this war."

Convictions? Course, I had convictions. I'd even explained them—or tried to—to my grandfather, to Betsy, to Jeremiah, to lots of folks. Yet in the face of all that, I'd bumped into toplofty words and bothersome skunks, into soldiers too, soldiers no better than vermin, and some, right outside, more caught up in having a lark than in fighting a war. Convictions? They were hard to put into words.

"Let me put it to you another way," the Colonel resumed. "You are a Marylander. Maryland is a border state, still in the Union, yet a slaveholding state as well. Strong ties to North and South both, yet neutral, not committed, officially, to either side. Where does that leave you, Shipley?"

"I, uh, don't know what you mean."

Colonel Davis smiled and stroked his goatee. "Well, neither Abraham Lincoln nor Jefferson Davis will roll a bandwagon past your door and insist that you hop aboard. You are free to make up your own mind where you stand. Unless, of course, you lack convictions and stand for nothing."

I purely did stand for something! My backside, for some reason, was finding it hard to sit still.

"I'm a Southerner, Shipley, from Mississippi. Can you imagine what my family, my friends, think of me now? Yet here I sit, arrayed in the blue of my Country. My Country! Your Country, too!" Now the Colonel himself was red in the face.

"You can hang your talk on the hook of states' rights or on the certitude of the Constitution," he pressed on. "There are worthy arguments for both points of view, I admit. But a true patriot must cut to the core!" He made a slashing motion, then looked away, dismayed, I think, by his volley of words.

I had a weighty notion myself: "Sometimes you can't cut to the core. Sometimes, knowing your convictions is like peeling an onion, gradual-like."

There was a touch more respect in the Colonel's eyes. "Shipley, have you peeled the onion?"

"Maybe. A little. I know there's more to this than political wind. Slavery! Isn't that what's at the core of the onion?" Making sure that he saw it, I raised my arm and slashed it down.

I waited for the Colonel to voice or nod understanding, and waited some more. He put on a frown, his fingers at work on his goatee. "I cannot disagree with such cogent reasoning," he said at last. "But isn't there something you have left out? Something even more compelling?"

I shrugged my shoulders.

"You have left out the fact that the South will never fight to abolish slavery. And if slavery, as you seem to think, is at the core of it all, at least some people in the North have already cut their way there."

The hot, stuffed smell of the canvas made it hard to think. I tried to recapture my father's face. What would he have said about slavery? G'Pa, Jeremiah, Betsy, and Brother Russell—their faces, their words, were clear in my mind. My father's—?

The Colonel wouldn't give up the attack: "Shipley, there is a question you haven't answered yet."

The tent was stifling. I squirmed on the stool.

"You were holed up at the ironworks with a Confederate soldier. How come? More to the point, why were you there at all? The truth now!"

Yes, the truth. But wouldn't the truth brand me a Southern sympathizer, maybe a Rebel myself? There was another truth, though—a truth building somewhere inside me, a truth that cut through all the talk, close as a heartbeat, clean at the core of my own understanding, beyond what I felt or thought about slavery, more important than Johnny Shipley becoming a man. G'Pa was in danger! He himself had touched on the fact. And Jeremiah, he'd told me so! Me, I'd been too took up with myself to listen or care, to be nothing more than a little curious about Barbara Reel's ominous words—a killer, gunning for Shipleys. G'Pa, now all by himself. And me, fussing and fuming with scarecrows, with bluebellies, unable to help. I had to get home! Somehow.

The Colonel kept coming back to the ironworks: "You know the place. Correct?" Why was he so up in arms about the ironworks? Did he intend to go there? If so, why? Didn't matter. The ironworks was on the way home!

"I, uh, I work there, part-time, sometimes." I looked the Colonel in the eye briefly, then took great interest in his papers and maps. "When I'm not in school," I thought I should add, while crossing my fingers. "There's no schoolmaster now. He went off to the war."

"And that Confederate soldier at the ironworks?"

"He was a deserter. Really caught me off guard. He took my food."

"Yet you remained behind, side-by-side with this Rebel deserter, after everyone else had fled the place. Explain that away if you can."

Pleased that my imagination was working so well—it wasn't so awfully much of a lie—I reckoned I should add the clincher: "I was way over by the barge canal, loading nails onto a flatboat, when I, um, sprained my ankle—you must have seen me limping when I came in—and by the time I got back, every man-jack had high-tailed it out of there, because the Rebs were coming."

Encouraged by the officer's nodding, I hurried to make one more compelling point: "I figured I'd wait till morning, though, till my legs…I mean my ankle…were better. Then that deserter threw down on me and snitched my bread, because he was starving. I felt sorry for him, so I just let him be."

I felt I'd told the story so artfully, I nearly believed it myself. Colonel Davis continued to stare at me. "You find any merit in what I was saying? About our Country? About patriotism?"

Patriotism. Yes, surely it was important. But not nearly as important for me, at this very moment, as getting back to G'Pa. I began to nod my head, tentatively at first, then, I hoped, with convincing assurance.

"Splendid!" The Colonel beamed and gave his fist an exultant shake. "Exactly what I hoped for! Now I'll get to the point of why I called you here. Come with me a moment."

Stepping outside, Colonel Davis took me to a spot where the slope bumped up into a little rise. He handed me his field glasses and pointed to the south, to a lofty green eminence on the far side of the river. "Have a look up there," he said. "About halfway to the top. What do you see?"

I swept the hill. "I see oceans of trees and some big craggy rocks and—Wait! They're waving flags. White flags. Are the Rebs up there surrendering?"

The Colonel gave a humorless chuckle. "They've been at it, off and on, for hours. Surrender? We're the ones that likely will have our arms in the air and soon! In all probability, they're signaling to their own forces. Up there." He turned and pointed to more elevated ground, a long way up past the city of tents. "Gentleman by the name of Jackson, I believe."

I gaped at the hazy strip of trees in the distance, then forced my attention back to the high green hill across the water. The flags had gone to flapping like pillowcases in a blustery wind. I heard the Colonel gasp, quickly followed his eyes to the north, where banging had been going on since morning, where smoke hung in tatters in the cloudless blue sky. Immediately, I had the field glasses up, but the officer snatched them. "Heaven help us now," he groaned, then hissed through his teeth.

Slowly, he handed the binoculars back. I grabbed them, brought them to bear on rooftops down in the town, then out to the river, at last trained them on the splinter of bridge supported by boats.

All this should have nothing to do with me. But that bridge did. And so did the Colonel's cavalry troop. Maybe my only way out of this mess?

Blue figures came pouring across the bobbing pontoons, flooding into the town. A few seemed unable to move very well, and a few of them spilled into the river, thrashing, floating.

"Checkmate." The Colonel's voice sounded weary. "They've got us on every side. Now, with the bridge all but lost—"

He took the binoculars from me. He studied the wild procession for a minute or more. When he brought down the glasses, there were sparks in his eyes. "No! By the eternal, there's still a chance!"

The weariness had vanished; he was looking hard at me, his eyes so calculating I had to look away. I was in for it. I knew it. Not just because of the ironworks, either.

Something more. Much more.

I stole a glance at the man and saw him start to open his mouth. *Whoosh.*

A great rush of air smacked by our heads, the ground heaving and shaking, nearby a volcano of earth and smoke shooting up. I blinked and spat; dirt gritted my eyes and fouled my mouth. No flags waving now, only tiny puffs, little white flowers blossoming fast as they punched out of the green where the flags had been. All around us tents quivered and jumped; some lost their support and flopped to the ground. The booming grew louder; my eyeballs tried to bounce in my head. The Colonel was yelling, I couldn't hear what, and nothing made sense: some men for some reason weren't moving at all.

Suddenly I was on my feet running, running after the Colonel, and the Colonel was shouting at me and at people who'd stopped chasing rabbits and had thrown down their playing cards, and finally,

I heard what the Colonel was shouting, and I obeyed without thinking: "Run! Run!"

Caught in a clot of scrambling feet, I tumbled down a shallow ravine that cut through the slope. I could do nothing but tumble and roll covering my head with my arms as I rolled, my ears rammed full of shouts of rage and disbelief, shouts that contended with whizzing metal a few feet up. I looked up at the sky and saw something angry flash orange and come all apart, and a huge hand grabbed the ground and shook it, flinging more dirt.

Where was the Colonel? What had he been about to tell me before the world went to pieces? I couldn't tell where he was. I had squeezed my eyes shut and clamped my hands hard over my ears. Seeing the elephant. Wasn't that only for soldiers?

*****

My hands had gone stiff; my ears were numb from pressing so long. I opened my eyes. The light was stabbing. Stiffly moving figures had already begun to crawl and stagger up the ravine. I waited, almost till last. No telling what you would see up there. Daring myself, I hooded my eyes and took a quick look. Drat! So much for daring myself.

Not ten feet away, a tight group stood craning their necks and cocking their heads at a form on the ground. The arms and legs were crooked, as if caught in the act of running, running as I had been running but coming up short by just a few feet.

The face, thankfully, was hard to see, turned away as it was. But I saw enough: a young face; maybe, like me, too young for a blade. And a few inches away, a dog-eared volume, the words "Dick Turpin" still visible where the cover was creased.

Watching from a safe little distance, I sighed my relief that the youth was even more nameless than the Winchester Reb. But then came the murmurs: "Jeremy, it's Jeremy, Jeremy James."

I got bumped from behind. But for that, I might have gone back down the ravine, to get away from the sight, from the sound of the name, from the memory—short-lived though it was—of Jeremy

James. And in spite of it all, I couldn't help wondering: Where had the fatal metal struck? Was there blood to be seen? And I couldn't help thinking: could've been me.

I had no trouble finding the Colonel. His Sibley still pointed straight up; most of its neighbors were drooping or down. He stood stiffly erect, his elbow atop a folded arm, his chin atop a fist. Spying me, his demeanor changed abruptly: "Shipley! Did you take a hit? You look a bit gimpy."

I braced myself and shook my head.

"Good, I'll get right to the point. There isn't much time." He steered me inside, rustled his papers, and singled one out. "Here's the situation," he said, smoothing a map with particular care, "and it involves you." He looked up, his goatee pointing straight at me. "Here we sit, in a bowl. Jackson is up there behind us, on Bolivar Heights. The enemy is also on our immediate flank, on Maryland Heights, right above that pontoon bridge." He stabbed the bridge with his finger. "No need to tell you, I think, that they have well-sighted guns on all of those heights."

"So, there are heights all around us. Aside from the fact that nobody can get out, what does that have to do with me?" At once I was sorry I asked. I wasn't sure I wanted to know.

The officer began to breathe faster. "It has everything to do with you! At least for me and my men it does. This garrison is surrounded, penned up, doomed! Tomorrow, if we hold out that long—and it may be sooner—that plunging artillery fire will only get worse. Fact."

"I still don't see what—"

"I have already proposed to Colonel Miles, the post commander, that I saddle up my cavalry troop and break out of the bowl! My troopers and mounts—all fifteen hundred of them—are champing at the bit! Because if we don't escape this sorry mess, we'll all be captured or cut to pieces! Only two things need to be settled. One, Colonel Miles refuses. Says not a single man may abandon his post!"

My stomach was knotting up fast. Somehow, incredibly, I was part of a scheme that already had gone down in flames yet a scheme with very live coals. Still, if it had something to do with getting me out, with getting me back home to G'Pa—

"Shipley, there is a shot I haven't fired yet. It could be dangerous. But it is essential. I'm convinced of it!" He paused; his look was unsparing. "On top of the arguments I have already made, I aim to make a case for military necessity. That's where you come in. The ironworks! You know the place intimately! Our intelligence operatives report that the Confederates are about to seize the complex. It is also reported that the ironworks is the only hot-furnace facility hereabouts capable of forging steel bands for Parrott guns!"

The ironworks. A dangerous plan. All because I'd said something about loading nails onto a flatboat. "P-Parrott guns?" I hoped the Colonel didn't see my expression.

"Cast iron and rifled. Tubes strengthened by a wrought-iron band shrunk to the breech. Parrotts, they're called. The South would dearly love to get its hands on the place. Their best ordnance comes from what they import from Europe or capture from us. Shipley, the ironworks must not fall to the enemy!"

The Colonel had gone to pulling his goatee. "Shipley, my men are the only Federal troops with the logical and logistical capability of reaching the ironworks before the Rebels seize the place and fortify it. But if we can get out, over that bridge, and get to the ironworks before they do, we can maybe shorten the war. We can blow up the foundry!"

My belly was pretty empty, but whatever was in it wanted out. The Colonel didn't seem to want to look at me when I told him, hopefully, "Colonel, this, uh, blowing up the foundry has nothing to do with me, though."

As if talking to himself, he said, "Chances are the secesh will come after us, but if my plan falls into place, we'll have maybe ten minutes to set the charges and hotfoot it away. Do you get the picture?"

I was getting the picture. I desperately wanted to get out of the tent. What did I know of the ironworks? I would quickly get lost. That bridge? It was already lost.

"That's where you come in, Shipley. You are the only one I can turn to who knows the ins and outs of the ironworks. It sprawls all over the place. We've got to make straight for the foundry, know the right entrance, get a fast fix on the set of the furnace, and blow the thing to kingdom come! All in ten minutes. All in the dark. Without you, it simply cannot be done!"

I had a serious urge to get up and get through the entrance. Colonel Davis placed a restraining hand on my shoulder. "I know you are man enough for the job," he said. "And the fate of my entire troop rests in your hands. Now, if I can only convince that ornery, aimless post commander."

I was convinced that he would. The Colonel must have been convinced as well. He drove a fist into his palm, again and again and again.

It was only then, when things couldn't get any worse, that something crashed into my mind. The Colonel had said that only two things had to be settled. Convincing the post commander was one of them. He hadn't told me the other. I had an ominous feeling.

Chapter 10

"The secesh, up on those heights, above that bridge." The Colonel spoke as if to himself. I attempted to catch his eye; he made a point of looking at his map, drumming it with his fingers.

Finally, slowly, he lifted his eyes. I tightened my bowels. The second thing that had to be settled—I knew that pin was about to drop.

"No moon tonight." His terse words sent my bowels to quivering. "But as long as the Rebels are up there—" He suspended the sentence, his eyes looking straight into mine.

I took a deep breath. "As long as they're up there, all those cannons aimed at us and aimed at the bridge. We'll never get out." Though my words came out in halting, short little bursts, I knew I'd said what he wanted me to.

"Shipley, you've got it! But there may be a way to get the enemy off of there, if—"

The Colonel had a knack for leaving things dangling. I said, "It has something to do with me, doesn't it?"

He dropped his eyes, resumed his drumming, and stroked the point of his beard. "Although you have seen the fires of hell already today," he said, still looking away from me, "there may be a way for us—for you—to get those people off of there. Quickly. Of their own accord."

I tried not to squirm and crossed my legs; my upleg wanted to swing up and down.

The Colonel climbed to his feet and began to pace about the tent.

He had sent out a detachment the previous night, he told me. A Capt. Charles Russell and nine other men of the 1st Maryland

Cavalry. He repeated the name, told me not to forget it. It might "legitimize," he said, my showing up suddenly, when I—

Without finishing the thought, still pacing, he said, "If those ten men—or any of them—got through, they must have reached Federal headquarters by now. Their orders are to tell General McClellan—or anyone with the good sense to listen—that we cannot hold out here more than twenty-four hours."

This still had nothing to do with me...

"Twenty-four hours, Shipley. Then we surrender, all fourteen thousand of us here. Unless their artillery ends things first. "No, I will not give up my cavalry troop!"

Start-and-stopping his pacing, he said, "Captain Russell left at nine o'clock last night, which means the twenty-four hours will be up—" he brought out a pocket watch, "will be up four-and-one-half hours from now. Possibly the post commander will wait till morning before trying to run up a white flag. I can't wait to find out. I will not wait to find out!"

The Colonel stopped his pacing; his eyes blazing, he came and stood right over me. "All of which means we must get the secesh to pull out, fast! 'cause me and my men, we're gonna bust loose. Over that bridge. Tonight!"

"What about that Captain Russell and his men, their going for help?"

"Hopefully, the Captain's tidings—if he gets through—will turn the trick and get us that help. Way too iffy. And time's a-wasting. But we know, from our last patrol, that General McClellan, our estimable but cautious army commander, has—can you believe it—got his hands on a copy of the Confederate plan of battle, back near Frederick Town. Special Orders No. 191, dictated by Robert E. Lee himself. The secesh up there are badly outnumbered. There are Union forces—an entire corps—not an hour's march from their backs!"

I was becoming more and more baffled. He must have noticed: "Shipley, the Rebels have divided their forces. One small piece of their pie is up on those heights. Divide and conquer, that is a basic rule of warfare. We have them in the palm of our hands. Divided! And they have no idea we know their pie is cut!"

I opened my mouth, closed it, tried not to look stupid.

"Shipley, what if they did know we've got their battle plan? What if we make sure that they know?"

I could not sit still any longer. I got up, looked longingly at the Sibley's open flap, and took a step toward it.

One more time I tried to remember my father's face, but his features were dim, far dimmer right now than the Colonel's, his goatee pointing straight at me again. I heaved a sigh and sat back down. "So, Colonel, you want me to—"

"We must get the Rebels off those heights, which means we must give them a good swift kick. Shipley, you've got a stout pair of boots. I want you to take that news that those graybacks up there are about to be pounced from behind and kick it square in their Rebel teeth!"

Colonel Davis might just as well have asked me to abolish slavery or to end the war. I wanted to tell him that none of this had anything to do with me. But for some unearthly reason, he'd already made up his mind that it did.

*****

It made sense, sort of. If the Rebels learned they were about to be jumped from behind—their only route of escape—by an overpowering Yankee force, they would have to skedaddle; they would have to abandon their craggy perch and haul away their wellsighted guns. But it had to be bloody fast!

Colonel Davis was a cagey one. He reminded me that I'd been jailed up with Confederate prisoners, down by the river, prisoners who might accept me as one of their own. Wouldn't that make me sympathetic to the plight of "our" Rebel comrades up on those heights? Wouldn't I be heartbroken, in fact, to have discovered— quite by chance—that "our" compatriots up there were about to be crushed?

I nodded my head, though there still seemed to be loose ends that—

"Shipley, feature this. We send you back to the jail. You contrive to break loose. But those other gray jailbirds are chained. They give you the password through Confederate lines—"

Again, he left the thought dangling. But I was getting his drift.

"Boys run into trouble," the Colonel said levelly, "but when you're a man, trouble has a way of running into you." Yes, if I were a man—

I stilled my jiggling leg, looked up at the Colonel, finally got to my feet, and stuck out my hand. Just before he took it, a shocked expression came to his face. "Shipley, I forgot to ask, must have took it on faith. You, uh, do know how to swim?"

*****

"Those ropes you have on me, they better not be too tight, or I'll never get loose," I charged the same smug Lieutenant who'd marched me up from the jail. "And you'd better be real sure, when you chain up those Rebs, that their locks won't come apart!"

"Yes, yes, the Colonel explained it all to me. You'll slip the knot, no problem. But if you ask me, he's taking a mighty big chance risking the whole show on the likes of you."

I frowned over at the two soldiers he had with him, as they marched me back down to the jail. They gave me a smirk, then gave the chains and shackles they carried a taunting little shake. "You know, you don't have to jab me with that pistol till we get back down there!" I blurted, making sure the scorn in my voice reached the lot of them.

One thing continued to nag at me. I had assured the gray-eyed Confederate Captain that I could be trusted. Yet Colonel Grimes Davis, a Union man through and through, thought the exact same thing. A double-edged sword.

Still, delivering the Colonel's "good swift kick" would save those Rebels up on Maryland Heights from being wiped out. Oh, their gray cavalry patrols might smell out that truth—the Colonel had informed me of that with a cheery clap on the back—but not smell it soon enough to get their Rebel brothers off of there just after dark, when the Colonel was determined to break out of the bowl. For me, the best of both worlds!

Helping both sides! No damage done! Best not think of the ironworks. 'Course, it's hard to think of a place you know nothing about.

A couple of things to remember. A name, Doctor McVay, loyal Union man, many a time come to Harpers Ferry to treat the Colonel's cavalry troop. A place, Sandy Hook, a hamlet, really, where the good doctor resided across the river just about where I would run smack into the Rebel picket line.

All I had to do was get free of my ropes, make it across the river somehow, raise a hue and cry about Yanks closing in, find Doctor McVay—big sign out front—and wait till Colonel Davis's men came there to fetch me. Yes, right. That's all I had to do.

We jangled to a halt outside the jail. Much darker now. White water rushing out there behind the tumble of bricks. Current could sweep me away. Cold as ice water, probably. Legs hadn't lost their watery feel. Quaking down in my guts wouldn't stop. Act like a man. Act. Yes. The pistol jabbed into the small of my back.

Loud objections as the chains went on, the shackles snapped and locked. The gray-eyed Captain, indignant at being chained like a slave, glared at me. "Why are you here? And where are your chains, if I may ask?"

"They thought I knew something about the ironworks. Hey, I don't know a blessed thing about the ironworks! But I got 'em convinced I'm not a soldier. So, no chains."

I grinned. Telling the truth wasn't so hard. "I guess they don't know what to make of me, though. My pa was in the Stonewall Brigade. Remember?"

He'd better remember and pretty darn fast.

"Still and all," I went on, as I'd rehearsed, "I'd much rather be here, than over there." I pointed my chin across the water, lifting it toward trees and rocks higher up, where fires were beginning to flicker, the barest essence of smoke beginning to find its way down to the jail. I peered through the gloom and tried to read the Captain's face.

Blinking, quizzical. Yes. Good.

"You would rather be over here? What do you mean by that?" The Captain was good at asking questions; the voice, though, didn't question; it accused.

"You wouldn't believe the hubbub up at their headquarters," I said, pausing just long enough, I thought, to stretch the suspense. "They were running around like schoolboys, because they've captured a copy of your...I mean, our battle plan. Special Orders No. 191. Our pie is divided, and the bluebellies know it! They have scads of troops on the march, closing in on our boys up there, ready to put a cork in the bottle. It could happen any minute!"

"You can't possibly know these things! They would never say them in your hearing!"

This was going so well I couldn't wipe the grin off my face. "There was so much whooping and hollering. I'm surprised you didn't hear 'em! I might've been a rabbit in a bush for all they cared. Besides, I was right outside the headquarters tent, and the guards, they were all took up with playing, uh, poker, I think."

It seemed like a good time to play my best card. "They sent their chief scout and some couriers—Captain Charles Russell and nine other men from the 1st Maryland Cavalry—to the Yank high command, to rush 'em the news. Uh, Captain! Think I'm loose."

I stopped talking and made a show of flexing my fingers, of being absorbed with picking my nose.

"This Russell, these couriers, what about them?"

I waited a few seconds and closely inspected a fingernail. "One of those ten men, they reckon, is bound to get through, and their message is for the Yanks to attack. Tonight. Before the Rebs...I mean, before our boys over there discover their fat's in the fire."

You'd think I'd just branded the Captain with a red hot poker: he stood there, like a wide-eyed statue, for over a minute.

At length, he looked at me keenly, looked across at the heights, looked over at the guard, and looked back where I stood brazenly rubbing my wrists. Finally, he turned and looked out at the water.

Things were moving fast but not fast enough. Best shake my arms, really relieved at being untied.

"For God's sake, don't do that! Turn around! No, get behind me! Hide your hands!"

"Huh?" I looked as bewildered as I could.

"Your father. You said he was a Confederate officer?"

I nodded vigorously. "A Captain. In the 27th Virginia Infantry. He was killed at—"

"Killed at Kernstown, yes, I remember. You, uh, value your father's memory, his sacrifice?"

I didn't have to act, not now. "It means more to me than anything, almost."

The Captain's eyes went darting again. When they came to rest on the filthy soldier who talked too much, it seemed he must have arrived at the same poser as Colonel Grimes Davis before him: "Alvin over there says he can't swim a lick. Is it true what you told him? That you swim like a fish?

*****

The Captain put stock in me, no doubt of that. His wedding ring was safely jammed in my pocket. And another confidential, vital fact to remember: his brother-in-law, Major Jack Taylor of Cobb's Brigade, 15th North Carolina Regiment, Lieutenant Colonel William McRae in command; he was up there, somewhere among those flickering fires.

"Paddle like fury. Just get across!" the Captain charged me. "Grab the first Confederate officer you find and tell him exactly what you told me. Give him that ring and urge him by all that is holy to get it in the hands of Major Jack Taylor. He and his sister picked out that ring for my marriage. He will know, from the inscription, that it came from me and that your message is genuine. Can you remember all that?"

I repeated it, nearly verbatim, I think. "There is one more thing you had bloody well remember," the officer said. Yes, there was always one more thing. "Lorena," he said.

"Lor--?"

"The password. Lorena. You will need it to get past our pickets the other side of the river. Sometimes soldiers shoot before asking questions."

That was easy to swallow: the ironworks, the Winchester Reb.

Those jailbird Rebs were pretty good actors themselves: squabbling like hogs fighting for slops, kicking, jangling their chains—all the diversion I'd needed to slink behind a pile of bricks, skid down an embankment, take two or three anxious breaths, then slide into the river.

In the gloom, the white water appeared almost black; it congealed my clothes to my skin; it oozed deep into my boots, soaking the wadded-up paper it found there, numbing my toes. The sky, dark as the river, cloudless, no moon. Stars pretty soon?

Already, stars looked as if they had fallen to earth. Across the river, high in the rocks, under the trees, it looked as if dozens of candles were dancing. Rebs. Snugged next to their fires, guns at the ready, waiting to pick off anything sneaky, suspicious.

Swim like a fish? Dog paddle mostly. Out there in front, just out of reach of my clumsy, loud-splashing hands, bright yellow pins had dropped from the heights, nipping the water, wiggling reflections, watching me splash. Farther in front, a waterbird skittered and flapped for the Maryland shore.

More current, sweeping me right, back where I came from. Paddle like fury. Yes, I could do this! Didn't even get that gray Captain's name. Diversion still going on? No, don't look back. Look inside yourself. Look to the fact that you're not a boy anymore, not walking in your father's footsteps anymore, because you can stand on your own now, and come hell or high water you won't turn your back once you've given your word, and you can look at—*look out for the bridge!*

An anchor cable snagged me, tangling my foot, pulling me under, icy water sucking me down, sap gone out of my arms, legs waterlogged pieces of wood, lungs protesting, pleading, head banging the bottom of a pontoon boat, spluttering up, flailing past.

Sudden swift water, bones of a black railroad trestle above me, water impatient and whirling; another river—the Shenandoah, yes—foaming in from the right to push me and pull me closer to— *whing splat crack.*

The air whined, the water snapped, a sharp, silvery swirl past my eyes, the echoing clap, the current insistently pushing me nearer to—*crack splat.*

A ribbon of flame from the shore, no, not from the shore, from the towpath beside the canal, too close to miss.

Gotta dive deep, no, bad idea, gotta make myself heard, gotta find breath, even with spume in my mouth, stealing my breath, filling my silent, screaming lungs sucking for air, coughing it out: "Lo-re-na!"

A musket clumped on the towpath; arms came toward me, pulled me to shore.

One final, watery wheeze to make sure: "Lo-re-na."

*****

"Don't hang on me so tight—like, y'all gettin' me soaked!"

I let go of the Reb's shirt, lowering my shaky hands to the pitch of the saddle. My legs must belong to somebody else; they plopped like dead things, in rhythm with the slow-plodding horse. I looked to my left. Every house dark. How to find Doctor McVay?

Small stabs of light ahead. A stark silhouette: a stone cross on a peaked roof, a dimly lit chapel of fieldstone, a small pot over a low fire sending up steam quickly lost in the night.

The Reb slid off his horse. "You tol' me the first officer I could find. Well, he's in 'ere. Fact is, he's the onliest officer. All t'others is way topside all them trees an' rocks."

The door to the chapel stood open, the windows as well. The place seemed woeful and sickly. Because of the smell? If death and dying had a smell, that smell was fleeing from this tiny stone building, poisoning everything that stood in its way.

Three men were inside. No, wrong, more than that, maybe a dozen all told, but only three that weren't mostly flat on the floor;

some were completely covered over with blankets, though blankets were maybe in short supply: for one poor soul only his goldbraided uniform coat, pulled high to cover his face.

The Reb—a corporal, buck-toothed and pimply, I could see from the flare of two lanterns—shoved past me. "Excuse me, suh," he lisped at a bent-over man, "this-here feller says to get 'im to a officer. Almighty important, he says."

The officer didn't look up; he bent to his task on the floor: a soldier, the upper part of him crimson, glistening, jerking, the mouth working feebly, noises a newborn puppy might make.

The officer wiped his hands on the apron he wore; the white cloth looked as if he'd been wiping up buckets of strawberry jam. "Not now, Corporal, not now." The words came out slowly, dead-weary. "This is almighty important, too." He reached up; an orderly handed him something sharp-looking, shiny.

I moved further into the chapel, my boots shuffling, acting as if they wanted to go backward instead of ahead. More men than I thought. I'd missed the ones laid out on the high-backed wooden pews.

"I'm sorry, sir, this can't wait." I moved closer to the puppy noises, the indescribable smell. "The lives of all your men on the heights up there—"

"I have no control over the lives of those men. Only those you see sprawled on their backs. At least, some of those you see sprawled on their backs."

"No! You do control the lives of those men! If you don't help them, right now, they'll be captured or killed!" My hand made a grab for the ring in my pocket.

The man rose stiffly to his feet, a slow, painful unwinding; there were deep circles beneath his eyes; his hair was dark and lank, plastered damply against his skull.

"Son, I am but a poor surgeon," he said. "These men are dying, most of them, and I have precious little help as it is." He turned, looked at a tall, elderly man with a gray mustache, bald as an egg. "Inasmuch as my learned medical colleague over there refuses to join forces with me, I am compelled to ply my trade assisted by a single orderly, who, I feel sure, hasn't washed his hands since sometime last week!"

He was breathing heavily; his fists were clenched. "Christian charity and the Hippocratic oath be damned!" He shook a fist at his learned medical colleague.

"I have stated my reasons. I'll not change my mind." The tall man stood rigidly before the altar, his black attire mirrored in the large, shiny gold crucifix behind him; the glimmering flame from one of the candles reflected off the man's bald head.

Excuses. Arguments. No time for that! If this surgeon wouldn't listen, he would have lots more blood on his hands than he already had!

Despite my shivering, I recounted the Yankees' discovery of Confederate plans, Capt. Charles Russell's hell-for-leather ride for help, a walloping blue monster with deadly jaws closing in. "It could happen any minute!" I told him. "I'm the only one who could get away, to bring the news, and I'm c-cold and s-s-soaked to the skin, and I got shot at too, and… and just look at this ring, because it means—"

The man kept shaking and shaking his head. "Ring? What in the deuce are you talking about?"

I kept trying to explain, but my words, like fresh-born pups, wanted to tumble over each other.

The surgeon seemed torn between studying his patient and inspecting the ring. At last, he dropped the ring in my hand. "Very implausible! You can't authenticate any of this. And names, you haven't given me names. This Captain who supposedly gave you this ring, what is his name?"

I shuffled my feet. "I don't, I mean, he didn't tell me his name. Only the name of his brother-in-law, and he can identify—"

I gave it up. The surgeon had gone back to his knees. Again, the orderly handed him an implement; again, he was hovering over the form on the floor.

I wheeled away. But even with my back to the man, I had to let him know: "This ring, that Captain's brother-in-law, he'd know I'm telling the truth. He's Major Jack Taylor of Cobb's Brigade, Fifteenth North Caro—"

The surgeon must have jumped to his feet, for he'd seized my shoulder. "Did… did you say, Major Jack Taylor, of Cobb's Brigade?"

"Fifteenth North Carolina, Lieutenant Colonel William McRae in command." I knew my stuff, and this man should know it! But he wasn't looking at me; he was looking at the elderly man dressed in black.

Finally, he did look at me, a crestfallen look, his face the color of chalk. He said, "Major Jack Taylor, I am very sorry to tell you, died twenty minutes ago, of a chest wound." His eyes went to a form nearby on the stone floor, the face covered over by a gold-braided uniform coat. "And I believe I could have saved him. Yes, I could have. With a little humanitarian medical help! Isn't that so, Doctor McVay?"

*****

My teeth still chattering, my legs wobbling beneath my sodden pants, I stumbled outside to the fire, nearly running into another man who had just gotten off a horse; he was stumbling too. He was clean-shaven, pale, lacking a hat; he held a small volume in both his hands. As he bumped by me, I detected the sharp odor of whiskey.

"Ex-excuse me," the man muttered. "Oh, this is dreadful, I have not seen the like, I… I have never seen—" The man's voice trailed off then picked up as he mumbled, "I suppose I must… I must—" He lumbered into the dead smell of the chapel, muttering words I couldn't make out.

Dr. McVay came out and stood next to me. Stretching his hands out to the fire, he said, "All that you told the surgeon in there, is it true?"

I merely nodded. No use talking. I'd failed, failed miserably.

Dr. McVay let out a heavy sigh. "My grandson was not much older than you. But he was killed, two weeks ago, Bull Run, artillery fire, killed by gray soldiers, like those in there."

"So you won't try to help them?"

"I cannot. I simply cannot." He drew himself up, a little more rigid, smoothed the front of his black coat.

I figured that it was safe to tell him, quietly, so that no one could hear, who I was and why Col. Grimes Davis of the 8th New York Cavalry had sent me there and even directed me to seek out the Doctor's own house.

I glanced up from the flames. The Doctor was nodding.

It was probably safe, too, to tell him why my message was so critically important, that it might save thousands of lives, including fifteen hundred blue cavalry troopers.

Yes, still nodding.

And since it was safe, I could tell him some other things, too. Like my pa being killed by Yankees, and why I'd run off, but that vengeance and glory—even emulating my father—had given way to something more important than all those things, "because... because this war is really about... is about..."

I felt I was choking, then felt the tall man's arms come around me, and he wasn't so rigid and was sort of quaking himself, and the steam from the pot on the fire kept curling up, watering my eyes, and it must have got in the Doctor's eyes, too, because we both were rubbing our eyes and our noses.

"Perhaps... perhaps I can be of help here," the Doctor said. "And for my friend, Colonel Davis, thanks to you. Perhaps it isn't too late."

The surgeon was up off his knees, staring down at the unmoving form at his feet, the face not yet covered over, no coat or blanket to be found for such use. "Assuming this youngster is telling the truth," he said, looking at me now, "we have nowhere to turn. A credible officer would have to carry the news. I cannot leave, for obvious reasons. I have no idea why you changed your mind, Doctor McVay, but both of us are required here, just as you said."

The surgeon yawned and knuckled his eyes. "Orderly, some coffee for the Doctor and me. For the boy, too."

As we stood there, I looked to the altar: a lone figure reflected in the gold of the crucifix.

I reached in my pocket and brought out Betsy's tiny gold cross. Turning my head to the source of the reflection, I fastened my eyes on the newly arrived man, leaning against the side of a pew, the little volume uplifted before him. Clearing my throat, I pointed.

The surgeon, frowning, pondering, followed my finger; he shrugged his shoulders. "Chaplain!" he barked at the man whose lips were aquiver with silent words. "Over here, man! And be quick about it!"

The chaplain cast doubting eyes in our direction. He didn't move, at least no move beyond a quick jerk of his head. The surgeon steered himself around some recumbent and curled-up figures, grabbed hold of the man's arm, and dragged him back with him. "I have an errand for you." But after looking the man up and down and wrinkling his nose, he said, "No, not an errand, Lieutenant, an order!"

He explained my message, or tried to, as the chaplain looked toward the door. One hand still clutched his volume; the fingers of the other were tapping a place near his heart.

"Blast you, you're supposed to be a man of faith!"

"I... I believe I have lost my faith," the chaplain mourned. "All that death up there...down here..." He glanced at the gore on the surgeon's apron and quickly turned his back.

"Faith or no, I have given you an order!"

The man sagged, the little volume pressed to his breast.

There was no time for this! Col. Davis had trusted me, had enlisted me to deliver a good swift–

Without further ado, I aimed the toe of my boot at the chaplain's hindquarters and caught them flush. He dropped his volume, snatched it up, and whirled around. "You gotta have at least an ounce of faith!" I hollered at him, surprised more by my voice than by my accurate foot. I held up my gold cross, where he could see it. "Faith without works is a dove without wings!"

"All right, I'll do it!" He was still holding the volume tight to his breast. And he still reeked of whiskey.

"Lieutenant!" I thought the surgeon might be holding out his hand, but he was holding out coffee. The chaplain drained the cup, gulped another, and was out the door. The hooves of his horse were sluggish at first, then quickened in the breathless night air.

I felt the warmth of smiles turned on me. I couldn't smile back. What I truly needed was an ounce of the faith I'd just spoken of and an ounce of knowledge about the ironworks, scant miles up a road that pointed me home.

Chapter 11

I cupped a hand to my ear. Grinding, screaking, almost like a distant, discordant chorus of frogs. Where from? Way upriver? Not that far, and not on the water; it was quiet out there, except for the determined rush of the river past Sandy Hook.

From the concealment of Dr. McVay's front porch, I gave my full attention to the persistent, metallic grinding sound. Upriver, yes, on this side of the Potomac, on the high ground above it. Wheeled guns. The Rebs had taken the bait!

Nothing to do now but wait. At least my clothes were dry, if a tad too large. Dr. McVay's grandson must have been taller than me.

A couple slabs of pork and tart apple cider, from the pantry cooler, just where the Doctor had said they would be. The house key safely back in its hiding place. Oh, to have a hiding place…Hidden away from the world, maybe I wouldn't have to keep wondering. Why did Jeremiah have a debt to G'Pa? Why was his other finger cut off at the tip? What about that big-booted man? Doesn't hurt to wonder, I guess. But my grandfather's safety, that was something to worry about. No, I couldn't stay hid.

Shadowy pickets, on the towpath beside the canal. Others closing in, dodging between stubby railroad cars resting on tracks that ran through town. The sky dark, now full of stars. And Harpers Ferry, now full of Yankee cavalry troopers, waiting, just like me.

Maybe not like me? On the move, maybe? Col. Davis, he wouldn't stay put, not after hearing that persistent grinding echoing down from the heights.

No earthly way to pick up the clicking and clacking of ironshod hooves, the nervous jingle of bridles and bits, not this far away. I could imagine it, though: a long column of horsemen hedged in by empty buildings, the slow procession, the sound of it bouncing off grim-staring walls, catapulting out to the dark-water gorge, rebounding up to where candles still danced.

One of the pickets froze. Another came, the two close together, watching, listening.

Again I cupped my hand. A soft, hollow clopping, a good way off? Upriver? On the river?

The pickets, too, must be listening: hundreds of jittery horses striking on boards balanced on boats, lots of Yanks sneaking across, the whole shebang of Col. Davis's cavalry troop.

Moments later, a horse came pounding in, and with it, a single voice, all undone: "They're comin'! Good God a'mighty, they're comin' across! Hunnerds of 'em, I swear!"

Within a minute, a cluster of horses drummed on the roadway you'd have to take to get to Sandy Hook, then opposing little stabs of flame, from the towpath and the railroad cars, the drumming closer, hammering the roadway, a voice hollering...

(Any real reason I had to go? Hadn't I already done my part? Maybe I could make it home on my own? Maybe the Doctor could loan me a horse? Maybe I could stay where I was, safely hid with a man who'd just lost his grandson, who'd had his protecting arms around me, who surely wouldn't care if I went to the ironworks, or stayed where I was?)

Hollering, "Shipley! Shipley!"

(Maybe G'Pa didn't really need me, didn't need his arms around me? Maybe a deadly man with steel-tipped boots wouldn't come?)

The ironworks, I'd given my word.

"Shipley!"

I didn't have to be told to holler or run, but I seemed to be doing both: "Here! Here I am!"

A gauntleted hand grabbed hold of my arm and pulled me up on a horse's rump, other horses quickly around us, the horses wheeling, pelting back the way they had come, a few shots behind us, fading fast.

We raced past a pool of light from a little stone chapel. No one came out. They must have been too busy to look.

Near the bridge end, a trooper sat holding reins for a riderless horse. Willing hands flopped me up into the saddle; the reins were tossed at me, a couple of times.

The night was alive with horse noise; the bridge planks rattled as the last of the column made it across. Luminous light still licked the water, the fires still burning, far above us. But Maryland Heights was emptier now. The wheeled guns and gray soldiers were clearing out. And so were we.

With some bumping and grousing, we formed column of twos; some of the horsemen appeared confused, heading off in the wrong direction. A horse nudged in front of me. The Colonel. He turned in the saddle: "Shipley, I knew you were a man we could depend on! Our Country is proud of what you did!"

I wanted to grin back, but out of breath, my mouth hung open. It didn't help that they'd given me an overlarge horse; my legs spraddled out before they went down. I searched vainly for stirrups. Not a good time to grin.

Col. Davis was still on a high: "Shipley, I don't mind telling you I pleaded my case with admirable eloquence! The post commander was so taken up with my ironworks plan that he broke out glasses and offered me whiskey! Which I declined with admirable restraint!"

I couldn't grin and couldn't speak. The shudders had me. Because the saddle hammered me where I lived, and my boots kept flopping and stabbing for stirrups? Uh-uh. Worse. Much worse.

The sudden collision of hooves and stones rebounded off the escarpment hard on our right. On our left, ghostly reflections glanced off the face of the barge canal. In front, fireflies frantically played with the road—no, just sparks from horseshoes striking the rocks. And still I shuddered.

Abruptly, we cut sharp right. My horse faltered as the road pitched up. I whiteknuckled the mane. It seemed a long time till we got to the top. And then we were cantering, galloping, my backside pounded by marble-like leather, my fingers trying to fist horsehair because—

"Colonel, my stirrups!"

Shouts ahead drowned me out. Dim figures by the roadside sprinted away and vanished into the trees and the fields. They had no sooner gone then flashes came twitching out from where they had gone. Hunching down for our lives, we swept on by. "Colonel, my stirrups!"

The two of us fell out by the wayside. He cursed, fumbled with the stirrups, and got but one of them hitched. "Make the best of it, Shipley. Back in the saddle, back into line!"

It wasn't long before bundles of matchsticks and boxes littered the roadway in front of us, but as we got closer, they grew into fence rails and overturned wagons impeding our way. It spooked the horses. We had to slow down. But no shouts, nothing with bite spewed out of the darkness. More obstacles waiting ahead?

We broke to the left, busted through brush-tangled pastures and fragile worm fences, plunged past black-as-ink farmhouses, and scudded off cross-lots, then back to the roadway again.

The horse to my left gave a small bleat, seemed to lose balance, to hobble. The rider lurched toward me, got hold of my coat, swung himself over, and knocked me sideways; he threw his arms around me, an immediate deadweight, and me with a foot hanging loose.

I'd lost track of where we were but not of where we were going. Practically there.

My own mount started to grunt, to labor. Blast that man at my back! Blast the Colonel's admirable plan! Know the ins and outs of the ironworks? I knew as much about the moon. The Colonel, heedless, held his back straight as a stake.

For a second or two, I was ready to haul on the reins and call off the charade. Instead, hugging the horse with stiffed-up knees, I freed up a hand, reached for my pocket, got a grip on Betsy's cross, and squeezed it hard. "I'm sorry I lied, dear God. I'm sorry. I'm sorry!" I didn't say it aloud. Probably, it wouldn't do any good.

The shudders still had me. I combed my memory. The ironworks, if only I could remember...

People I'd seen there: Brother Russell, sitting his mule, and the Winchester Reb, crumpling just short of the pines. People, yes, but what of the place?

A stone bridge, just past the place, an overturned casket of nails, some kind of chimney–no, more than one chimney—but one very tall.

Hot furnace facility, capable of forging steel bands for Parrott guns.

A sprawling place, a sawmill, a gristmill, a furnace. My nose remembered the smells, and I could trace them—some of them—to buildings with chimneys.

A very hot furnace. A very tall chimney? I recollected a smoke-stack, brick, and stone at the top, and somewhere it must poke up from a building.

Before I knew it, hooves cobbled the bridge, and we were over and past it; we hardly slowed. I slid from the horse. "Ten minutes!" The Colonel slapped my behind. "It's all in your hands, Shipley!" I shuffled my feet.

"No! Double time, Shipley, double time!"

I lumbered ahead. "Colonel, it's hard to see—"

"Never mind that! Get to the furnace!"

I raised my eyes, found a chimney, across a field, tall, massive, black in the gloom. I started into the field and began to run. I stopped and looked back. The Colonel was not far behind me; he was holding a sputtering torch; some troopers ran with him, straining under the weight of some bags.

Yes, that chimney was tall, so there must be a building.

I pushed my boots over grassy patches and weedy places and found solid dirt, then the earth cut away, tripping me up, and it must be because—

Ruts. A deep-rutted track–from hauling wagonloads of heavy stuff?–made straight for the chimney. Heaving for breath, struggling for balance, I ran down the ruts—and ran into a wall. Where was the building?

When the Colonel caught up, he pushed me aside and smacked a hand against the wall. As I waited for him to smack me down, our shadows played over the bricks and stones, as if gesturing helplessly. I was afraid to look at him.

All at once, Col. Davis began to chuckle; then his arm came around my shoulders. "Shipley, you've done it again. You've saved the day!"

Couldn't possibly be. There was no building. I brought up my eyes to the light of the torch. There wasn't a wall, and the torch told me why. A huge casement of brick and stone was built into the base of a hill. And the three curved openings close to the ground must be for—

"Must lead deep into the hill, to the furnace in there. With all our paraphernalia, Shipley, it looks like a very tight squeeze for a full-grown man. You'll have to do it."

"Uh, do it?"

"Of course. Get all the gunpowder bags in there and set the fuse."

*****

The night again knew only the sound of horses, as the two columns stretched out at both ends. The Colonel's back was ramrod-stiff, his head fixed; he didn't utter a word. No one, it seemed, wanted to be the first to speak up.

We continued at a swinging trot, riding into a freshening breeze that stirred up the dust. You would think what had happened would stir up some protests, anger, something.

The horses slowed to a walk. Col. Davis broke the silence at last, over his shoulder: "It's not your fault, Shipley. You got us there in fine style, then scraping around in the very bowels of that dungeon, without any light. But I should not be too surprised, I guess, that the gunpowder—"

The trooper still hanging to my waist growled his own explanation: "Army contractors, sir. Trusty as rattlers and stingy as sin! But you'll have to admit one thing, Colonel. The fuse worked!"

Col. Davis caught me off-guard with what he said next: "It's enough to take the patriot wind right out of your sails!"

He was right. Like him, I'd felt the wind go out of my sails when the powder fizzled. I'd come close to striking a blow for beliefs

I'd finally got in my craw. I was still trying to hold fast to the memory I had of my father. But my father had fought for a side that would keep the Jeremiahs of this world in an agonizing pit of despair. The Colonel had said so, and the Colonel was right. But in a sense, he was wrong. His patriot wind—preserving the Union, whatever the cost—would blow itself out when, eventually, the fighting stopped. And black folks would still have lashes ridging their backs, even be flogged, or worse, for learning to read.

I sat up straighter and took a deep breath; my voice had to cut through the clattering hooves: "Colonel, patriotism may be important. But it isn't enough!"

The officer's head jerked up. "Sergeant," he directed the soldier beside him, "fall back and trade places with the boy there."

There were a few things I needed him to explain: "Colonel, why do you think the Union is so almighty important? You said you're from the South. Don't those people have patriotic wind too?"

"Patriotism and politics go hand in hand, Shipley. But the states that have remained united are united in more than political theory. They are united out of necessity. If the fabric of our Country may be cut to shreds whenever rebellious hands lay hold of a knife, then the lifeblood of our people may as well flow through a sieve."

"I don't get what you mean."

"I mean that we as a people, a culture, cannot survive disunited! Right now, we've got Rebels ahead of us and behind us, and us'ns, we're in the middle, the meat in the sandwich. But at least the Brits and the Frenchies aren't the ones nibbling the bread, which could easily happen, if the South is allowed to set up for itself. Can you imagine a South made up of eleven separate nations, with separate jealousies and separate governments—even, God forbid, with separate armies? That's what a confederation of states comes down to, when all is said and done. And that would make us terribly vulnerable."

"But what about all the slaves down there? Isn't slavery just as important as any of that? Didn't you admit that slaves are at the core of all this? Don't they deserve to be free?"

Col. Davis moved up and down in the saddle, composed, at one with his horse.

But he didn't answer. I blew out my breath and waited. Still no response.

"The slaves?"

"All I can tell you, Shipley, is that I stand foursquare behind the Commander in chief. Lincoln believes that saving our Country is paramount. Yet he is opposed to slavery as well. So since saving the Union and freeing the slaves, at one stroke, would be politically ruinous, he favors emancipation on a gradual basis. Maybe the government buying blacks their freedom from their legal owners."

"But even if that happened, could those bought-up slaves do what they wanted and go where they pleased?"

The Colonel adjusted his hat and rode on a while. Just when I'd about given up hope of getting an answer, he said, "The President contemplates a refuge for the negroes. Like Haiti. Or Liberia. Panama perhaps."

"How's about the Black Hole of Calcutta, Colonel!" brayed the man from the rump of my horse. Hoping that my elbow was as sharp as the trooper's remark, I jabbed it backwards, my full weight behind it.

An outraged "Oooph" was all that I heard before the earth went thump, as if a millstone had hit it. Troopers around us began laughing but Col. Davis thrust up a hand. He went up in his stirrups, intent on the trooper pounding back from the head of the column.

"Lights up ahead, sir," the soldier reported. "Looks like a town." The Colonel turned to me. "Your town, Shipley?"

"Yes, sir. Sharpsburg."

"And if we stay on this road?"

"We'd go straight on through, then… then right past where I live."

"The Federal army is reputed to be somewhere near Boonsboro. What road do we take to get there?"

My thoughts had already turned to a different place, a different road. "Boonsboro, Shipley?"

"To the center of town, then sharp right, east, I think, then down a long hill to a bridge. Pheasants used to nest—"

"Bridge?"

"Across Antietam Creek."

The Colonel kept talking. But Taylors Landing Road was almost in sight. I'd made it full circle back, why I'd jumped on the Colonel's bandwagon at all. Now, he didn't seem to know it was time for me to jump off.

(What about the other reasons? What about my newly discovered convictions of what the war was about? Wasn't it about right and wrong, pure and simple, as Betsy had said? And where did that leave me? Already I'd spouted off at the Colonel, patriot winds, and such, and I'd elbowed a jackass off my horse. What more could I do? How long was this mission supposed to last? Forever?)

We reined to a stop near the center of town. St. Paul's Church loomed up on my left. All but a few of the houses were dark inside, the blinds shut tight. I could swear I heard barking, a few houses away.

In a flash, thoughts of houses and barking went out of my head. A hundred yards in front of us, the night came alive with tongues of flame, dozens of them. I ducked as something went *whizzz* just past my head.

The Colonel went tall in his stirrups, shouting, waving his hat in the direction of big trees back down the street.

Uh-uh, not the way out of this mess... "Gotta go that way, sir! North!"

"Where does it go to?"

"Goes to Hagerstown!"

Horses were rearing, men hollering. "Shipley, show us the way!"

I broke to the left, orange flames licking after me—hissing, buzzing—a cry of pain close by me, the shriek of a horse.

We hammered along the Hagerstown Pike, pelted past the Piper farm (*Jeremiah, are you out with your hoe?*), scudded by the mouth of the sunken road (*was the fox out after chickens this night?*), a dead-on dash by the Dunker Church (*pale as a ghost standing watch by the woods*), Mumma's, and Miller's quickly behind us (*rest easy under your rocks, Ol' Ty*). We slowed to a trot.

Suddenly, I was struck by a daredevil notion. I could throw myself from the horse, just tumble away. I'd done my job! No one would stop me, and no one would care. Our cottage, I could make it there without breaking a sweat.

Did I still have a mission? Did the Colonel still need me? Would my pa have turned tail when the going got rough? Course not! I thrashed my head and lifted my chin to the wind in my face. My mission, it hadn't played itself out.

My horse's stride became more of a lurch, the panting and huffing a painful thing to listen to.

This mission—whatever it was—where would it take me and when would it end?

Chapter 12

"**S**hipley, y'all got more muscle than that! Go ahead. Rip 'em off!" Col. Davis's voice had slipped into an easy Southern drawl. I found it easy to believe that this Yankee officer had, as he'd claimed, been reared in the deep South. But why rip off his shoulder straps?

Figuring that it must have something to do with all the wagons grumbling on the turnpike ahead of us, I gave a final yank that left behind only a few stray threads on his dusty blue tunic.

A few minutes earlier, we'd come mucking up out of a bog onto the Hagerstown-Williamsport Road. A trooper riding point had come hot-spurring back, flailing an arm in the direction of whining axles a half mile ahead. A hurried conference as the noise grew louder. A deaf person could have heard the corkscrewing sound, and a man needing spectacles would have had no trouble detecting the dust cloud, rising yellow in the gray dawn light.

"How many wagons?" the Colonel snapped.

"Several dozen at least, sir. Rebs, sure enough. Six mules to a wagon. Haulin' heavy stuff, appears like."

For nearly a minute, Col. Davis sat silent, his fingers consulting his chin whiskers. His eyes flashed. I knew the look. He wouldn't sit still very long. And now, the shoulder straps.

"With no uniform, Shipley, y'all could sho-nuff pass fer a Reb," the Colonel drawled, his shoulders now bare of insignia. "Care to try it? It's still dark enough fer some gov'ment work!"

Government work? Pretend to be a Reb?

He must have mistook my silence for sober hankering to string along. "Foller me," he said, as if he did this sort of thing all the time. "I'll do the speechifyin'. Jus' try to look secesh!"

I wanted to tell him I wasn't a soldier, couldn't even look like one. If I had me my foxtail hat, maybe. No, maybe not—that might change me on the outside but not on the in.

"Ready there, Mister Shipley, suh? Then how's 'bout us cuttin' loose with some Rebel racket, so's to show 'em we're legit!" As the wagons came into sight, he laughed, then whipped up his mount, bawled some high-spirited "H'yah's!" and went tearing right up to the first of the wagons, completely unnerving the slow-plodding mules.

"What outfit y'all with?" Col. Davis boomed in a voice that brought the rumbling wheels to a stop.

"Gen'l Longstreet's reserve amm'nition train. Headed fer Williamsport. 01' Virginny, carry me back! Yanks done busted though the mountain passes, so's we gonna—Hold on a minute! Who're you?"

"Cap'n John Sims," the Federal officer sang out with not the slightest hesitation, "Barksdale's Brigade, Twen'y-fus' M'ssippi, Cunnel Humphries commandin'. If y'all fixin' fer the Potomac, best head t'other way. Enemy cav'ry's at the rivuh crossin' in force. Gobble yuh up down 'ere. Gotta go north t'get round 'em. We're goin' thataway our ownselves an can ride escort fer y'all. Can't be lettin' the enemy snooker them amm'nition wagons!"

Dutifully, the driver began turning his wagon and g'yupping his mules, not, however, before hollering word back up the line that they gotta go north, 'cause of enemy cav'ry.

The Colonel and I sat our horses in silence, watching the wagon train gather a host of dusty blue outriders as the duped wagoneers lashed their mules with unbridled energy.

I wished the moment could go on and on. There was hardly anything I wouldn't do for this Southerner who fought for the North, who addressed me as "Shipley" this and "Shipley" that, who could be sternly efficient one minute, warmly good-humored the next.

In high spirits, I let my curiosity out: "I finally reckoned why you didn't want them to see your shoulder straps. But that other stuff, Captain John Sims and all, why did you--?"

Col. Davis smiled ruefully and worked a finger to the corner of his eye. "Well, even though I'm a Northerner now, including my normal inflection of speech, I had to pick someone from Mississippi, my native state. These secesh, you see, can tell what state you're from by the accent you have. Captain John Sims?" And again, the quick jab at his eye. "Why, I grew up with the fella. He, uh, just happens to be the best friend I have in this world."

The Colonel's words struck a chord in me. Or was it because his finger was still at work on his eye? Searching out the wedding ring still in my pocket, I gave it a squeeze. The ring, too, struck a chord: Major Jack Taylor, Cobb's Brigade, 15th North Carolina—he would never set eyes on that ring again.

*****

I thought I'd got rid of the shudders when Ty's rocky mound had vanished behind us. Maybe it was because of the chill dawn air or maybe because I was completely alone. The Colonel was off with his cavalry troop, riding into a jubilant cockcrow morning, victorious. I was off on my own and maybe lost.

He still counted on me. He told me so, squeezing my shoulder. Then he turned away and rode north, while I posted south, the roadway gray and grim in my path. I gnawed the inside of my cheek and turned for one last look.

From a mile's distance, I could no longer hear the wagons. For several seconds, I squinted in the direction they'd gone. The cloud of powder the wheels had churned up appeared almost golden in a low slant of sun; but it was melting, even as I blinked, into an endless gunmetal sky.

I rode another mile or so. I had never seen this ground before. A way opened on the left. Left was east. Boonsboro, where the Union army was supposed to be, where Col. Davis wanted me to go. I had his written message in the toe of my boot. He'd told me, "This is your home turf, Shipley. It is imperative that someone get through. Headquarters needs this information, badly. Can you do it?"

It took me a few seconds to realize I'd halted the horse and another few seconds to realize that this new mount was high-strung, insisting on jerking the reins, stamping the roadway, urging me to move on from where we'd stopped.

How long since I'd had any rest? I wasn't sure where Boonsboro was. Sharpsburg was straight ahead, down this very road. Yes, the sleep that I craved, that I deserved.

Still, Col. Davis, he must be exhausted himself and still in the saddle, steady, in firm control of all those captured wagons.

Imperative that someone get through.

I ordered myself to not fall asleep and reined to the left.

Chapter 13

A bugle sounded. My eyes snapped open. I looked up. Apple trees. Odd. Every last apple must have been picked. And something had been draped over me; it stopped short of my knees.

"Welcome back to the land of the living! Total collapse of body function, the good Doctor said. In a word, exhaustion. Good timing, though, laddie, we're bellying up on suppertime!" A Federal officer had come sauntering over, flashing a smile from under a droopy yellow mustache. "Don't be unkind to it," he said, as I flung off the cover. "That-there's the General's own cape. By the by, to my friends, I'm 'Autie'." Fingering a long blond ringlet, he added, "Behind my back, they call me 'Curly.' I wonder why!"

My memory had a huge gap. Dimly, I recollected following a meandering track through the woods, finally allowing the horse to find a way for the both of us. Seemed like I may have tied off the reins and wrapped my arms around my mount's neck, resting my head, just for a moment.

A faint vision too of dust disgorging unending columns of bluecoats, jabbering, bringing foul air as they swung by, a hazy glimmer of wagons trundling past, of cannons, tubes bouncing, wheels churning dirt, the spokes a blur—the whole thing a blur. And then, trying to explain the Colonel's note, even before I forced off my boot. I barely remember the stiff boards and jittery wheels that jarred me to this place where all the apples were gone from the trees.

The officer was still watching, still smiling. He reached down a hand. I managed to get in a standing position. "Are we still in Boonsboro?" I asked him.

"Nope. Boonsboro is a good five miles back thataway. Thisaway's the end of the line."

We were in long orchard shadow, downslope of a large brick house. It looked vaguely familiar. Men in blue were clustered up near the white-pillared porch. They kept palavering, pointing. One went over and looked through a telescope tied on a stake; then they palavered and pointed some more.

Curious, I turned to see where the telescope and fingers were pointed. I should have known. Still, I sucked in my breath.

Autie chuckled. "It's all my fault, laddie. You gibbered some when you unburdened yourself of that note, even babbled a bit about cuttin' for home. So it was either leave you there or bring you here. It maybe won't hurt my career none, neither."

"How come?"

"On account of the General sparked right up when I told him I done got us a real live person knowin' the lay of the land hereabouts. 'Cause we gotta know it, every nook and cranny of it."

I must have looked puzzled; he chuckled again. "I want you to explain to the General how you mean to get yourself back where you come from. The heres and theres, the ins and outs of doin' it. 'Cause, mark my words, that's where all the fightin's gonna be."

He turned and looked intently at the hummocky fields that bumped up and away from Antietam Creek; he raised his eyes to the tips of some buildings I knew, where they poked up from behind a ridge I knew, dim in the distance.

Autie said, "You know more about what's over there and betwixt and between than anyone among us that's partial to blue. Our esteemed Generalissimo, cautious soul that he is, was delighted to hear of my enterprisin' discovery. And anything that pleases the General tickles me plumb to death!" His chuckle returned: "Hell of a homecoming, what!"

*****

General McClellan prodded me out onto the porch. Two miles away the rooftops of Sharpsburg glittered in the twilight. I glanced at the figure beside me. He stood with arms clasped, as if hugging himself; his dark mustache bristled like a paintbrush fresh off the shelf; he jerked his head right to left, jutted his chin, and puffed out his chest. "I mean to pinch up the secessionists in a vise," he declared, pointing south and north. "Then," he added, jabbing his arm straight ahead, "I will cave-in what is left of their center with my reserve and the cavalry. A classic touch, I think. Reminiscent of Marlborough, or Frederick the Great, perhaps of Napoleon himself."

The General had a faraway look in his eyes. Though we stood side-by-side—he wasn't much taller than me—he seemed to be talking down from much higher up.

I wanted him to know that I wasn't a soldier to be talked down to or ordered about. I said to him, "I only live around here. You don't need me!"

"Oh, but I do! The better to see every hill and hollow, of which there is a plenitude. Captain Curlylocks says that you were not totally unhinged when you claimed to know this ground."

I nearly told him that, absolutely, I did know this ground: it's where I'd hunted a fox and gone after pheasants, where I'd patched up a fence and had trouble with ants, where a black-furred head used to nuzzle my hand, and a black man chopped at weeds with his hoe. But I didn't answer him straight-off. I held back, just long enough, to let him know I wasn't about to dance to his tune. Finally, I did tell him, "Yeah, I guess you could say I know my way around these parts, better than anyone you might know!"

He turned to me and called me by a name I had never heard before. "Master Shipley, I require that you draw me a map. Sound planning necessitates that we leave nothing to chance. Especially when, like at present, the enemy have us terribly outnumbered. Preparatory to your cartographic efforts, however-"

"My, uh, cart—?"

"Cartography, of course, map making. Kindly articulate for me, before you take up pencil and paper, the number and location of roads, their direction, points of intersection, the noteworthy improvements relative to the predominant topographic features." He was going pretty fast.

I felt angry little gusts blowing in my chest, demanding their freedom. Talking as fast as I sensibly could, I began throwing fact after fact at the General, rattling off roads, farms, bridges, and patches of woods. I told him that Sam Mumma's farm was chock-full of limestone to trip you up or hide behind, that wild animals made war on each other out there, that David Miller made war on his trees, so they lost their sap, that his cornfield was so big and the corn so high you could get lost in it if not on your toes, and that the Dunker Church was over by higher ground but the crawl space underneath it was too creepy to articulate about.

The General tried to cut in a few times, but I raced right on, secretly pleased that I was disturbing him to where he looked fretful, pulling at the stiff brim of his cap, finally reaching for one of the pillars. I wanted to finish off with something important, something that cut to the core of why we were there. I said, "General, do you know what this war is really about?"

The man almost lost his footing by the steps. By the time he recovered, he had the disgruntled look of our mule when I was a couple hours late with the feed. "You're spouting nonsense," he said. He'd got his boots back in line with each other, his hands clasped behind him, before he went double-timing after my question of what the war was about. "Union! Nothing more, nothing less!" He was speaking so loudly that people down by the telescope looked back up at us. "And anyone who diverts public consciousness from the central issue of abiding by the Constitution is guilty of rank and open treason!"

Col. Grimes Davis had thought much the same thing but had said it lots better.

He'd taught me some other things, too, which had helped me come to believe in myself, to stand up for beliefs now part of myself. My mission now was heaps more important than drawing maps or discussing topographical features, more important, maybe—for a little while anyhow—than getting myself back to G'Pa. I had me a mission to trumpet the news! And so I flat-out told the General, "That sounds toplofty to me! Slavery has to be the central issue. And slavery's wrong!"

General McClellan continued to run his eyes over the fields across the creek, almost as if he and I weren't sharing the porch. After a weighty pause, he proclaimed, "There are many unfortunates who, like yourself, fail to grasp that this conflict is for the minds of a people, not a contest for the bodies of billy goats! Institutional hegemony is required if the dynamic of our civil government is to persevere and endure. We therefore must coexist with disparate views, allow reason to prevail over sympathetic weakness, promote mutual tolerance which—"

"But what about the slaves? They deserve to be free!"

The General lifted his chin another inch or two. "Our purpose must be to coerce the Rebels into removing to Southern soil, not to destroy them as a people, or to overthrow what they deem fundamentally pregnant to—"

"So they should be allowed to keep all their slaves? Treat them any way they want?"

"In a word, yes! Slavery is incidental to the disciplines required of national sovereignty. In fact, if any slaves come within our lines, I will send them back to their proprietary owners straightaway!"

Jeremiah.

The General again had that faraway look in his eyes. I'm not sure he even knew I was there. "Slavery was regrettably ordained," he resumed, nodding to no one in particular, "and remains a black cloud obscuring the sun. But the sun itself must continue to shine." He rocked on his heels, the leather of his boots seeming to squeak their approval; he must have been pleased; he gave every indication of not wanting to stop: "The President, no doubt, will shift his position from one of saving the Union to one of pious poppycock. He may be preaching Constitutional rectitude now, but I fear that soon he will be ranting and raving alongside all the other sniveling anti-slavery baboons.

"Indeed, I have it on excellent authority that he already has drawn up a proclamation of abolishment. He will not implement it, however, until I hand him a clear-cut victory on the battlefield, which, in the course of time, I suppose I am bound to do."

There could be no doubt that the General, at long last, had finished; he slid a hand through an opening in his uniform coat; his ruddy face wore a look of deep and settled satisfaction.

I needed no more incentive than that. I had a parting shot of my own: "If the Country's a good crop and slavery's a bad weed, there's lots of folks, like me, who know what to do with a hoe!"

The General appeared to have no need to argue the point or to waste breath on an answer, though he did cock his head and briefly bristled his mustache. He cleared his throat and announced that it was time to go inside, to address issues of substance. At that instant, the windows rattled; the house shook, followed by a single distant *boom*.

I was still on the porch and Gen. McClellan was halfway inside. He turned and, for a second or two, lowered his eyes to mine, a slightly shocked expression on his face. It could have been because of that boom. But I hoped it was because he'd formed an image of people, like me, who knew what to do with a hoe.

*****

Half-awake, I went in and out of a dream: Jeremiah swiping his hoe at armies of soldiers—blue and gray soldiers—who'd put down their muskets, the better to shrill their laughter at him. Was it a dream? I gave up on sleep.

Snugged under my blanket, I couldn't escape the sporadic gunpowder claps, up past the creek. As close to G'Pa as they were to me?

The nightmare memory of cackling soldiers kept my eyes open, staring at twisted apple tree branches. Now, my memory wouldn't shut down: The General fussing me into drawing a map, declaring his views about the course of the war, about God's own righteous hand sending a certain General to save the Country from a certain gorilla back in Washington, all of which had brought coughing and nodding and scratching from the assembled headquarters staff, except for Autie, who only smiled.

Sleep kept creeping close but dodging away. And when at last I began to drift off, Jeremiah, again, seemed to come with his hoe, chopping at weeds, and at soldiers who insisted on blowing their—

The blare of bugles jarred me awake; there was low-hanging fog; the porch seemed detached from the house, floating.

"But look, the morn in russet mantle clad walks o'er the lew on yon high eastward hill!"

I could tell it was Autie, even before I saw him come swinging through the apple trees. He was gesturing at the mist-shrouded hills with one hand, holding out a steaming platter of food with the other. "Not bad versifyin', eh laddie, for a man who graduated last in his class!"

Today, he was wearing a bright-red scarf; his blue eyes still sparkled a laughter that seemed part of him now. I hoped he had a serious side, because I had a need for serious talk, which I would certainly hunt out after taking care of those just-sizzled eggs and sweet-smelling ham.

Something about Autie triggered confusion in me. Thanks to Brother Russell—and maybe a few other folks I'd encountered lately—I surely was less absorbed with my father and, almost certainly, had a mind of my own. And yet this Federal officer—athletic, clear-eyed, and whimsical, never mind that his uniform was rumpled, his boots were too big, and his hat had the slouch of a flop-eared dog—he brought a quickening to my throat. He stood out from the crowd, like my father, and in much the same way. Pa had been a prankster but could be wrinkle-browed too, when he chose to be. Did Autie have a serious side?

"The General doesn't give a hoot about slaves," I threw out, not waiting till I swallowed a mouthful of biscuit. "He figures they're just—things. What do you think, Autie?"

For a moment or two, the laughter was gone from his eyes. But then it came twinkling back. "Philosophy and politics? Piffle! My voice is for war! And before this war is over, I aim to have stars on my shoulders. I mean to shoulder responsibility!" He fingered his scarf, keeping his eyes way from mine.

Clearly, Autie had his own mission. So did Gen. McClellan. But so did I! "This is serious," I cried out. "Why do you turn it into a joke?" Heads turned in our direction.

Probably, I shouldn't have asked the question. I knew the answer. Brother Russell had told me: to a lot of folks, a slave was no more than a bothersome skunk, best kept at a distance or in a cage.

Still, I held out hope that Autie could, like my father, put his jokes in his pocket, wrinkle his brow, and talk straight about things when I needed him to. I crossed my fingers and waited.

When Autie shrugged and merely looked out through the fog, I said, "I used to think there was glory in being a soldier, until I saw what war does to people. I saw what slavery does to people, too." Good. I'd managed to get his attention. "It would take someone wiser than me to offer ponderous thoughts about that," Autie said. "Some folks are wise and some otherwise, and I fear I'm the latter. Could be you're the wise one, laddie, and have our roles reversed. Still and all, since you're scrounging for answers, I'll give it a go, 'cause sometimes a wise man can learn from a fool, so long as it can be determined which is which."

"You don't make sense, sometimes."

"But sometimes I do, so I reckon I'll blather on a bit. I feel sorry for folks who think they know everything but believe in nothing. Maybe luck and selfish desire will take me where I hanker to go. But something—maybe my Methodist upbringing—tells me I need more than that. He who boasts of being self-made relieves the Lord of a lot of responsibility. No disrespect intended, General, I'd follow you anywhere!" He waved, airily, in the general direction of McClellan's headquarters tent.

"You still haven't told me what you think about slavery."

"I ain't no Black Republican, laddie. Here's why. What would happen if the slaves were freed at a stroke? Where would they go? Could they fend for themselves? Competing with us whites would be hot work!"

"A friend of mine told me that sometimes you gotta go through the fire, when the stakes are real high."

"Oh, we're goin' through the fire, no mistake. Now whether it's a fire for the Union, or a fire for freein' the slaves, or maybe both, I guess that's for each man to figger hisself. Course, in official circles, abolition is on the back burner, for now."

Autie's face wore the ghost of a smile. But then his mouth and mustache drooped. He sighed, sat down on a rock, and propped elbows on his knees, steepling his fingers. "Tell you one other thing, just 'tween us two." After another sigh, he said, "Be true to your own beliefs. Tuck 'em away down here," he tapped his chest, "but before you put 'em there, before you stand up for 'em, hell or high water, remember one thing. The good Lord constructed us humans to get on our knees before we get on our feet."

I looked down at my hand, a little amazed. I'd been unaware that I'd dug in my pocket. From the corner of my eye, I saw Autie turn and look down, too. I'm sure he must have seen Betsy's little gold cross. But by the time I thought to get his attention, he was far away, intently regarding his bright red scarf.

Chapter 14

The light was dying. Facing the town across the valley, I lifted my face to the wind and watched the clouds building. Even without the wind and the clouds, I knew that rain was just over the horizon. I'd smelled it before, blowing up from the Potomac and the Blue Ridge beyond it. What was happening over there? G'Pa, Jeremiah, Betsy...

I smelled more than rain: sulfurous smoke, a sharp reminder of what had been going on all afternoon, in David Miller's woodlot, his farm, in Sam Mumma's fields. The smoke had turned the sun red, its last rays striking the brick house behind me, apple tree shadow long on the grass, as the world around me turned gray.

Nowhere to turn: my comings and goings walled in by masses of men with their muskets and long-barreled cannons, the tubes no longer glinting in sunlight, dark and menacing now. I could still see them, across the way, some pointed at me.

I felt a twinge in my bowels. Quickly aware that my shudders had already reached a part of me leaving no time to ponder, I made a dash for a bush, dodged behind it, and dropped my pants. A secret place. For precious seconds, nothing and no one could touch me. I peeped over the bush. The General was at the telescope; a black-bearded man stood next to him, ramrod straight.

"Fitz, I don't like it," the General was saying, as I strained my bowels and tried to make myself part of the bush. "I am afraid we will lose the element of surprise," he continued. The black-bearded man nodded like a puppet on a string. The General stepped away from the telescope and looked around him, as if searching for something. His eyes came to my bush, moved on. I let out my breath. Still, if I hunched down the slightest bit more.

I shouldn't have moved. "You, there!" the General snapped. "Yes, you with your trousers down!"

As I hitched up my pants my hackles went up. Earlier, I bad been "Master Shipley." Now, I was nameless. I came out in the open; he beckoned me closer.

"You have intimate knowledge of the ground around here," he told me. "That being the case, I desire you to follow on the heels of the First Corps, that way, north, and find General Hooker. Present my compliments and advise him I have sent you to explain, in details with which he is as yet unfamiliar, the lay of the land over there. Since he has no written orders, enlarge upon what you delineated on your map, if you please, and then—"

"But I've never been that far north, except in the dark, on a horse, going real fast. Besides, I don't have a uniform. If the Rebs caught me, they'd maybe think I'm a spy, so I can't—"

"Can't, you say? Nonsense! You live over that way. Or so you claimed. Were you lying? Your patriotic ardor, is it a sham?"

I searched for words, couldn't find them. If only I could make the flame on my face go away.

"It's settled then," the General resumed, his chin lifting. "You live over there and indisputably know the ground better than General Hooker or anyone with him. In the dark, you say? On a horse, you say? Well, it is getting darker by the minute. And you will be on a horse. As for your attire, Sergeant Daniels!" With a sweep of his chin he summoned a man standing nearby.

The Sergeant came bounding, saluting with one hand, clutching a sloshing tin cup in the other.

"Issue this youngster some military garb," the General directed. Turning to me, he said, "Now then, once you have located General Hooker—florid-faced man, drinks brandy and water—make plain to him the character of the ground over by that little white church, or whatever it is, across the way, I assume you know the one I mean, and explain how it sits on ground that falls away to the woods, including those limestone ledges you informed me of. That is the ground he must take. Can you remember all that?"

I told him I could, but he wouldn't believe me and made me repeat it. He again struck the pose of thrusting his hand in the front of his tunic. "Very well, there is one more thing I want you to say.

Say to him I have decided there shall be no campfires. We must not divulge our intentions. Say to Hooker—I have told him already but it bears repeating—say to him that he must launch his attack at earliest dawn. I repeat, earliest dawn! I am sending Sergeant Daniels here with you—he is known to Hooker as one of my couriers—so he will know you are credible. Be advised the password is 'Bonaparte.' Any questions?"

They all stood looking at me. My mind in a whirl, I couldn't remember exactly what the question had been. I shook my head and decided I'd better give it a nod. The General nodded back. Yet he continued to stare at me for several more seconds. At length, he whispered behind his hand to the Sergeant. It didn't matter. I had plans of my own.

Home, so close I could almost reach out and touch it.

As I turned away, General McClellan fired a parting shot: "Young man! The latrines, you should know by now, are out behind the house! A good bivouac is a clean bivouac! I'm sure General Porter here would agree." The man next to him nodded that he most certainly did agree. Impulsively, I, too, bobbed my head up and down— looking for all the world like a puppet on a string.

*****

"Sorry, it's the best I could do. Not all the supply wagons are up." The Sergeant fingered the blue sleeve that flopped a good two inches over my wrist. When I gave the blue kepi a tug, it wanted to go down around my ears.

"The General, he's been busting a gut," Sergeant Daniels said through a crooked smile. "Seems he's more hot and bothered about those supply wagons than he is about the Rebels strung out along all those hills over there."

The clouds had thickened; the night had turned black. The wind blowing up from the creek didn't smell so much of sulfur now, or even of old grass or new hay or plowed earth, but of something I had never before known, sickly sweet, something that prickled my backbone, my scalp.

145

We swung to our saddles and walked the horses slowly down-hill. The animals were skittish as we ghosted into a ravine that crumpled quickly into folds that fell to the creek. And again that smell.

I turned and looked back. A small group of men stood in front of flames darting from a big metal drum. Even at a distance, I could see that one of them, his bushy white beard illuminated by the flames, appeared to be making fretful little gestures, as if pleading; then his arms just dropped.

I nudged the horse forward and turned my thoughts to the man riding beside me. Could it be that, unlike other Yankees I'd talked with, political wind hadn't blown him away from the truth? What slavery could do to a man?

I tried to make out the town, a steeple, something I knew. Nothing but darkness and a few flashing pops, way up by farmer Miller's trees.

A sprinkling of other lights now. I could almost hear, barely, the sound, very faint, of voices, broken and thin, singing.

Fragments of song whiffled in with wind coming down over the fields and up from the water, the voices nearly dying as the wind, for a moment, stopped brushing my cheek, then, briefly, coming alive: *"Look awayy... look awayy..."*

A fleeting image of my father wormed a tightness to my chest: that singing; those Rebs; my pa, sparkling in his gray uniform—he might have sung that look-away song—and me, tricked up in ill-fitting blue, on a mission for a puffed-up Yankee General...

More wind. No song in it now. A snifter of rain. The night wasn't cold, but the shudders were stubborn. I tugged at my cap; it still wouldn't fit. Touching my heels to the horse, I tried to search through the darkness. I couldn't see where I was going.

"We gotta be too far north!" Maybe the Sergeant would listen this time. I'd already voiced my suspicion, but he'd plodded on and kept to himself. I wanted to know where we were. More than that, I needed human sound between myself and the uncertainty that lay in our path.

A path. Less certain than a road, it worked away from the water, going west. But no signs of Hooker. No signs of life. At least I couldn't see them or hear them or smell them. Yet I could feel them, feel them with my neck hair, feel them as surely as if someone came whooping the name "Dick Turpin" straight in my face.

A burst of bangs stippled the night. Pickets? Hooker's men? Stonewall's? Whose side was I on?

Somewhere ahead of us a dog began barking. And now, a low murmurous thrum, like faraway waves cuffing a shore. Yank voices? Bouncing in the saddle like a cork on the sea, I blinked into the void. It had started to rain.

The night wasn't just dark; it was the color of ink, the rain drizzling down, the air charged with that sickly sweet smell. And with something more now, something rank, almost like hugging a pig. All at once a truth struck me. The new smell: human flesh that was unclean but alive and the other, flesh that—

Suspicious, I stood in my stirrups, reached a hand inside my pants. Good. The wetness near my crotch was only the rain seeping through.

"What do you think, Sergeant?" It was less a question than a plea for personal human sound.

"Hooker might have cut across the fields," Sergeant Daniels replied, "instead of holding to the roads if there are any roads. Maybe we should bear off to the south."

South. Miller's farm, Mumma's too, farther on. I could make it home from either place blindfolded.

Hunching my shoulders against the rain, I tried to shake the sop from my shirt, the same as Ty used to shake himself when out in the rain, wanting to be someplace else.

Someplace else? No place anymore that wasn't chock-full of guns and Yankees and Rebels.

Rebels. A deadly, big-booted man tromping in with them, like Barbara Reel had feared?

"Why are you here, Sergeant?" I had to say something. Besides, I needed to know.

"Same as you. The General sent me."

"No, I mean why are you in this war at all?"

"I'm a Massachusetts man. Plenty of us up there hold strong beliefs about right and wrong, which is pretty important when you're fixing to fight for those beliefs."

I almost laughed with relief. Something more than political wind or selfish ambition must have drawn this man into the war, which was at least one up on certain Generals and Colonels and Captains I could name pretty fast. They hadn't got past the Union or having stars on their shoulders. Jeremiah, he could tell you what kinds of whips and sticks had made a cruel map of his back!

"What do you mean by 'pretty important'?" I couldn't let the thought get away easy.

"Well, what really put a bur under our saddles was the evil of slavery."

My heart began hitting my ribs as fast as the rain was hitting my face. "So you think slavery is a low-down, rotten thing, and that slaves, even when they run away, they shouldn't have to go back!"

"I mean to say they have as much right to their freedom as you and me have a right to ours."

Didn't the night seem a little less nasty? If this man felt that way, maybe some, maybe a lot, of those Yankees out there felt that way too? I had to get the thought all the way out in the open: "You mean they should be free like us, have the same chance as me and you to do what they want with their lives. Right?"

"Well—"

More shots, much closer, like hands clapping hard. Too close? Too far forward? Had we gone past the blue pickets? More important things first: "For everybody to be free and equal. That's what this war really comes down to, huh, Sergeant?"

"That way, though, the darkies would be your equals in everything. Living right next to you. Like a... a neighbor, competing for the same job even."

"But you said they have a right to be free!"

"Sure. Free from bondage. Free from getting whupped all the time."

"But they should be able to choose what they do and go where they want. That's what freedom is all about, isn't that so?"

"They should be free, yeah. But I can't say I want them tossing their hats in the ring with me, even-steven. And what about respectable employment? I'm planning on being a lawyer. Can you feature a darky lawyer?"

Now I was sure where we were—not that I'd been here before—but I knew. This gloomy, rain-drenched field, surely it met up with grass and dirt and woods that knew the weight of my boots, and surely it could take me where I needed to go—the Smoketown Road; it cut through Hooker's whole cursed corps!

I shook myself, blinked the rain from my eyes, and sat bolt upright in the saddle. I had to get free of all this, free of bluebellies who paraded their patriotism and fancied respectable employment but hadn't the foggiest notion of lashed backs, of blinded eyes.

Strange. Why had it taken me so long to come to the truth—truth as bright as the flash over those looming woods up ahead, as sharp as the clap that followed that flash—that my grandfather's anguish had a much stronger pull on me than jawing with Yankees or with anyone else, and even if he clammed up at times and ignored me at times, he cared about me all of the time, and cared about—Astounding! G'Pa—Barbara Reel too, I'd take bets—had been hiding and helping slaves who were running away! Like Jeremiah, who, because of some great crushing debt, wouldn't run anymore.

Sergeant Daniels again had gone quiet. Thinking about becoming a lawyer? And all those other blue soldiers—wherever they were—thinking about their own white skins? If only I could rid myself of these Yankees, fly away on a wind of my own.

My blue woolen shirt was ungodly soppy, too itchy for words. I squirmed, scratched, and hunched myself.

Sergeant Daniels had nudged his horse nearer and was watching me closely. "What's the matter?" I threw at him. "Why're you looking at me all peculiar-like?"

"On account of you're acting weird. Besides, the General told me on the QT to keep a close eye on you. He said you were young and likely to scare up real easy and said—"

"Oh, he said that, did he? Well, he doesn't know the half of what I've been through! Neither do you! Neither one of you care about anything that doesn't—"

"Pipe down, you'll spook our pickets. We might have circled around our flank, gone beyond our lines."

The Sergeant wasn't too quiet; he talked too much! Enough of his babbling! His presence was as much a hindrance to what I had to do, right now, as the soggy blue thing that stuck to my arms and clung to my chest.

He'd moved in front of me. Now, because he couldn't watch me as much—searching ahead of us, as if unsure where we were—I yanked off my cap, sailed it into the night, then tore at my shirt, blindly ripped at buttons that tried to elude me, and the horse was no help, lurching, shying away from the voices that had closed in around us, so I gave the horse a smack of my heels, went lickety-cutting past Sergeant Daniels, and shoved myself free.

Free! Even the buttons knew when to give in, letting me peel off the shirt. Sliding side to side on the saddle, I tightened my knees and wide-opened my mouth for the joy that I had. "Bonaparte! Bonaparte!" Just the right thing to be yelling—the word from McClellan's own mouth—so they'd keep their hands off me. Yes, I could vanish like smoke down that road that I knew!

Even the rain seemed to know I was free, bringing gooseflesh as it flushed off the feel of what I had worn. And because I was free, like a flyaway goose, would it do any harm, holding fast to the reins, to hold out my arms like the wings that they were?

Men rose up, their hands snatching at me, their throats cutting loose, as I leaned into the forward push of the horse.

"He's vamoosin'! Grab 'im!"

Clinching my knees as hard as I could, I raced on past, raised my face to the rain, and let it plaster my hair, and suddenly, the road was before me, and I knew where I was. Those trees looming up, they were girdled old friends, would take me in, would—*pop… pop, pop—Whump.*

All at once, I truly was flying, nothing beneath me, and my side was on fire as I slammed to the earth. The fallen horse's scream bounced off the trees, and one of its forelegs kept kicking and kicking the air. My own leg, yes, I could move it. I tested my belly, my side, where an outcropping of rock had raked me raw.

Get away from here! Run somewhere! Run? I hoped I could walk.

More noise, rustling through bushes, coming my way, low branches yielding, twigs snapping. I lay stock-still. For certain, "Bonaparte" didn't belong here. My horse had gone eerily quiet. Now I could tell I was surrounded by gurgling, croaking, calling for "Mother," for "God."

Swishing sounds. Closer now. Twangy voices. Col. Davis, he'd know what state they were from.

"Come straight from that Yank picket line yonder, arms a-stretchin' out like some ol' bird."

"Crazier'n a hoot owl, screechin' somethin', an' belt-up nekkid, seem like. Cain't be lettin' 'im run loose 'mongst our boys. Sure we drilled 'im?"

"Ifn he ain't holier'n thou already, we'll put 'im dead t'rights pronto. Cock yer pieces, boys."

I heard a series of *clicks*, no more than a dozen paces from me.

But I was no Yank. I'd got rid of the cap, stripped off most everything blue, so surely these niggling secesh would understand, would—

"See any sign of 'im, shoot 'im, first an' fast."

These drawling creatures wouldn't care who I was, who my father had been, or what would happen at earliest dawn. They had but one thing in mind. I was no better off than all those other nameless souls mewling beneath the dripping trees.

Jeremiah, he'd know what to do... and so would his brother, the fox...

A sudden thought: the fox carrying scat in his mouth, tricking his enemy, pretending to be something he wasn't...

In seconds, my tortured breathing would give me away, not to mention my rollicking case of the shakes. They were certain to see me—no, they were certain to hear me. Pretend to be something I wasn't? Play stone-cold dead?

Couldn't do it. Too cold. Too bruised and bloody to be that still. Swiftly, I sent my hands to my pockets and brought them back out. Something to hold onto. On my own, I couldn't get through this—but maybe with help. A tiny gold cross balled in one fist, a gold wedding ring clutched in the other.

Before I could capture more air, a spatter of drops, other people sucking for breath. A toe prodded my side; it slipped, something slippery down there.

"Got 'im dead t'rights, jus' like I tol' yuh, Eb."

Another foot—this one shod—stabbed under my back, pitched me onto my belly. "He's done fer, let's get back inna corn, safer in 'ere. More Yanks comin', prob'ly."

They began to shuffle away. I tried to hold in my breath, but the pain wouldn't let me. I bit back a sob and opened my eyes to be sure they were going. Couldn't see, I was turned the wrong way. Still, I had a dreadful sense of – Yes. One of the Rebs had stopped and was coming back.

Wheezing over me, he kicked me faceup, leaned down. It was only my mouth taking air, but the fume found my nostrils, filling them; my throat started to quiver. A hand dove into my pocket, fishing and bumping, the other pocket too, both of them rifled, both of them empty. My fists in a death grip, it seemed like my life now lived in my fists.

A starburst, a *Bang*. My insides jumped as light flooded the woods. For a few seconds, my tiny festering space became a pale imitation of daytime. A firecracker frenzy brought yells from the corn. The Reb straightened, turned. My breath came out in grateful little gasps, now that…*Clonk*.

A single swing of the Rebel's boot caught me square on the side of my ribs.

Instantly, a white hot coal consumed my insides and ignited the loudest scream of my life. The woods went dark.

I rolled away, my flesh crying *No!* But I rolled again, into a tree. I knew this tree! I knew the limbs I'd lopped from it, the woodpile I'd fashioned from it, and just enough space behind it to squirm myself. But not enough time.

Yellow flashes stabbed through the rain, etching tree trunks in stark relief. The Reb stood looking down, his musket pointing. Even if he didn't squeeze the trigger, that sharp thing on the end—

More flashes, more popping. Some leaves went *clip-snip* close overhead, and something went *thunk* into the tree. I dared to look up. The Reb was gone.

Lots of jabber outside the woods. I would never make it into that cornfield, let alone through its acres and acres of crispy stalks. Only one way to go.

Chapter 15

Still short of breath, I inched along on knees that had scuffed through my pants, poking at underbrush and rises of earth, trying to aim myself away from the Rebs and their jabber and muskets out in the corn. I pocketed the wedding ring but kept the cross firm in my hand. It might not help, but G'Pa would approve.

My fist bumped into something. It seemed inclined to give way. Too soft for a rock, too solid to have come from the ground. I lost my balance. My face plopped down on whatever it was.

In only a second, I knew what it was; it was human—or had been—and it reeked, and it moved, not on its own, but because I made it move. Shocked to the roots of my teeth, I tumbled away.

Above the trees another shell came apart, leaching everything white. My jaw dropped like a well bucket. Not because of the deathly stink and not because of the corpse my fist had discovered but because of the ashen figure, an arm's length away, hunched on the ground at the dead creature's feet. Rocking and swaying the figure was. Shards of bone showed through splotched corn leaves holding an ankle together, as the figure's unblinking eyes stared at the corpse.

"That-there's my pa," the figure muttered. "Don't you be messin' with my pa."

I scrubbed my contaminated hand on my pants, wanting to holler that his pa was gone, that he couldn't hang onto his pa anymore. The naked truth! But I only crawled away. And as darkness returned, the muttering returned, calling for, "Pa…Pa…?" Sucking for more breath, I crawled out of the woods.

Barren fields stretched darkly away, bumping away, pitching down and away, till stopped by the water, far beyond the range of my eyes. Barely I could make out the lumpish hills on the far side of the creek. I took a long breath, looked left and right, again straight ahead. Everything was black, except for a single flicker of light, a good mile off.

No, no campfires tonight. Even Gen. McClellan's headquarters up on those hills was dark. Except for that tiny yellow flame. It was the last place I wanted to go but the only place I could go and only by crawling. How else to get back to sheltering apple tree branches, where a flickering metal drum stood alone in the rain? But then the cruelest truth of all hit me. The General's message—what would he do when he learned I had failed?

*****

The little cross was warm in my fist. Something heartening to hold onto, nothing else to hold onto, even memories of my pa slipping away.

Tentatively, I reached down a hand, tried to feel how broken I was: a sticky reminder that misery had hounded me since I'd shot down poor Ty, misery that had followed me to Harpers Ferry and back, a deadly reminder of the Winchester Reb, of Jeremy James, of Major Jack Taylor. Their blood somehow had dulled my memory, sidetracked it from the blood shed by my father. It wasn't fair!

My misery finally boiled over: "God, help me!" I waited a few seconds for something to happen. Nothing happened. Not even another flash from the sky. Again, I started to crawl.

In less than five minutes, I collapsed on the grass, rolled onto my back, and stared into the void. I looked across at the hills for a flame from the drum. Just as I found it, it flickered a few times and went out.

Breathing was better, so were my ears: sobbing, pleading, cursing; the sounds kept coming at me from places I couldn't see. I could hear the misery, could feel it myself, because the misery came back repeatedly to the same precious thing. Water.

Another sound. Not imploring or raging...muffled, not a misery somehow. Best not move. Best not get too close to a sound I couldn't see. I had to move, though, and after renewing my grip on the cross, I was back on my knees. Now, strangely, I was drawn to the sound.

Crawling closer, my own parched throat as insistent as all the others out there, I cried out my need, silently, cricket-clear in my brain. *Water.*

The creek. Water down there. But a trip and a half for somebody down off his feet and out at the knees.

The sound, I heard it again, a few yards away. A snort, no, a snuffle. Lordy, I'd found me a horse! And now that I was close and screwed up my eyes, I detected a rider, slumped, swaying in the saddle. I stopped crawling and stared. I needed that horse!

The animal thrashed its head, lowered it, and lapped at something. Water? Had to be, I could smell it almost, could reach out and feel where it seeped from the ground where the earth may have fractured, maybe from all the infernal thudding, and now it was leaking, more than farmer Miller's trees I'd just got flush of.

The horse's nose was soft against my hand. The rider must have sensed my presence: "Water…"

I didn't respond. I needed water. And I needed the horse. Dropping the cross in my pocket, I cupped my hands, winced as water escaped through my fingers.

"W-water."

Uh-uh. No stranger to slow me down, not now. I dropped to the ground, faced away from the man, this nuisance that stood between me and the horse. Trouble was this man couldn't stand between me and the horse. Couldn't stand at all. Kind of like me.

I drew up my knees, rocked back and forth, tried to find something to help me know what to do. Something prodded me, like a thorn in my side. I made a grab for the irritation. The cross, it insisted on jabbing me. Again, the horse snuffled. I looked up and tried to make out a face. Too dark, he could still be a stranger.

I struggled to my feet, a little amazed that they could support me, and went to the horse. I searched with my hands, my eyes. No canteen. Nothing to hold any water, not even a hat.

Once more I cupped my hands over the seep: it was like spooning up broth with a fork.

The creek. Water aplenty. For both of us.

After two or three tries, I got a grip on the saddle, clumsily swung up a leg, and flopped myself back of the man. Had to be in back, he was starting to tip. It was only after I got the horse moving that I realized I could have satisfied my leathery throat by using my tongue, just like the horse. Yet I was riding away, propping up a man whose face I still couldn't see.

My arms and legs cramping up, I labored to hold the man upright. I couldn't find the reins. Good thing the horse didn't seem to need steering; it moved with little urging, following the downhill sweep of the land, picking its way over patches of rock, sidestepping other faint shapes, some of which made secret little noises.

The man swayed in the saddle. I scrunched up my mouth when something wet found my fingers where I held to a shoulder. He didn't speak but every so often made feeble utterances, almost like those rising up from the ground near where the horse's hooves cobbled the rocks. It wasn't talk. Still, the man could listen, and the night was dismal, and the rain was clammy, and Sergeant Daniels had come a cropper when it came to listening. Talk, even one-sided and only briefly, might shield me from the grisly things I'd seen and heard and smelled and tasted since I'd run off, especially since my father's face was much dimmer now.

I rambled on about Kernstown, about a runaway slave and a quick-witted fox, about lighting out for Harpers Ferry and coming full-circle back, about how I had to get back to G'Pa. Rambling talk mostly. But my arms seemed to find comfort as I clung to this man whose face I couldn't see.

The man said nothing sensible, not until the horse abruptly stopped. The creek. A bare whisper then: "Think...you've come... wrong way."

It was too dark to see this soldier's colors. It was beginning to dawn on me, though, that, instead of helping him out of harm's way, I'd delivered him up to something maybe more wretched, delivered him up to soldiers in blue. Yes, wrong way. Wrong for me, too. Almost at once figures came at us, rifles raised.

"Bonaparte!" The word came out high and scratchy. But the rifles went down. Two Yanks, one holding the reins, led us across a stone bridge, past a lonely-looking gristmill, up a soggy ravine, to a large brick house on a hill. Nearby, a big metal drum sent up wispy smoke through the dim glow cast by the coals.

A mocking voice came from the dark recesses of the porch: "Hark! Yon comes a woebegone fella. Methinks he forgot to take his umbrella!" A pause, a shuffle of boots, and the voice turned serious: "Yee gods, laddie, what have you got yourself into this time?"

The boots clumped on the stairs; a lantern flared, and Autie's lean face was looking down at my near nakedness, unbelieving. Yet in an instant, he shifted his gaze and narrowed his eyes. "It can't be!" he blurted. "Is that really you, Ol' Rob?"

My bewilderment grew as the man I was holding murmured, "Really me, Ol' Fanny...and never been...in sorrier shape." He started to fall. Autie thrust up his arms, steadied the man, and eased him to the ground.

Immediately, he was all business. "You two," he snapped, "put down those rifles and carry this man to my tent. Carefully, now! Then go fetch Doctor Letterman and bring him there, on the double!"

"But sir, the Doctor's been cutting and stitching all day and the General ordered him to get some sleep. Besides, this-here's a Reb!"

"Are you deaf, man?" Autie snatched off his floppy hat and took a swipe at the soldier. "On the double, I said!"

I attempted to get words in edgewise: "Horse ran away, shucked off those blue duds, lotsa shooting, Reb nearly kicked me to pieces."

I might as well have been that metal drum, cold and wet and lifeless, for the attention I got. As he led the way to his tent, Autie held the lantern low, inspecting the wounded man's colorless face, clucking his concern for this soldier who was supposed to be his enemy.

Minutes later, a wiry man in a crumpled blue uniform pushed his way through the tent flap; his dark mustache drooped; below his eyes were the darkest circles I'd ever seen on a man.

"My apologies, Doctor," said Autie as he took the man by the arm and ushered him across the tent, "but this problematical officer here happens to be a very dear friend of mine, despite his low-grade intelligence in choosing up sides." Autie hovered over the half-conscious form sprawled on his cot. He pulled at his mustache as he studied a shoulder of the gray uniform where a small ragged hole was oozing. "Pray acquaint yourself with Major Robert Pescud, CSA," he said. "A gentleman of Virginia and late of the United States Military Academy. A scholar and a speechifier to boot, though a bit shy on speech at present. Would have graduated near the top of his class but took French leave when his native state jumped out of the Union. You look a mite poorly, Rob ol' boy. You can help him, can't you, Doctor?"

The sight of the wounded Confederate did something peculiar to my insides. A Confederate officer. A scholar and a speechifier. So much like—

(There had been a time I'd watched my lawyer father argue a case. There had been tears in that courtroom, tears worked up by the wistful but compelling voice of my father, scholar and speechifier that he was. And now my own eyes were tearing up, because my father's memory was still alive—his face more vivid than in any dream I'd had lately—and on top of that I'd talked close-up to this Confederate officer, my arms around him, a hug almost.)

"A clean wound, I think" the Doctor observed, probing carefully. "He has lost a lot of blood, and we are short of medical supplies until all the wagons are up. I will dress the wound as best I can. Mainly, he needs rest." He reached into a black bag he'd brought with him and lifted out a small bottle of amber-colored liquid. "I'm sure this brandy will ease his pain." He looked over at me. "Some for the boy too, I think. He looks like—Well, give him some brandy."

After attending to Robert Pescud, the officers turned their attention on me, which made me feel fine as silk! They peered and puttered, Autie calling for dry clothes, Doctor Letterman calling for a fresh basin of water, finally wrapping clean cloth around my middle before announcing, "Keep this on, young man! Your ribs don't appear to be broken. However, another tumble could turn you into a charming medical specimen!"

I looked over at Maj. Rob Pescud. The brandy seemed to have worked wonders on him: his eyes were open and focused, resting on us for several seconds, shifting to a table piled with papers, lingering there.

Autie heaped thanks on the Doctor then nodded at his Confederate friend. "I'll take the Major's parole. He can stay with me till he's more fit. Assuming, of course, his friends don't come calling and knock my good intentions into the creek yonder."

We followed the Doctor outside. Even though the Major inside had qualities that brought a lump to my throat, I had to know: "How can you be friends with the enemy? Back over there, he'd have tried to croak you! Now he's calling you '0l' Fanny,' and you're giving him brandy! It wasn't like that at Kernstown, I can tell you that much!"

"Easy does it, laddie. Here, take another swaller. I'll even join you. As to '0l' Fanny,' Rob and some of his waggish cohorts tagged me with that, plus a few other unmentionables, when we were at West Point together. Just tongue in cheek, you understand, trying to get my dander up. Rob, though, was a tad more serious when it came to orating about Southern rights, hurrah. Still and all, a friend is a friend."

Maybe Autie was right. Col. Grimes Davis, hadn't there been a catch in his voice when he'd spoken of Capt. John Sims of Barksdale's Brigade? Still, I had a notion that gunpowder—when it worked— blasted friendship to kingdom come when battles were fought. I opened my mouth to argue the point. Autie beat me to the punch: "I have it on the highest authority, laddie, that a man can have no greater love than laying down his life for a friend. Not for his Country, mind you, for a friend!"

"What did the Major orate about?" I asked. Maybe knowing that would help me understand my father's convictions.

"Know it all by heart practically," Autie said, as he led me back inside the tent. "Maybe if he hears me orate about him, it'll perk him up some. 0l' Rob really used to lay it on me and my Northern brethren. Specially the part about the Northern colonies—early on anyhow—turning a deaf ear when Virginia, the beloved state of his birth, kicked up a fuss about the evils of slavery. Can you believe, laddie, that the Old Dominion appealed to the British Crown twen-ty-three times in a vain attempt to put the vile practice down?"

I drank in the words. Maybe my pa, without my knowing, had taken a stand like that.

Apparently enlivened by my rapt attention, Autie took a deep breath, looked over at his friend, and plunged ahead: "Alas, the South went bumping every which way, trying to get rid of slavery on a grad-ual basis, within the context of law, not overnight and not, I might add, by repugnant violence that makes leaders out of West Pointers before the ink on their commissions is hardly dry. Course, that was all before Mr. Eli Whitney changed everything by inventing the cot-ton gin, which made keepin' slaves a tad more profitable, leastwise farther down south. How'm I doin' so far, Major Pescud, suh?"

The Major's eyelids fluttered, but he must have been listening: he let out a heavy, perceptive sigh.

Autie bobbed his head in what I took to be self-approbation and hurried on: "But it was not because of slavery per se that the South finally took up arms. It was because of Honor, me lad, and because of the violated sacred right of self-government reputedly signed, sealed, and delivered by the Founding Fathers of us all. Not to mention the fact that given its growing industrial and political clout, the North was near to unleashing on a genteel and sensitive South its pugna-cious hordes of...uh...uh—"

"Robber Barons!" Rob Pescud's voice was a bit quavery but had conviction behind it.

"Saints preserve us, the patient perks up! Steady on there, Ol' Rob, I know the litany by heart. And so, laddie, as a result of these threats to its health and prosperity—nay, to its very survival—the South had no choice but to strike the first blow. To preserve its gene-alogical assets, you might say."

Autie hesitated and pulled at his mustache, pondering, it looked like, then bobbing his head, as if he'd made up his mind about something. "And the Rebels," he went on, "have done passing well, wouldn't you say? Even here, they have us exactly where they want us. They have an excellent defensive position, and they got us way outnumbered, now that all of Jackson's forces are up from Harpers

Ferry. But I digress. We were talkin' about Major Pescud's highfalu-tin' falderol!"

I'd been watching Autie but throwing glances the Major's way. Was it my imagination? Hadn't the Confederate's eyes gone enor-mously wide when hearing that all of Jackson's forces were up?

Autie appeared not to notice: "Now, here's the part I fancy most, laddie. Having slavery was like having a wolf by the ears. You have him, but you're afraid to let go! And here's Rob's kicker. There was a stronger legal and moral imperative for the South to secede than there was for the Declaration of Independence! There, how'd I do, Major ol' boy?"

Rob Pescud's eyes were closed, his chest rising and falling, slowly, sleepily. Yet seconds before, I could swear his eyes had been those of a hawk.

I found myself studying both men: enemies one minute, friends the next. Which meant the reverse could be true.

As I listened to Autie chatter on about his Confederate friend—not that I savvied everything he said—I seemed to rediscover memo-ries of another Confederate officer, almost as if me and my pa, even briefly, had put our Shipley heads together. I filled my lungs with the breath of fresh recognition: how a life could change because of a friend—like Jeremiah and me—and how my father might have cho-sen a side because of his friends, which was maybe the wrong reason but made it easier to understand and forgive.

All this because I'd denied myself water and steered an enfeebled soldier away from a place where trees got shot. And all that because I'd been drawn to a sound hidden in darkness, while squeezing a tiny gold cross, as if my very life depended on it.

My eyelids kept sliding down, and though I fought to buoy them up, seductive waves kept enfolding me, blurring my vision and fuzzing my thoughts. Autie's jawing finally damped down, along with the lantern, and I was but dimly aware when a warm nubby blanket came under my chin.

Through a wisp of dream—a man staring through cobwebs, another man clutching a hoe—I felt someone shake me. Now why in the world would Autie—

"Son." A low whisper, a hand placed lightly over my mouth. Autie, he never called me "Son."

"Listen carefully," murmured Rob Pescud's voice, soft but distinct. "From what you told me—Kernstown, your father—I know I can trust you. And I know that somehow you'll get through to your folks, over there, real soon. Take this note with you. Guard it with your life if need be. Hard to read, done in the dark. But more important than you can possibly know. And when you do get back, place it in the hands of the first Confederate officer you find. Now where can you hide it?"

All at once a sour taste came to my mouth (*the first Confederate officer you find: that sounded eerily familiar*). Turning away, I drew down in my blanket. This was none of my business. I wasn't a Reb.

Pescud shook me again. He must have sensed my reluctance. He said, "Your father's memory, do this for him!"

This man, he'd called me "Son"...

I let several seconds go by, then rolled back toward the Major, got an elbow beneath me and braced myself up. I still wanted no part of his message, didn't want to know what it said, and would only be doing the thing to honor a memory, a memory that had new life because of this man.

"I... I can hide the note in my boot, up by my toe," I whispered. Little did he know that, a couple days past, I'd hidden a Yankee message up by that toe. After squeezing my shoulder, the Major went back to his cot.

For a long time, I listened to raindrops spatter the canvas. I listened to sharp little *bangs*—how far away?—and listened to light snoring across the tent, snoring that did not come from Rob Pescud's cot.

I listened, too, to what my conscience was asking me. Had I taken a stand? Done anything that might make a difference? Hadn't I been helping both sides? Whose side was I on? And even if I figured that out, what could I do?

Chapter 16

I thought I heard guns. When the earth shivered, I knew I'd heard guns, big guns.

I reared up from my blanket. A canteen rattled against the tent pole and not far off: something went *Whamm Clank*.

Rob Pescud stirred on his cot; he looked over at me intently. A moment later, Autie poked his head inside and beckoned to me. "Up'n at 'em, ol' top! The General desires your presence out of doors!"

The General wanted to see me? Uh-oh.

"The General's not going to get any more of me!" I fired back. "This war's not going to get any more of me. I'm going home!"

"And how do you propose to get there, laddie? A morning stroll through the meadow, perhaps?"

"I… I don't rightly know. But I'm going. Somehow."

"Well, before you take leave of us, you should know that the General's lathered up to a fare-thee-well. About your exploits last night, that is."

I attempted to cover my head with the blanket.

"A courier made it back here early this morning. Seems you caused quite a ruckus!"

The blanket was too small to get all the way under.

"Never seen him in such a tizzy. Seems he's singled you out for special treatment."

Maybe if I curled myself up, the blanket would—

"He's near ready to give you a medal. Short of that, a letter of commendation. Well done, laddie!"

I opened my mouth but couldn't find words.

"If I had your modesty, laddie, I'd still be a shavetail lieutenant! Thing is, your mad dash into enemy lines allowed Sergeant Daniels to get back inside ours. He was able to deliver the good General's message, thanks to your quick-thinking diversion. Course, the message itself made no more sense than a cow with a musket! Now as to your going home, humor me first by getting some food in your belly before—"

Whamm Whamm Clank.

Wanting desperately to plug my ears, I started to squirm under the blanket. But that wouldn't do, not with Autie waiting, watching, and Rob Pescud doing the same. I shrugged off the blanket.

My fingers searched for the note in my boot, shoved it further down near the toe, and all innocence, asked Autie to help me pull it on.

"There's a good fellow!" Autie gave me a quick smile before pushing through the tent fly, not looking back.

Avoiding Rob Pescud's eyes, I worked my toes, tested the feel of the paper, and finally hitched my way outside. Gen. McClellan was nowhere in sight. I was secretly pleased. A letter of commendation was the last thing I deserved.

Ground-hugging fog discovered my face. "Why are they shooting?" I asked as I licked at the moisture. "Can't see a blasted thing!"

"We pretty much know where the enemy's at," Autie replied, "and the General's got fond of bringing guns of position to bear, a tactic he prizes highly from studying the arts of war, over in the Crimea, I think."

Autie paused, his eyes mischievous. "Those are twenty-pounder Parrotts," he said casually.

Not about to be suckered into a childish inquiry about large birds, I said, "Yeah, with wrought iron bands shrunk to the breach!"

Feeling some of the tension melt, I stole a look at him and detected a wide grin. Best not be taken in by Autie's wiles. I put on a frown. "What does the General want me for this time, besides a letter of commendation?"

"Need you ask? To expound on the lay of the land! As if you haven't done that already. Did I mention that the man is a mite cautious?" Autie made no attempt to hide a smile. "Since, lamentably, he's off somewhere on his high horse, I'll third-degree you myself. That will tickle him no end." After fingering his red scarf, he said,

"We know the enemy's there." He aimed a finger. "You can catch glimpses of 'em through the fog. Look a bit like ants scurrying around up there, don't they? Up by those yonder woods."

"Last night, I almost got myself killed in those yonder woods!" I waited for some sympathetic words. They didn't come.

"Thing is, we're not certain what kind of cover the enemy's got." Autie was studying a notebook now. "Hollows, fences, rocky ledges, that sort of thing. Details, that's what we need. Now, this-here map you drew for the General, it's got a major thoroughfare running south to north."

"The Hagerstown Pike."

"That's the one." Autie traced the route with his finger. "Good access for infantry and artillery both. What they'll use to move troops north when Hooker hits 'em." He kept squinting through the fog, a hard set to his face. Without looking at me, he said, "Make no mistake, the Rebs will deploy in the fields just the other side of that Pike. That's where we're probing with our long-range rifled guns. With a tube elevation of ten degrees and a two-and-a-half-pound powder charge, they can hurl a twenty-pound projectile well over a mile. Now then, any other roads they might use?"

I looked away, roaming my eyes. I tested my legs: a trifle more steady. But our cottage was a staggering long way to go. Course, there was no way to get there.

I looked back at Autie; he was waiting, his eyes expectant: roads, yes.

"Well, there's this funny old cart path, real sunken down, I fell into it once, and it goes all zigzaggy past the Piper place. That's where my friend Jeremiah—"

"Sunken, you say, not in good shape, maybe fortified. And it goes from where to where?"

Even as I was explaining that the sunken road shot off the Boonsboro Pike, going this way and that like it couldn't make up its mind, that the farmers used it for hauling grain to a mill by the creek, and that their horses knew it so well the wagons didn't really need drivers, I had an alarming sense of another road that went north, of a white-framed cottage sitting all alone at a right-angle bend in that lonely road.

Autie, still making notes, said, "What about those other things—hollows, fences, rocky places?"

"Sam Mumma's place, it's chock-full of things like that. Just to the left of those woods up there, where—"

"What is it, laddie?"

I narrowed my eyes to be sure. Yes, I was sure. "That black smoke churning up, past all those trees, that *is* Sam Mumma's place! I've barked my shins on his fences and tripped on his rocks dozens of times!"

The Yankee Captain's field glasses went up. He briefly inspected the smoke, moved the glasses away from it. "What's directly the other side of those woods?" His voice was flat, no warmth at all.

"A real big cornfield," I said, trying to wring some warmth from that voice. "Some rails rotted through there, and I fixed 'em. And David Miller, he girdles his trees in those woods so that they—"

"What about farther west? There's another big patch of woods over near that Hagerstown Pike. True?"

"Yes!" I felt flame rush to my face. This Yankee cared not a whit about folks like Sam Mumma, like David Miller, whose homes were getting shot up and burned. Didn't give a hang, neither, about folks like Jeremiah. Just like the General. Autie was all wrapped up in hollows and fences and guns of position, in getting stars on his shoulders. To him, I was no more than "the lay of the land," and to Col. Grimes Davis and Maj. Rob Pescud, no better than a pair of boots to carry a note. My face grew hotter.

Intent on his notebook, Autie seemed not to notice. Not looking up, he said, "Back of that little church, roundabout those westerly woods, that's where the Rebels will stage up. I take me an oath, it'll be Jackson! Yes, back of those woods, that's where the enemy will conceal their forces. And that is where our Parrotts will concentrate their fire. By jings, we'll reduce that ground to rubble!"

I felt the blood sluice away from my face. And I felt Autie's eyes.

"Now what, laddie?" His voice, finally, had a touch of concern. But that didn't matter much anymore.

"You said, back of those woods—"

"Yes? So?"

"That's exactly where me and my grandfather live."

Autie said something, but my ears were ringing, my heart beating crazily, so I wheeled away, began running, stumbling, pain seizing me where I'd been hurt up in those very woods, near to what used to be Sam Mumma's place. I willed my boots to move faster and willed myself to ignore that my bandage was oozing. Whatever it took to put distance between myself and anyone with a blue uniform on.

Autie was yelling, but I was puffing, couldn't make out the words, and so kept pushing myself, pegging across open ground, over a ridge, plunging into a pocket of trees on the reverse of the slope. I seized a low-hanging limb and flopped to the ground.

Wheezing like a bellows, I made a peephole through the branches. The gun carriages of the Parrotts were bucking like wild horses, the tubes darting bright orange tongues, huffing smoke whiter and thicker than the hovering fog. The cannons lurched and rumbled, a thunderstorm of battering drums. And now—nobody could see me, thank God—I jammed my fingers in my ears and if only there was a blanket to hide myself under.

I squeezed my eyes shut, opened my mouth, choked back a scream, squiggled my fingers, and shoved them deeper. It seemed that my fingers were too small for the job: the guns of position kept *p-p-pounding* into my head.

I began to have a coughing fit. Nowhere to go. How do you hide from smoke?

Behind my eyes, my head belonged to the throb of the guns. Maybe I should have stayed put with Autie? He at least, at times, helped keep the emptiness from getting too close. But emptiness, that wasn't enough to make me go back. So I lay on my side, curled up my knees, and squiggled my fingers some more.

Soon, I discovered that with some creative squiggling, I didn't hear the guns as much. I discovered, too, that by humming a tune that I knew I could almost pretend it was some other time, some other place. A tune my mother had sung long ago (I was only a boy), a time when her laughter was the best song of all (wasn't Betsy's laughter sort of like that?), and she had called me "Johnny jump up" and crooned to me after I'd said prayers and was cozy abed, making up words as she went, and that sure enough had tickled us both! Now, I had trouble remembering the words.

After the fever cruelly snatched Ma away from Pa and me, I tried not to think of her laughter and found pain in her songs. But now they were back, at least part of a song, and now, rocking myself (almost as if she were the one doing the rocking), I was moving to and fro to the sound of the tune my ears could hear, so long as my fingers didn't squiggle too hard.

A few minutes of that and the tune lost its allurement. My chest, then my throat, went tight, and all at once I felt the pain—the emptiness—I'd felt when my mother was gone. The pain had discovered a place right next to my heart. Then came Kernstown and that place was waiting, and the pain, it seemed to know exactly where to go. And now it was back—a special place, a secret pain.

But Pa had special feelings, too. Long before Kernstown, before the war tore us apart, I could see the way he carried the pain of my mother's quick, untimely death. Even at six years of age, I could feel his pain, almost as much as I could my own.

He filled up his life with lawyer work—or tried to—which lasted maybe a month, before his days and nights were taken up elsewhere. Drinking and cards, and other things, G'Pa had offered, his mouth so grim I couldn't look.

G'Pa carried pain as well—losing Gramma way too young—but he covered it up and carried on, leastwise till that brutal news from Kernstown. After that, he distanced himself from practicing law, betaking himself to an out-of-the-way farming town called Sharpsburg, which I'd never heard of.

No one seemed to know what he did out there, way across state. I was left with my Aunt Marcie in Baltimore, until her husband, a Union man, was killed at another place I'd never heard of before.

G'Pa didn't always have the glums. Every so often, he took me fishing—no hunting, though, he hated guns—and it was during those times that I got the smokesmelling, fish-sizzling memories of the Eastern Shore in my blood!

Sun-drenched beaches that made my nose mad with delight, whispering forests that marched down to the driftwood, rocks that grew barnacles, tempting places for bare feet, so you could wiggle your toes when the sand was warm, squish them into slick banners of kelp, pitch up rocks, and watch little blue crabs go scuttling off, even make them scurry over your feet. All of which wasn't nearly as much fun as hunting—shooting pintail ducks, say—which you could do only if armed for the purpose, I reminded my grandfather knowingly.

G'Pa's eyes went up, as if searching for V formations of birds. When he brought them back down, he astounded me by saying, "Pintails. That would be *Anas acuta*. No harm in learning their biological name. Why don't you try it?"

I sensed a long weekend of biological names stretching before me. I said, "I guess I'll just walk on the beach a while." Which would have been all right, except that I became a bit flustered and scoured my foot on a barnacled rock.

"Here, stand in this tidal pool," G'Pa quickly insisted. "The salt will do wonders for that nasty abrasion. Now," he went on earnestly, "what do you see down there?"

"Huh?" I felt the sting of my stupidity, as well as the sting of the salt, as the water turned pink.

"Below the water. What do you see?"

"More barnacles, on that rock, by my big toe."

He pointed to another rock, crusted white, high and dry in the hot summer sun. "See any difference between the two, between barnacles that are drinking in water and those that are drinking in sun? Can you learn anything from that?"

"Sure. Wear shoes next time."

He smiled, as grandfathers do, and launched an explanation of how a barnacle stands on his head and eats with his feet. "Look closely. Observe how this barnacle fellow has a sliding door that keeps him covered up when the tide is out. But when the tide comes back in, he opens his door and out come six pair of feathery feet, and he is all business, sweeping in food. But he is very creative. He keeps enough seawater behind his closed door to stay cozy and moist until the tide washes over him once more. Can you learn anything from all this?"

I was more interested in spying ducks on the wing and had a faraway look, I suppose, and didn't answer right off.

"Well, there is much to be learned," he answered himself. "A barnacle, of the Order *Cirripedia*, has tenacity, endurance, and patience." He poked his fingernail at a barnacle's base, where it sat staunchly glued to a rock. "Would that we had such selfpossession and adaptability in dealing with life!"

I sat down, took painstaking interest in sucking blood from my foot, and kept sucking and spitting till G'Pa finally stumped off to a lean-to he'd fashioned from pine boughs and driftwood and began to dabble with his watercolor paints. I figured that, and a decent lunch, would put him off asking more questions and spouting nonsensical Latin names. I was mistaken.

Maybe it was because we'd taken our meal (his own concoction, a portion of which consisted of greens he'd gathered from the margin of a nearby beaver pond) in the shade of a short-leaf pine (*Pinus echinata*, to be more exact) that stood next to a series of intersecting trails, though he called some of them "runs."

"How many signs of animal life can you detect, Sonny, from where we are sitting?"

I wasn't real surprised by the question, only at his calling me "Sonny." Of late, it had been "Johnny," unlike when I'd been young, when he was "G'Pa" and I was "Sonny" (pretty close to the "Son" my father called me and my grandfather called him), but I had enough presence of mind to point at a dull black bug at the root of a tree, then to a chittery squirrel, hard to miss in the sun-spangled branches directly above us.

"That is a horned fungus beetle by that root," G'Pa offered sagely. "It will feign death, trying to resemble fragments of rotted wood, when disturbed. Care to put it to the test?"

When I shook my head, he started in on the *Sciurus carolinensis*—that is to say, the gray squirrel—which actually leaves a trail, or skyway, in the limbs it uses day after day. And speaking of trails, he was actually rapt as he pointed to one of them—well trodden down and sort of squared up at the sides—that he said was a deer trail and had been in use for maybe a good hundred years!

Surely, I was a disappointment to him. I flat failed to detect a northern walking stick on a low branch, or a white-footed mouse peeking from a bush, or a wolf spider scurrying along its own little trail. He had to be stretching it, though, when he tried to bring me around to the notion that a really good Nature Tracker not only could locate a trail but identify the animals that used it, how old and how healthy they were, not to mention their gender, where they were coming from, where they were going to, and why!

It all seemed disarranged. What got me pumped up, though, was what he said next: "A true naturalist can size up an animal so well, he can become that animal. I would wager to say he could figure out how to reach out and touch any animal of his choosing."

I told him he'd pulled my leg enough for one day. "No, I mean it, Sonny," he said, perfectly serious. "I will wager that even you could do it, if the stakes were high enough." He fell silent then. I think he knew he had me.

After a tension building few seconds, he said, "What animal captivates your fancy?" Without giving me time to reply, he said, "I know. Pintails!"

Suspecting that he likely was playing me like a fish, I nevertheless leapt at the bait: "You expect me to touch a pintail? Even when they skim in and hit water even when it's way out from shore, over my head?"

"I said you could do it, if the stakes were high enough. What is the greatest desire of your heart?"

That would have been having my lonely, wifeless father back to his normal old self, of course, but I knew that was not what he had in mind. I told him, "A shotgun. Of my own. Just the right gauge and just the right size!"

G'Pa didn't even blink. Getting me to think like a true naturalist must have been really important to him, hating guns as he did. There was, naturally, a string attached to all of this. If I lost the wager, I would have to submit to a whole month of nature study, taught by him. Almost as an afterthought, he added, "Plan well, Sonny. You get only one chance!"

Though I was hardly one for being rash, I accepted the bet on the spot and stayed awake most of the night concocting a plan: how to touch a pintail duck? And I kept asking myself: why was he doing all this?

Well before the sun licked the waters of Chesapeake Bay, before the seabirds flashed their wings and screeched above the beach, I shook G'Pa from sleep, though I'm not sure, but he was waiting for me. No matter, I had no more than a half hour to get to the beaver pond, to get the ball rolling. And he had to be there to witness the wager and lose it!

I'd forgotten how chilly Chesapeake air could be before sunrise. Then it got strikingly chilly when I stripped myself naked and even more chilly when the gelid black murk of the pond encountered my flesh, but it became teeth-gritting tolerable once I'd immersed myself in pond scum up to my chin.

I looked back at G'Pa. He was watching from behind what he called his "witness bush." It wasn't easy to see him back there in the darkness. It looked like he might be grinning at me. Course, I wasn't grinning myself because there was too much at stake and I was still plenty cold.

I jammed on the tall crown of marsh grass I'd devised, a little surprised when the soggy stuff wanted to clog up my nose and get in my mouth. Pushing along the muddy bottom on the balls of my feet, I found that as I progressed farther out it wasn't deep by any stretch. I could actually walk straight out to where pintails soon would be dabbling up to their breakfast – my head!

I had planned perfectly. Just as the sun softened the tops of the pines, three birds came whistling in, low and fast, slapping the water and assorting themselves a few yards away. Steadying my breathing, I readied my hands.

The pintails appeared to be nibbling the water. One of them, serene as you please, started gliding my way, as if to nibble the grass, and—Yikes!—something nibbled my foot! I yanked it away, lost my balance, and thrashed my arms. The pintails whistled away faster than they'd flown in.

G'Pa, I think, had hoped I would succeed. Still, he didn't seem awfully surprised at how things turned out. He was back to his unsmiling self a little later as he explained: "*Chelydra serpentina.* Better known as the snapping turtle, sometimes weighing as much as forty pounds. They like to bury themselves in the bottom mud, you see."

He watched me a while, giving me time, I suppose, to compose myself. Then he said, "Sonny, do you know why I have been filling your head with nature, challenging you, pushing you?"

I had, of course, been wondering that very thing. Numbed with cold and devastated with defeat, I merely shook my head.

"Because," he said, "whatever things are true, and noble, and pure, and lovely, we are told to meditate on these things. You will then discover that God's creatures are interconnected. Consider: a flea bites our friend gray squirrel, who races out on a limb and chirps his annoyance at a blue jay, who flies away and screams his displeasure at a bug-eyed frog, who urgently leaps into the beaver pond. Plop! First thing you know, the large-mouth bass dodges away from your baited hook."

"But I'm not fishing! I can't find my boots, and I'm shivering to death!"

"True. Yet moments ago, we both of us heard a chirruping squirrel, a raucous jay, and you may not have heard through your chattering teeth, there are still rings in the water behind you, where—"

"But that has nothing to do with me!"

"Ah, but it does! We humans condition ourselves to block out what our logic tells us does not exist. We cut ourselves off from our natural instincts, from the interconnectedness of God's grand design. We are all brothers, you see."

While talking to me, all warm and dry-clothed as he was, G'Pa kept fingering something at his throat. A cross. I could just make it out through the thin fabric of his shirt, as he rambled on, trying to connect things up by telling me—staggering my belief—that we were more creatures of spirit than of logic and that slaves, too, were our brothers, and I should learn something from that!

Learn? I'd learned only one thing: make no more bets with G'Pa! Course, I had to make good on my promise, a solid month of plants, animals, and Latin names that wanted to pintail right out of my head. Still, one thing jumped out at me, once I'd collected myself over a driftwood fire. G'Pa had jumped me through hoops, but the warmth of the flames, the warmth of his presence, fixed a truth in me: his dogged, longwinded rambling was the only way he knew to show his grandson how much he cared.

Nature study wasn't all bad, as long as it lasted. Before my month was up, G'Pa began to spend more and more time away, in the western part of the state. I came to miss the learned flow of his words, even the laborious Latin. Maybe even more than I missed the shotgun he came so close to giving me. Finally, after another bet that I won, I did get the shotgun. Yet I still cherish that singular, pond-splashing time with G'Pa. Better, even, than the noise my shotgun made when it—*Whamm Clank.*

I snapped my eyes open, felt the sun on my face, and peered out from my hiding place in the trees. The fog had lifted. Smoke hovered around the Parrotts and lazed over the distant high ground where the cannons were aimed.

Long blue lines, stretched taut like shoestrings, were moving slowly up the rolling brown hills. When the guns let me hear—for a precious few seconds the Parrotts were quiet—I thought I could pick up, from somewhere far off, the sound of shouting, or yipping, before the Parrots got going.

Later—it must have been later, the shoestrings had gone—lots of figures were struggling back toward the creek, along with horses, some carrying riders, some only saddles, ragged smoke following, drifting on past.

If only I could go back to dreaming, but my nose wouldn't let me. Harpers Ferry had had air nearly like this: hard and sharp, it grabbed at your lungs. But something else had invaded the air. I struggled to my feet and went out of the trees.

My nose urged me to the brow of a ridge. Below me, sprinkled like pepper on the grassy flats, Yankees clustered around fires sending up sweet-smelling smoke. Meat!

My belly spoke to me; my mouth went watery. I leaned forward, toward the Yankees and the savory smell. My feet seemed unwilling to move.

Now, two more columns—blue beyond number—began to snake up the sere grass slopes. Little cotton balls low in the sky seemed to wait for them there. Suddenly, the cotton flashed and came all apart.

For long seconds, I forgot that my feet wouldn't move, gave no thought to my watery mouth, or to plugging my ears. G'Pa was over that way. And I was not.

I fixed my eyes on the blue lines that blocked the way I needed to go. Maybe, if my legs let me, if I went way around to the left—

Acting as if they knew my thoughts, the columns quit going forward and probed to the left, going down into hollows, slithering up and over humps in the earth.

The Parrotts cut loose all the more. Every so often, I could follow the arc of a shell. One shell would hiss; another would shriek. Every burst sent the ground jumping through the soles of my boots.

The columns veered once again, every man facing the Rebs that must be there at Mumma's, or Piper's, or in between, a road like a trench. For a breathless moment, they all stopped moving. Had they come to their senses? No, they went on, flags and banners higher up now, finding a breeze. A band, tinny and thin from so far away, found wind of its own as more cotton balls punched at the sky. I trudged away from the ridge.

Through stinging, half-hooded eyes, I detected a lane; it was nearly hidden by brambles and trees. But it led away from metal still hissing and shrieking through a sky gone crazy with cotton.

Ducking under branches, I slapped at bugs, went a dozen paces further, and stopped. I tilted my head. Hard to figure. Here in the trees, where the lane dipped and swung around big crusty rocks, I could hardly pick up the sound of the guns. Why not just stay there, curled up on a rock? Surely, sometime, the madness would all go away.

More insects, the air thrummed with them. No, a different kind of thrumming, getting close fast. I threw myself from the rock, back into brambles.

A wheeled gun—six horses pulling, three soldiers riding, hanging on for dear life—plunged around the bend, wheels churning, whipping the leaves, the horses' hooves chewing up chunks of the grown-over lane, the grime of it gritting my eyes, laying into my hair, then suddenly gone.

More buzzing nearby. I readied myself to bat the nuisance away. I studied the thing, black and yellow, inches from me. It was going drowsily about its business, flying away, coming full-circle back, poking into and out of a clutch of blue flowers, buzzing off, coming back.

("In the fall, Sonny, the whole colony, maybe up to three-hundred, will probably die. Except for the queen. She will seek out a place to hide and rest for a time. Of the genus *Bombus*. Be careful with them, but know them. Their stingers are barbless, so they will sting again and again. Know that they never give up. What you do not know, you will fear.")

I picked a cluster of flowers, held it as still as I could. Moments later, the bumblebee came to one of my flowers—its legs looked to be burdened with pollen—and squiggled right into it. Slowly, I dared myself to reach out a finger and barely touch the bumblebee's fluff. The bee didn't flinch; neither did I! Seconds later, it hummed away from the quiet, away from its own little slant of the sun, in the direction of Parrotts. I climbed to my feet. But something was coming.

I knew that wheel-churning sound. I backed away, squatted down to hide myself from the powdery dirt that was sure to attack me.

Only two horses this time, an open carriage. Nowhere near as fancy a rig as the one Judge Crockett had whirled up to our place with Betsy aboard, a lifetime ago.

The driver shook the reins and yeehawed the horses. He was no soldier. Decked out in tweeds, he sported a long yellow kerchief and a broad-brimmed hat with a feather stuck in it.

The horses slowed at the dip in the lane. The driver bawled even louder. His face lost in shadow, he half-turned and reached out to steady some sizable objects that wanted to go bumping around the carriage. I stood up to see. Yes, large wicker baskets, filled to the top. I knew food when I saw it.

The man appeared as whipped up as his horses. But why all that food? And why in a direction a sane man would fight shy of?

I made a move to go after him. If he thought he was as free as the wind, to go anywhere he wanted, he was in the dark about what exploding white cotton could do.

I sank back in the brambles. Let the man fend for himself! And yet... that halfturned face...

Suddenly I was on my feet, freeing myself of a thornbush, tromping over wheel ruts, scrambling after the carriage, because, incredibly, I knew that man!

"Wait! Wait!" The man didn't hear. Now, the carriage was moving out of the hush that lay behind the trees and the rocks and the dip in the lane, charging into what must be the most ear-splitting sound on the face of the earth.

The horses hesitated, tossed their heads, and stamped their hooves. The driver fought for control and thrashed the reins. I yelled one more time. Not near enough loud. Those Parrotts could make a man deaf. I pumped my legs harder.

The carriage slowed. I nearly got a hand on it. But my wind was gone, my fingers were weak, and the bandage around my middle was loose.

The driver stood, shaded his eyes, sat back down, and again lashed the reins. He appeared to know where he wanted to go. He turned the horses to take them up over the ridge and down it, clear around those cook-fire Yankees down on the flats.

As the carriage wheels swished through the tall brown grass, the man's yellow kerchief streamed out like a flag. He was headed for the Boonsboro Pike, where a stone bridge waited at the foot of a hill.

I had no wind to go farther. But I knew that man. I had to keep him from making a dreadful, deadly mistake.

I sucked in my breath for another go. One last try—the most hurtful, hard-fought shout of my life: "Brother Russell, you idiot!"

The man heard that! He yanked the horses to a stop, whipped around, his ample red face aghast. I staggered up to the carriage.

"You... you gotta be batty!" I managed.

"Bats have been living in my belfry for years, Mr. Shipley. But I have seldom known them to fail once setting a course. My immediate course took me through that unaccommodating lane. Alas, the quickest way here from Keedysville."

"You look real different."

"You behold a new Brother Russell, changed inside and out! One thing, however, remains the same. He held up the cross, near big as his fist, which hung from his throat. "And you, Mr. Shipley, you look rather different yourself. Perhaps you have tasted the acidulous dregs of purgatory?"

"How's that again?"

"You look like you have been through hell, Mr. Shipley."

"Oh, nothing much has happened to me. Just had a Reb from Winchester snitch that bread you gave me, before he got killed in front of my eyes and was jailed up by Yankees for being a spy and got clobbered by cannons at Harpers Ferry and was shot at while swimming across the river down there, before the bluebelly cavalry came and got me away and bent over backwards to blow up the ironworks, that place where you went off and left me and had a horse shot dead while I was on it and, oh yeah, a Reb in those woods up there tried to croak me last night. Like I said, nothing much has happened."

Brother Russell shook his head slowly, his mouth a thin, firm line; it quivered up quickly, and he laughed out loud. Though it was hard to hear him over the ground-jarring guns, he said, "Your stomach, however, remains constant, I see. You keep casting covetous glances at my collection of biscuits and hams!"

The man must reckon he had me all figured out. Probably thought I hadn't grown up an iota since he'd last seen me, despite all the details I'd just dished out with what I thought was a good bit of flair. I forced my eyes away from his food; in a few seconds, though, I was ogling it again.

Brother Russell laughed even more loudly. "Pray help yourself, Mr. Shipley. In moderation, however. This fare is bound for those needing it far more than you." Shading his eyes, he looked to the west, to the hills where all the blue soldiers had gone.

I followed his gaze. The sun-scorched ridgetop was seething with smoke. As we stared, all the Parrotts seemed to go off at once. Shock waves hammered the carriage wheels; the wicker baskets squeaked; then the guns suddenly stopped.

I felt a familiar shudder in my bowels. I pointed. "That way... it's impossible! What makes you think that you--?"

"At long last, I have taken it upon myself to follow my own conscience not that of my father, whatever the summons, wherever it leads. I take it on faith that service to others is the rent we pay for the space we take up in this world. Here and now, Mr. Shipley, my service is *there*!" He aimed his finger at the long line of smoke, now a half mile of puffballs and pinpricks of fire.

"No!" Having climbed slowly aboard the carriage, I now made haste to get off. "You'd be right in the thick of it, you'd never get out. Stonewall's stirrups, you'd never get in!"

I had one leg out of the carriage. Brother Russell laid a hand on my shoulder. "I have a powerful ally," he said. Again, he held up his cross. "Perhaps the time has come, Mr. Shipley, to put your faith to the test. Where do you feel impelled to go at this moment?"

That was easy. "I want to go home! But you're flapdoodle nonsensical to think you...we...can go over there! That's what hell must be like! How'd you get so unhinged?"

"Perhaps the door to my soul is back on its hinges and has swung open at last. I have been stubborn and self-absorbed far too long."

"What's wrong with being stubborn?"

With a rueful smile, he said, "Pharaoh taught me that stubbornness and doggedness are two different things. After years of mulish argument, my four-footed colleague came unhinged himself, from what we encountered at Harpers Ferry. He learned, as did I, that the stubborn-hearted are far from righteousness, that they have no hope."

"Why didn't you kick some sense into him? That's what I did, when an unhinged chaplain lost his nerve."

"Oh, but I tried! Pharaoh resolutely refused to go forward, then obstinately refused to go back. Perhaps it was because that pontoon bridge was so crammed with commotion and was swaying so much that—you seem to find this all amusing, do you?"

Fighting back the urge to laugh wildly, I only shook my head.

"Yes, I gave him the swift taste of shoe leather," Brother Russell continued. "I should have known that, lacking righteousness, he would respond in kind, seeking retribution from the offending appendage. Pharaoh, you see, remains stubborn-hearted and is unschooled in the Bible. He believes that one good kick deserves a kick in return. Regrettably, in my stove-up condition, I could not go preaching the evil of slavery nor the evil of mules. And so, here you find me, *hors de combat*, but alive and still kicking. That is to say, wheeling my newfound righteousness on an errand of mercy."

I eyed the smoke across the valley, burst after burst, then looked at his cross. "Your faith is a lot bigger than mine." I held up my own tiny cross. "Betsy, a friend of mine, said it might not even fit me."

"Might not, you say? Have you tried to find out?"

I fiddled for a moment with the fragile chain, raised it to my head before dropping my hands. "My head's too big. The chain's too small. It won't fit!"

"Try, Mr. Shipley! Put your faith to the test!"

With reluctance, I raised my hands, squiggled the slender gold links, and wiggled my head. Finally, the chain slipped over my ears onto my neck. Brother Russell's eyes were approving. I asked him, "Does this mean I have faith?"

"It means nothing of the sort. But at least it is a symbolic beginning, for faith without works is—"

"Is a dove without wings!" I cut in, more elated with my memory than with any faith I might have.

"Faith before works, Mr. Shipley! But our faith is constantly tested. You must have the courage of your convictions!"

"Like you?"

Again he turned to the west and shaded his eyes. "My courage is also being tested. Sometimes there is courage in numbers, so long as we don't lose sight of Him, who is leading the charge. Shall we put our faith to the test? Together?"

Looking down, I let my hand brush my throat. Gingerly, I adjusted myself on the seat. If only I had more time to figure things out. Too late. Already the wheels were rolling.

Chapter 17

Field grass gave way to the charge of our wheels, seadheads bending, breaking as the carriage cut through. As we raced by the Yanks on the flats I caught a glimpse of a butchered cow off to one side. I could breath-in. almost taste, the frizzling meat.

Now, my nose was a-tingle. My guts insistent, I attacked one of the baskets and crammed my mouth with biscuit and ham. Before I could swallow it all, the carriage skidded hard right. We were on the Boonsboro Pike. The horses, given their heads, careened downhill. Clouds of dust enveloped the carriage.

"Cover the baskets!" Brother Russell called out.

"With what?"

"Off with your coat!" Brother Russell struggled to do the same with his tweeds.

"There's three baskets. We have only two coats!"

"Spread-eagle yourself on the other. Those Federal troops that went up those hills over there must be famished. They deserve, at the very least, untainted food!"

From my awkward position, I caught a glimpse of weatherworn buildings, a straw roof, wash on a line. Normal things. We spanked on by.

Knots of blue figures clustered around the front of the bridge. As the carriage bowled toward them, the knots came apart. "Hold on! Restricted area! No civilians!" Sunlight flashed on the Yank's bayonet.

Brother Russell hauled on the reins but not very hard. "Official business!" he sang out. "Stand aside!"

"Official business? By whose authority?"

Brother Russell merely held up his cross and thrashed the reins. Goggle-eyed, the soldiers backed off.

Near the middle of the bridge, I turned and looked back. The dust was settling, just enough. I braced myself, stood up, and jabbed a finger at the tiny gold object that danced at my throat.

Clattering off the bridge, we churned up more dirt. Brother Russell jabbed his finger at the uncovered basket. I flopped back down.

More Yanks sat their horses by the side of the road. One man had binoculars trained up the hill. All had their eyes riveted on a gun battery scudding the Boonsboro Pike into powder a few hundred yards up ahead. The wheeled gun that had near mowed me down?

Bunches of blue-clad soldiers were lounging around Josh Newcomer's farm. Some got to their feet and hurrahed us as we barreled by. Goosebumps prickled my arms; my insides turned shivery warm. I grinned hugely, rose up, and threw them a wave.

I scrubbed at my eyes and squinted at the tracks made seconds before by the fastmoving gun, not as fast as the carriage. We were closing the gap.

"Why did those Yankee cannons go quiet so fast?" I wondered out loud.

"To avoid hitting their own troops, like as not. But do not lose sight of a cruel truth. The Rebels also have cannons. Pointed this way, I do believe!"

On the spot, I believed him. Something slammed down between us and that gun.

Instantly, the turnpike spewed up gobs of earth. Split seconds later, the roadside fence went to pieces, flinging parts of itself at the gun battery horses and the riders that rode them. I hated to look but forced myself. A horse and rider were down.

Even at a distance of two hundred yards, the horse's shriek was higher, more piercing, than any artillery shell that had punished my ears. The fallen animal jackknifed its legs, one of them senselessly striking a blue rag doll, the head askew, the eyes open, staring down the distance at us. It had closed to fifty yards.

One of the soldiers had cut the traces from the fallen animal, freeing the battery, and was quickly back on his horse, flailing his heels. The battery lurched to the right, knocked through the remains of the fence, bounced into the field, and kept on going.

The air hissed around us, something went *zing* off a roadside rock. I let go of the basket, and hunched down behind it. Yee gods, now they were shooting at us! Abruptly, our near-hand horse stopped dead in its tracks where the road still smoked. Brother Russell whipped the reins. The unmoving horse just jittered its head; the other animal got the idea; neither would budge.

The jittery horse stood bugging its eyes, baring its teeth, and shivering as if standing in ice. A small red stain glistened on a foreleg, fetlock high.

"I believe Old Slim can still put weight on that leg, Mr. Shipley." Brother Russell sounded as if this sort of thing happened every day. "He is a saddle horse, however, not used to harness. Notice how long-legged he is, not close-coupled like that other cob. He needs gentling, I think. Are you up to it?"

"How can you talk about gentling a horse? We're about to get our heads blown off!" I felt good saying that, though the metal seemed to have stopped lambasting our space.

"Do you, then, have a better idea? If not, let me put it to you again. Are you up to it?"

"I dunno. Horses have it in for me. You better do it. Gimme the reins."

"Improvident. He cannot take my weight. It must be you!"

"You mean you want me to get up on him? While he's all fussy and foaming? No, uh-uh, I'll go turn 'em around. We gotta go back."

Brother Russell pursed his mouth and slowly shook his head. "Oh, ye of little faith, Mr. Shipley."

I glared, set my jaw, and slid from the seat. Taking pains to limp more than a little, I approached the wary animal.

"Steady as you go, Mr. Shipley. They appear to have stopped shooting at us."

"They're not supposed to be shooting at us! We ain't in the military!"

"True. But guns fired in anger hit saints and sinners alike, without partiality."

You'd think the man was preaching a bloody sermon! The least he could do was show some concern. Something about my gimpy leg would be good.

I reached up and stroked the horse's neck. It twitched as if hornets had hit it. I had a notion; it had worked on Ol' Poke, in farmer Reel's big barn.

Speaking soothing words, I let my hand fondle the soft nose and the velvety mouth, then tried to puff warm air in his ear. No good. Either Old Slim was too tall or I was too short. Still, I could stroke the withers, ever so gently, croon softly to him, "Old Slim" this and "Old Slim" that, and at least he wasn't baring his teeth.

I walked smartly back to the carriage and thrust out my hand, palm up. Brother Russell looked puzzled. "Your neckerchief. Hand it over. I think I can get us through that fence. You said 'Federal troops.' Well, they're thataway." I pointed where the gun battery had gone scudding off.

The man's expression seemed to have fixed itself somewhere between confusion and respect, which put a spring in my legs as I marched back, reached up on tiptoes, draped the cloth over Old Slim's eyes, and tied it off. I demanded the reins. Both horses were still quivering, so I cooed at them, stroked them, maneuvered them around the gaping hole in the road, then led the whole rig through the jagged gap where, moments before, posts and rails stood guarding the Boonsboro Pike.

"How's that for faith!" I relished the words but didn't say them. It felt better to tell him, "Gimme your hat!"

"Whatever are you up to, Mr. Shipley? Do you intend to strip me of my earthly possessions?"

I lifted my chin. "You said he's a saddle horse. Well, I aim to ride him!"

The man laughed louder than I reckoned he could. He offered me his hat with a flourish. With a flourish, I took it and capped off the uncovered basket. Walking more briskly, I went back and cautiously slid the kerchief away. Only a flick of the ears and a toss of the head.

Doing my best to hide my reluctance, I slowly swung myself up, clamping my legs till the ache in them stopped me. I balled the reins in my fists and whispered more soothing words; my heart was dancing a jig. A light touch of the heels. Old Slim stepped out, hobbling slightly… more willfully now, the other horse following, grasshoppers springing.

Something wanted to bubble up inside me as we began to move faster. I had a devilish desire to let it all out. Topside of a horse and faith in myself a grand thing to have, it all went rip-roaring out of my throat, because the Rebel yell had a mind of its own, because beyond what you felt or thought, Rebel or not, it simply was!

My chest fired up as I allowed the holler to have its own way— as piercing as panicky horses, as shrill as flyaway geese. I wasn't in the Stonewall Brigade, wasn't a Reb, and was not even a dead Confederate's son. I was my own man now, riding high and in control and heading home!

My body moved in harmony with that of the horse. Old Slim must have sensed it, his head and neck and legs working together. Brother Russell also was yelling. I refused to look back. But he kept yelling. I reined in, and we bumped to a stop. I whipped round my head.

"Your ears are no match for your lungs, Mr. Shipley. I have been trying to get your attention for nearly a minute!"

"Too much racket!" I fired back. Yes, way too much racket and not coming from us.

We were still several hundred yards from the shuddering smoke on the ridge, from a sound more frightful than Parrotts: like canvas ripping, again and again, a roaring mixed with it, the whole of it shaken together and hurled at the hills. Autie was right.

"Thisaway's the end of the line."

I slid down the side of Old Slim's ribs. "I'm going with you! All the way!" I hadn't planned it; my words surprised me.

Brother Russell shook his head. "We are each of us called according to His purpose. Our paths must go in different directions. I congratulate you, however, for putting your faith to the test. And for having the healthiest pair of lungs I know!"

His smile faded, his face a mask of concern as he turned to study the ridgetop. He reached for my shoulder and squeezed it. "God willing, we will meet again. But whatever may come to pass, please remember one thing. Courage and faith are not one and the same. Keep your chin up and your knees down. Hopefully, not in that order."

I gave him the reins. He shook them gently, as if they were fragile. The carriage lurched forward. He had his hat back on. There was no dust now, only smoke drifting toward us. For a moment, he took off his hat and held it aloft. I couldn't smile back. My eyes misted over, not from the smoke. I was alone. Again.

The carriage, moving up the brown sloping ground, was getting harder to see.

Lifting my eyes higher, I hit upon haystacks, bumping up yellow through the dirty, drifting haze. A green flag—looking tiny up there but as green as the grass must have been before the sun burned it brown—bobbed up, went down, and bobbed up again.

It had turned warm, yet a chill reached all the way to my bones. Good thing I had no need of my jacket, still atop a wicker basket. I looked again. The carriage had been swallowed by smoke.

Chapter 18

"*Ovah theah! Git 'im! Head 'im off!*"

A cowpath cut through trampled grass up behind Henry Piper's henhouse. It was sloping ground, five hundred yards or so from a sunken road that used to shelter rats but now was clogged with screaming men and smoke. No more than a mile and I'd be home. I tried to run.

"*He's a-runnin'!*"

The meager path went in the right direction, and it seemed a tempting way to go. Unexpectedly, though, a clutch of rifle-toting figures—some in gray but mostly in butternut, the color of washed-out dirt—had come up onto it from behind the henhouse and began to run themselves, in my direction.

I changed my mind about the cowpath and looked for another way. My iffy leg began to cramp.

"*Got a limp on 'im. Maybe shot or somethin'!*"

If I could get free of Piper's, get up to the Hagerstown Pike and across it, David Reel's lower fields were the only impediment that—

"*Naw, he ain't shot. Shirkers is natch'lly unsteady on they feet!*"

I girded myself to make it up the slope. Not far past a water trough and some spindly trees behind it, the turnpike waited. Dried-up cow dung and rabbit burrows kept trying to trip me up. I failed to sidestep far enough, fell, bunged my leg some more, managed to right myself, and made a feeble leap or two over a rusted rake and the carcass of a chicken.

"*Ornery as a ol' jackrabbit! Look at 'im hop!*"

Plowed-up ground, lumpish clods. Stomping over that like a three-legged horse brought me to a stop, seconds only, which got my heart down out of my throat and back behind my ribs. But getting past the pike at all would be like going barefoot over barnacles. The road was spiked with soldiers and horses and cannons tearing north. Just like Autie said they would.

I resumed my stomping, took no more than a dozen steps, grabbed my leg, and tried to blink away the sweat. Past the pike? How to even get that far?

I moved out again, tougher going, all uphill. No time to look but…why had all that hollering stopped?

No more furrowed dirt. Solid grass. Little grove of trees ahead. A place to rest, squiggle in, squiggle out, just enough time to—

I raised my eyes. A rifle barrel slanted down; a ragged sleeve tied with yellow cloth. The man hardly looked at me; his attention was on those rifle-toters farther down; he gave them a friendly wave.

The Winchester Reb, he'd put a truth to something. Chasers and deserters, they had their separate little war.

*****

Next to the pike, more yellow-ribboned provost guards herded some sorry-looking souls into an area where rails had been thrown down to set it off. In their midst, an officer was dressing down deserters as they straggled in at gunpoint. The officer faced the other way. I knew him, though. Not so much by his crisp gray uniform and yellow sash, as by the clipped words, the tone of voice. My fingertips were tingling, a dreadful apprehension…

I reached for my pocket. Yes, this very officer's wedding ring. But if I up and gave it back, he'd know straight-off I'd failed to get it to his brother-in-law, Maj. Jack Taylor of Cobb's Brigade. No, not failure, really. I'd found the Major. But not before his coat had gone up over his face, on a cold stone chapel floor back in Sandy Hook.

I recalled the intensity in this Captain's steel-gray eyes when he had trustingly placed the ring in my hand. But hadn't me and that ring managed to flounder across that white-water river at Harpers Ferry? Hadn't this self-same officer, shackled up as he was, been a captive witness to all the wagons and cannons his Rebel friends had hauled away from those looming heights?

And yet, Maj. Jack Taylor, he'd been family to this Rebel Captain—whatever his name might be—and I had to be the one to break the dreadful news.

When he turned, there was astonishment in his eyes, a shade of doubt as well. I could hardly blame him. This man had seen—more truthfully had heard—his Confederate comrades beat a hasty retreat from Maryland Heights. But following that, he'd seen Col. Grimes Davis's cavalry beat a retreat as well. Across that same pontoon bridge I'd sculled my way under long minutes before. Thousands of troops on the move from Harpers Ferry. First the Rebs, then the Yanks. The one following the other as surely as rumbling Parrotts rocked the ground and me, square in the middle of that. The trigger, you might say, of all the hurry-scurry away from the place. The Captain's astonishment, his doubt, continued to cut through any assurance I had. Then what was left of it went into thin air.

The provost guard shoving me forward declared, "This here feller weren't with them other deserters, Cap'n Sims." At the name my toes curled up.

"Well, now—" The Captain, too, seemed at a loss. Seizing whatever advantage I could, I said, "Are you Captain John Sims, Barksdale's Brigade, Twenty-first Mississippi, Colonel Humphries commanding?"

The Captain's eyes went wide, then narrowed. "No, I am not John Sims. He happens to be my first cousin, however. I am Ashford Sims, from Hertford County, North Carolina. How do you come to know of my cousin John?"

Best not answer that! Any mention of my collaboration with his cousin's best friend, Col. Grimes Davis, of the Yankee army, and I'd be simmered for soup. Better to bang off in another direction. I curled my fingers around his ring and brought it out. He cringed.

"But—" His mouth seemed frozen open.

"I'm awful sorry, Captain. I got your message through, about the Yankees closing in and all. But I couldn't get it to Major Jack Taylor, because, well, I'm afraid it's because—"

For several seconds, Ashford Sims stared at the ground. Then, squaring his shoulders and lifting his chin, he was a Stonewall man again. And hadn't this Stonewall man asked me if I valued my father's memory, his sacrifice?

Taking a deep breath, I told him, "There's one more thing. Maybe even more important than… than Major Jack Taylor."

Ashford Sims glowered at me, waiting.

I had no idea of the contents of Rob Pescud's note, but as I worked my toes and felt the paper crinkle inside my boot, my curiosity began to build. And my need to rid myself of certain feelings, not yet resolved: I had helped both sides. At Harpers Ferry. But saving lots of lives in the bargain, maybe? Now, since I wasn't partial to Yanks or Rebs—until they looked slavery square in the eye—maybe, again, I could do something truly important, if only I—

I sat back down, stuck out my leg, and jabbed a finger at the extended foot. At once, Captain Sims wrestled the boot off; the note, freed of its prison, fell to the grass. I watched the Captain read.

From the look of the man, he might have been struck by lightning. He looked hard at me, then back along the way I'd come. Slowly, he nodded his head and ran a finger along the line of his jaw, before asking, softly, "Do… do you know what this says? Do you have even a glimmer?"

I shook my head. "I've got a feeling it's pretty important. I was told to guard it with my life."

"Small wonder," said Capt. Sims, looking me up and down, more critically now. "Do you know who EF Paxton is?" he asked sharply. "Ever heard of the Light Division?"

I kept shaking my head. And Ashford Sims kept giving me a calculating eye. "Can you read?" he asked.

"Course I can read!"

Ashford Sims smiled faintly; it was the very first time I'd seen his mouth turn up. "Then read *this*!" He handed the crinkled paper back.

I read:

> To: E. F. Paxton, AAG
>   I am captured and held at Fed. hdqtrs.
> Bearer of this, J. Shipley of Sharpsburg, may be

trusted. U.S. high command believes their forces outnumbered. Have no idea Light Div. still at H. Ferry.

        R.B. Pescud, Maj., Starke's Brigade, CSA

"Why is this so all-fired important?" I asked, returning the note.

"All it means is the success or failure of this army! Because it is our forces that are badly outnumbered. We are near to breaking, here and now! But McClellan believes just the opposite, you see. Which we now know, from this note. So if we can hold on, just a few hours longer, McClellan, soul of caution that he is, will draw back to redeploy and resupply, before he attacks again. Guaranteed! By then, A.P. Hill with our Light Division will have arrived from Harpers Ferry to shore us up. And this," he exclaimed, waving the note, "dictates whether we retreat, our tails between our legs, or stay and fight!"

I tried to gather my thoughts, to think like a soldier. But my mind went wheeling in another direction: Wouldn't it be a splendiferous thing to get a stamp of approval for all that I'd done? At least tried to do? Especially since this Rebel Captain excited memories of another Confederate officer, months in a nameless Kernstown grave.

Ashford Sims was studying me still, with, yes, an approving look. "And after what happened this morning," he started up, "up on our left flank—"

With tingles urging me on, I broke in to tell him, "I bet Hooker attacked your left flank at earliest dawn!" Seeing the man drop his jaw awful fast, I had an irresistible urge to race on: "General McClellan, he aims to hit your right flank too, then punch through the center with his reserve and the cavalry. He calls it a 'classic touch'!"

Ashford Sims snatched off his hat and ran a hand across his forehead. "You, uh, actually heard McClellan say these things?"

I flushed with triumph, I bobbed my head. "Like you said, he's real cautious. Still and all, he's got fond of using guns of position. With a tube elevation of ten degrees and a two-and-a-half-pound powder charge, a twenty-pounder Parrott can—"

"Yes, yes, I have no doubt." He went to his forehead again, with a handkerchief this time. "You must come with me!" he blurted. "Someone will want to talk with you. And at once, I think!"

Quickly, he got hold of a pair of horses, jackknifed his arm, and aimed his hand. In seconds, we were across the pike and into a field, pounding past surging columns of shouldered muskets, past wheeled guns, then scudding back into turnpike dust.

Far to our right, the crackling was constantly head-splitting loud. Pounding downhill we found a gap in the fence, swerved left, and headed straight for a belt of trees; a white splash of church was barely visible through all the leaves and shot-off limbs.

After several seconds of low-toned conversation with another officer, Ashford Sims motioned me forward. He led the way to a small group of soldiers sitting on their horses close to the woods. A slouched, drab-looking man held binoculars to his eyes; a bearded officer next to him squinted into a notebook, writing feverishly.

Ashford Sims dismounted, went over to them, and saluted smartly. He pulled my note from his pocket, held it out, talked a blue streak a few seconds, and then shut up.

My attention beginning to wander, I turned and ran my eyes up the slope. Reel's slope.

"We'll reduce that ground to rubble!"

Capt. Sims called out to me. It hardly mattered. I had far more important things to do. I prayed that Autie, he'd maybe been wrong. Reduce our cottage...to rubble?

The Captain called out again, more excited this time. For some reason, my attention was drawn to the drab-looking man. The man said, "Please elaborate on this note, if you will." The man's forage cap being pulled down low, it was hard to see his eyes, until he lifted them, ice blue, glittering with stormy intensity.

As I opened my mouth, my throat closed up. I stared back at the man and knew the truth, even before a voice called out the name. General Jackson? This draggle tail?

I felt a quick flare of excitement. Just as quickly, the flame went out. The man had the look of a cold-blooded killer! What convictions churned behind those flashing blue eyes, besides marching hard and killing? There was more to this war than that!

I slid off the horse, marched up to him, and fixed him with some ice of my own. "General," I threw at him, "do you know what this war is really about?"

It seemed that, for a moment, the blue eyes softened. It was only a moment. "Sir, we do our duty!" he answered in words as clipped as any I'd ever heard. Then, "Tell me of the note. If you please."

I went through it all, leaving out, naturally, how I had helped the Yankees. He would have no way of knowing why I had helped both sides: because of my father, because of Jeremiah, because of... lots of things.

"I believe he is telling the truth, sir," the bearded man said.

The General looked at me, back at the note, and back at me. "Perhaps you are right, Major Paxton." He called for pencil and paper, scribbled quickly, and handed the note to a man next to him. "For General Lee, with my compliments. Near the center of our line. Lose not a moment!"

The General was back to inspecting me with more calculation than I thought I deserved. "Your name is Shipley. Was, uh, your father a soldier by any chance?"

"Darn right he was a soldier! In the Stonewall Brigade!"

The General stroked his long brown beard then raised his eyes to the sky, as if lost in thought. "Yes," he said at last, "I remember your father quite well. Would I be correct in saying that he was killed, some months ago?"

It was time for the truth to be known, to stamp out for all time the ugly rumors about my father being a coward. "Yes!" I hurled at him. "He's a hero! He was killed at a place called Kernstown! That's spelled K-e-r-n-s—"

"Yes, yes, I know the place. What I—"

"My pa was a man of honor and courage and—"

The man abruptly held up his hand, then held up his whole doggone arm. It hovered there a few seconds. I was relieved when it came back down. For another few seconds, his fingers touching his beard, he studied my face; his eyes softened. He said, "A gallant soldier, your father. You can be very proud."

I lifted my chin—I grew a good inch! I was hardly aware that Gen. Jackson had reached for the notebook and was writing something. He folded the paper, leaned down, and handed it to me. "One good message deserves another," he said. And now the ice was gone from his eyes. "You have a remarkable memory," he added, "and a penchant, I believe, for being succinct, something we in the army prize highly. When you are of a mind and of an age, I feel certain a suitable position could be found. And now, if you will permit me."

Getting control of his stooped shoulders and curved back, he pushed himself erect. With a quick smile, he gave me a crisp salute.

I should have said something, but my head was awhirl. Curious, I unfolded the paper. At length, I looked up, to thank General Jackson. But he had moved away—nearly disappearing under the shade of the trees.

*****

Ashford Sims, his feet set apart, was sort of rocking on his heels. "That paper he gave you. Would you, uh, be of a mind to share it with me?"

Drawing a sleeve across my mouth, I managed to read:

"The gentleman bearing this, Johnny Shipley, is a true patriot and a special friend of mine. Please extend him every courtesy. T. J. Jackson, Maj. Gen'l CSA."

Had I misjudged the man? Well, I'd had my say and didn't regret it. Something told me to look to the trees. The General had disappeared. But tendrils of smoke were twining up beyond the trees. Gen. Jackson went clean out of my mind. What of Sam Mumma? What would he see and smell and what would he feel, when he went back to his home and found what had fueled that smoke?

I wheeled and looked the other way. A hand touched my shoulder. "You appear to be searching for something." Ashford Sims was smiling. "May I be of service? Escort you somewhere?"

I shook my head, running my eyes over ground that lifted away toward a farm I knew, a big hay-fragrant barn, an ornery mule.

"The horse then. Perhaps you should take—"

"No, thanks. I'll go back the way I left, by myself and on my feet." I looked down. There near my feet, a straight-shafted limb from a wind-blown tree, just as I'd left it. Some things, most things, had changed, but some things had not.

I shoved the General's note in my pocket. My pa, I'm sure he would have been proud of me. And G'Pa? I'd dug in my heels with the General, I'd had my say. Still, when it came to what the war was truly about, I hadn't made a difference or accomplished a thing.

*****

Reel's slope, that part of it not planted in corn, was mostly bare. A few runty scrub oaks huddled together, looking lonely, the leaves already crusting, some already part of the grass. Other things, too, lay on the grass: a canteen with a hole near the bottom; wrinkled playing cards tossed every which way; a swollen horse, one of its legs jutting up oddly; a single shoe, the sole yawed open for toes to come through.

I searched for another way to the top. I turned one way then the other, wrinkling my nose. The air smelled as if something lay moldering at the bottom of a well. Grassy places had been stomped flat. Where there was corn, countless feet had come trampling through it—cornstalks crimped, lacking ears, ripped away. My mouth tasted like metal.

The ridgetop hid Reel's stone-sided barn. I went on tiptoes, so that I—the roof. Where was the roof?

Plodding upward, I'd been absorbed with the ground. Surely, I should have seen the smoke wisping up, smelled the char. Stiffly, on the balls of my feet, I went over the ridge.

The barn was gone. No, not completely gone. The roof-supporting fieldstone ends, lacking a roof, pointed at the sky. Inside, mostly everything had been reduced to ash, still glowing in places. I recognized a few things, some still glowing, sending up smoke: a soldier's cap, mostly ash; a familiar bridle, once newly tanned, turned crispy-black; within arm's reach, a feed bucket, half-melted now: my hands had clutched it, many a time.

I felt an agony in my belly a split second before ham and biscuit came spewing up. Mopping my mouth, I backed away.

Off to the left, the farmhouse, much the same, thank God. And to the right, a road running north: that road, hadn't it known the beat of my boots, day and night?

A butternut Reb suddenly appeared from behind the fire-blackened fieldstone.

Raising his musket, he yelled, "Say there! Gen'l Early's men are s'posed to be stayin' put back up that-there road!"

This meddler knew nothing about that-there road! He deserved to be brought down a peg or two! "Did you know," I hurled at him, "that runaway slaves used to hide in that-there barn? Well, they did! Some of us folks hereabouts are partial to slaves, and we help 'em all we can! This-here is free ground!"

The young Rebel froze in his tracks; he looked to be nonplussed. All the same, he kept handling his rifle like he knew how to use it. He looked halfway intelligent, though. I reckoned he could read.

I went for my pocket, unfolded the paper, marched up to him, and thrust it in his impudent face. His eyes grew large, then went to blinking. I tried to put on an indifferent look but immediately had to fight back a laugh.

"I ain't with Gen'l Early," I told him. "But up there, yeah, that's where I'm aimin' to take myself." He still looked befuddled, but he lowered his musket, then his eyes. When we reached the roadway, I breathed in deeply. Something wasn't right.

Though the breeze was gentle against my face, there was a rotting-apple foulness in it and more: what had gagged me at Reel's burned-out barn. I began to run, fell, and looked up.

G'Pa's place, only some fissured beams remained. My belly wanted to convulse again. I fought it down.

The shed? Yes, almost where it used to be. It had little support now: it slumped, trying to reach out for a vanished cottage wall. The door hung open, supported by a single hinge. I lumbered toward it, quickly stopped. *Wham.* The sound something heavy might make when attacking a locked-up trunk. Leaning forward, I peeked inside.

The hugest man I'd ever seen was in the act of swinging back his leg. The flour sacks that had covered the trunk lay heaped where I used to lay my head at night. The man must have sensed my presence; he quickly turned.

I didn't look him in the face right off. My eyes went to his boots, home for what had to be the thumpingest big feet in all creation. There was metal on the tips. I took a guarded breath. I had to see his face.

I got no further than his hands. One meat hook alone could get around my entire neck. Slowly, I raised my eyes.

The narrowed eyes that bored into mine glinted out from under bushy black brows that met above his nose; his beard, however, appeared to be trimmed with exacting care. But the look in those eyes, hate-filled, yes, but incredulous too, as if in recognition of something.

The butternut stepped through the door. "What regiment y'all with, soldier?" he demanded of the giant. The rifle appeared steady enough; the voice, though, was on the wobbly side. Maybe because a huge hand had dropped to a whopping horse pistol jammed through a black and glossy belt; fingers like sausages dwarfed a handle the color of bone.

"I ain't no soldier, soldier boy!" the giant spat.

Other Rebs had come to gawk. The giant shoved past them. Halfway through the door, he whirled. For a chilling moment, he stared straight at me. I took a step backward. Those glinting black eyes, they could have been those of a deadly snake.

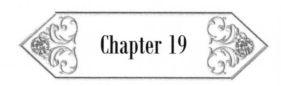

Chapter 19

Breathing fast, I gulped for air. It was only a half-dozen paces to where the front door had been. My eyes lacked the boldness of my feet. So hard to look. And yet—

The spindly doorjamb had given up, its scorched members leaning lazily to the left. My eyes wanted to shift away. Best look at the clouds, the trees. G'Pa, he sometimes shut himself up for days at a time. *In there.*

For the moment, a big-booted man—wherever he'd gone—he didn't matter; Gen. Earley's troops—sprawled in our tramped-over grass, face-down under charred apple-tree branches, squabbling for precious seconds at our water-lift pump—they didn't matter; the ache in my leg, the squeezed feeling in my chest, none of it mattered. Finally, I ordered my eyes back to the cottage, to take it in.

A few things I knew: a slat-backed chair, topsy-turvy, a leg knocked off; a bookcase, miraculously still upright, filled with crispy spines; a lantern that had seen too much flame, its fragile face cracked and smudged. If Parrotts could do that to wood, to leather, to glass…

Guardedly, I breathed the fume, looked again, more carefully now. No, no sign of anything truly grisly. Discovering that I'd been holding my breath, I forced it out and went limping among the drooping Rebs, firing questions. The owner here, had anyone seen him, did anyone know?

Leaning down, thrusting my face up close, I demanded answers. I jabbed a man: he flinched, gave an anguished sob, and hid his head. Nobody would give me the time of day. Well, if I shoved Stonewall's note in their witless faces, they bloody well would! I made a move for my pocket and stopped my hand. Uh-uh. No time for that!

I studied the road, where it hooked sharp left. No reason G'Pa would go that way, away from his friends. Maybe the other direction, back down the dusty way I'd come? The Judge's house? Too far. Too many cotton balls bursting, flashing, the roadway clogged.

Can't ponder too much. Not with that savage loose, that horse pistol a half-breath away from that monstrous hand.

Absently, I ran my fingers over the cross at my throat, recollected my grandfather's cross and Barbara Reel's, hers nearly as tiny as mine. Reel's? The barn was gone—but not the house. Not too far, I could walk. No, I could run!

The racket down at Piper's was coming in waves, thudding and rattling, growing louder the closer I got. My leg again was beginning to cramp, but I kept running, my suspicion building as I pumped my legs, swelling to horror, because now I saw: a hulking figure, a tall, gray-haired man, a small man with him, grasping a hoe, both backed up to the smoldering barn.

G'Pa! The blood sang in my veins. But he was too far away—a good hundred yards—and my leg was pleading; my lungs were spent.
"Healthiest pair of lungs I know!"

Heaving for air, sucking it down to the agony there, I caterwauled it back out. The giant spun, his arm like a log: that horse pistol, it must be as big as a cannon.

G'Pa flung himself; the giant dodged and lashed a boot. Above the racket at Piper's, I could hear the impact on my grandfather's ribs.

Jeremiah hurled his hoe; it glanced off the man's arm as the pistol went off, the slug snapping past me, the pistol still up, G'Pa gasping, lunging again, the pistol jittering into the grass—but a few feet away from the outstretched paw, a discarded musket. That horse pistol, if only I moved fast enough…

My gimpy leg, had it gone to sleep? It wouldn't work.

As G'Pa lay on his side, coughing blood, I willed my legs to move. Both had turned into dead things. Squaring my shoulders, I stood as a Shipley should stand—unflinching, defiant. The giant glared back. "You're a Shipley!" he growled. "I knowed right-off!"

Stand like a Shipley but don't even blink—I might betray what I saw—Jeremiah, his gnarled fingers inching closer to the only weapon he knew.

The giant, wild-animal quick, whirled, jabbed the butt of the musket; Jeremiah's head snapped back; he fell like a leaf.

"I'll finish you later, with my own hands, you murderin' black devil!" Raising the musket to his massive shoulder, the man stared down the barrel at me.

For a split-second I prayed that the rifle was empty that when the trigger was squeezed, nothing would – *Bamm*

A flash and the world exploded, the side of my face blazing, my head a molten, clanging bell, the ground whirling up, yanking me down, something salty creeping into my mouth, onto my tongue, strangely grown as big as a boot.

I still could see, could see the giant still holding the musket, half-turned from the shattered black man who somehow had got his hands on the hoe, who was spitting blood and bone from his mouth. I could see Jeremiah's single eye: it glowed like a coal, and it must have inflamed him with frightful power.

Quickly, he was up, planting his feet, swinging his hoe, a two-handed slash that sent the blade hissing before it struck. A near fountain of crimson spouted as the giant collapsed like a girdled tree to the ax.

The red haze was lifting; my cheek was still a firepan of cinders, but I could focus my eyes, could watch as a shiny black fly alighted on the toe of a metal-tipped boot, seemed to inspect it, before buzzing up to the neck, and inspected it too, before getting busy.

Elation raced through me. G'Pa and Jeremiah, real-bad hurt, but alive! Yet that monstrousness, that unbridled hatred. *Why?*

Guardedly, I raised a hand to the throbbing, a way to hold my cheek together. I allowed my arm to fall back. It was so much easier to let the dark-haired girl—come from the house?— press cool damp cloth against the thousands of hornets attacking me there. Looking up at Barbara Reel, I managed a smile.

G'Pa, still gasping for breath, tears damping his beard, supported my head. "Sonny," was all he could manage.

Hunched on his knees, Jeremiah gazed down at me. It looked like he wanted to speak; he kept opening his mouth, red froth coming out. I looked away. Later, I would show him how much I'd learned, how much I cared. Yes, later.

I looked up at G'Pa. "Why? Why?" I forced the question through the sodden cloth as bubbly blood bit into my wound and went up my nose, into my mouth.

"A ramrod, there was a ramrod in the barrel of that rifle, and it—dear God, your cheek is laid open, lay still!"

"No, I mean that man, why did he--?"

"Later, Sonny, later. Rest easy now!"

Barbara Reel had fresh cloth. Applying it, she exposed my cheek to the air. I clenched my teeth—a bad mistake—and shut my eyes as she set the dripping one aside.

With a catch in her voice, she said, "A press cloth, Mister Shipley. Constantly, until he gets stitching. But he must get it soon!"

"Have you lost your senses, Barbara?" G'Pa was still gasping, and now I noticed bright red spots flecking the gray of his beard. "Haven't we just spent hours in your cellar tending the wounded because there are no doctors to be had? Thank God we managed to haul a few poor souls from your barn before it gave way, but—" He began coughing again.

With her free hand, the girl ground at her eyes. "We must get help!" she sobbed. "Jeremiah, at the very least, he has a dreadful concussion, and you yourself, your ribs must be broken. We need a surgeon!"

"Perhaps down in town. But a mile away? With the road jammed up? How can we get there? And why would Confederates help us civilians—one of whom is black?" G'Pa's chest convulsed. This time, I refused to look at his beard.

I took a quick look at Jeremiah, on his side, his knees tucked up, the grass unspeakably ugly where he'd settled his head. I twitched my legs, tested them, flexed my fingers, and worked my toes. Blast, I could get up and walk! At least a little, if I had help.

Even if my mouth didn't work too well, I still could make words. I had to make words. Barbara was right. G'Pa and Jeremiah, they both needed help and needed it fast. G'Pa was right too. Lots of obstacles stood in the way. Only one thing to do. It had to be now. And it had to be me.

My head swirling like a dust devil, I hoisted myself to a sitting position. At once, G'Pa tried to restrain me. Pleased that I could at least mumble a bit, I substituted my own hand on the press cloth; stickiness oozed through my fingers. "You gotta help me up," I said more forcibly. "I know how to get us some help."

My grandfather began to plead, to cough, to protest with his hands. He looked at Barbara, beseeching her.

"I think he means it, Mr. Shipley. Besides, didn't you tell me that when it comes to stubbornness in the family, your mule runs a very poor second?"

"But there is no help. He can't possibly—"

I had made it to my feet and onto a leg that halfway worked. I took a halting step and another. And Barbara was with me, helping me, so that—

"Sonny, what are you up to? Where—"

"I can get us some help. Trust me this time."

I moved forward some more. I was afraid to look back, afraid I might see what I'd seen so many times: the doubt in my grandfather's eyes.

No, I couldn't look back. Not until I proved to those imploring gray eyes that I was as staunch as a barnacle glued to a rock.

*****

Less than a half-hour! I was still amazed at how Stonewall's note had put springs in the legs of Rebs who, minutes before, wouldn't even look me in the face.

As the long-bed buckboard lurched out of the ruts of the Landing Road onto the chewed-up grass of David Reel's barnyard, I held to the press cloth with one hand and made a grab for the warped wooden side with the other. Something familiar to hold onto. "The Sharpsburg Express," G'Pa had called it, when hauling me here after my train ride out from Baltimore.

The driver beside me urged on the slow-plodding horse. Three other Rebs rode alongside. One of the riders, an officer, his face grimed and crusted with blood, tugged gamely on a rope; at the other end, a mule dug in and hee-hawed its feelings at every two-footed and four-footed creature it saw. I was hardly surprised. Ol' Poke was like that at times. I wanted to smile, but the press cloth, it was there for a reason.

G'Pa, looking mightily relieved, gazed at me, then, incredulously, at the buckboard and mule.

The officer hauling on the rope was quick to observe; he dropped the rope, dismounted, and took off his cap. "Yes, yes, it is your mule, Mr. Shipley," he said, approaching my grandfather literally hat in hand. "The wagon as well. Your grandson here has made me, uh, painfully aware of that already. Terribly sorry. Just, uh, borrowed them, you understand. Yesterday, in fact. From a… a barn hereabout. At least, I think there was a barn hereabout. Frightfully bad manners. Dreadfully sorry. Sad to say, it is the only transportation I can offer you at present. The wagon and mule, that is. We are in dire need of the horse."

The man put his cap back on; he went and gave Poke one more tug; he shook his head. "Your mule, regrettably, seems a bit, uh, disinclined. Your grandson insists he can prevail over the animal, but he is in no condition to—"

"I can make him mind!" Making sure that I caught my grandfather's eye, I added, "Just trying to order him around, though, that doesn't work. He ain't a soldier! There are better ways to make him see the light."

There was something like awe on my grandfather's face. Sparkling, too, with delight and approval?

The Reb officer stood glaring at me. "And how would you make a better job of it?" he said, folding his arms.

"Not by pushing and pulling, or by hemming and hawing. He's real stubborn and stands his ground." I had to grin, press cloth or no. And since everybody was waiting and watching, I hastened to add, "If we had time we could beat some sense into him, because—and I should know—he learns things the hard way. But after he's been through a whole lot of hell, he catches on. Like seeing the elephant, huh!" I was talking to the officer, but my eyes were mostly on G'Pa. The mounted soldiers began to snicker as the officer fussed in the dirt with his boot.

"We gotta get us a move-on!" I tried to shout through the press cloth. "My grandfather and my friend are stoved-up bad. They need a surgeon. Isn't that why you came with me?"

"Yes, surely. And you need a doctor yourself, of course. But we must keep the horse. And this mule, it won't—"

"Just blow in his ear and talk to him gentle-like. He'll go. Want me to do it?"

"Not at all necessary, not at all." Hesitantly, the man went up to 01' Poke, leaned forward, as if inspecting an artillery shell that hadn't gone off. I felt sorry for him: an officer, wounded while leading his men—even now unconsciously swiping at the gore on his cheek— and his men were watching him with more than casual interest. No, that officer couldn't gentle up to that mule. Poke, flicking his ears while cropping the grass, was as disinterested as the soldiers were watchful. It was time to act.

I was mightily aware of G'Pa's approving eyes as Barbara helped me over to where the officer stood making fruitless clicking noises with his tongue. Raising myself just enough, I blew out a throbbing, thin puff of air. Poke began to move, but I stopped him. Looking pointedly at the Rebel officer, I said, "That man in the grass over there is coming with us. You'd better go help him into the wagon."

He looked over at a huge prone form more flies had discovered, then past it, to another still figure, dark as a shadow, nearly concealed by tall-growing weeds. The Confederate stared for several seconds. Keeping his eyes to the ground, he seemed to take renewed interest in what the toe of his boot could do to the dirt. I was feeling less sorry for him by the second.

"Well, now," he said finally, "you, uh, failed to mention any- thing about a...a...What I mean to say is—"

What you mean to say is that it'll take all four of you to make sure he's comfortable. *"Because he's a special friend of mine!"*

The officer looked up quickly. "Why, yes, that would undoubtedly ease some of the gentleman's, uh, some of his discomfort."

He frowned at the driver and the two mounted soldiers, then jerked his chin in Jeremiah's direction. The soldiers sat motionless, their eyes turned away.

"Move! On the double!" The men put on stem looks before stirring themselves.

The officer remained where he was, head down, eyes again on his boot. I opened my mouth to tell him there were only three men at the job. Uh-uh. If I said that, he might not be able to hold his head up again.

*****

G'Pa cradled my head in his lap. Wincing at even that effort, he nevertheless kept me from bouncing around the bed of the buckboard. I thanked him with my eyes. Not easy to do; they felt like hot stones, and my vision kept blurring. Good thing someone else was driving the rig.

You would think my grandfather was back in front of a jury; he wouldn't stop talking: telling me how much blood I'd lost, third-degreeing me about where I'd been, whose clothes was I wearing? Why had Rebel soldiers come to help us so fast? I kept trying to shake off his questions. More important things first: "That man, I caught him trying to kick open our trunk! And he was after all of us! How come?"

G'Pa coughed again, with agitation this time, it seemed to me. He averted his eyes, took a few seconds to watch the mounted men shoo other Reb soldiers out of the way.

Finally, after a long look at Jeremiah, who was huddled, trembling, under a blanket, he said, "Yes, I believe you should know. And our friend here, I'm sure he would agree. Especially since we, all of us, are Shipleys."

I jerked myself up. "All of us Shipleys?"

"It comes down to why that brute came back here, intent on his mischief, on getting into our trunk. The logical place for him to look, I suppose. But the story is long. And astonishing."

I had to know! Yet try as I might to search G'Pa's face, a dancing haze kept coming between us. I began to drift, to be lifted up by the rays of a sun that came out from behind a tiny white cloud that, miraculously, didn't burst all apart.

My hand dropped away from the press cloth. I felt another hand come in its place. As the world retreated till there was only the sun, I tried fitting my mind around words that seemed to come from G'Pa, and I fathomed the words, most of them, some of them, and tried to focus my eyes on the friend who had saved us with the only weapon he had and remembered the gnarled hand, the two tipless fingers, and I knew about one, his wife sold off, so far away, but the other finger, I still had to know, and G'Pa was matter-of-factly trying to explain about...

"Jeremiah's daughter, his beautiful Clemma, the only important remaining part of his life. The brother of that steel-toed brute ravished the poor girl. Allowed his drinking friends to have their way with her. With child, you see. Hanged herself. Jeremiah found her that way, and the letter she'd written. He'd taught her to write. He had to put an end to that lust-driven monster. No choice but to flee. Chased the whole way. Found his way here. In my debt always, he says, because of something I...I took upon myself to do."

The other finger. Because of his Clemma. Yes. Jeremiah cutting that way, I guess I understood, sort of, though that one more thing remained out of reach, and G'Pa's words seemed reduced to a mumble, and I was so awfully cold, no matter the sun came shafting through leaves as Jeremiah, moving awkwardly, tucked his blanket around me, lots of lumbering wagons, frightful noises inside them making me shudder and open my eyes to see something leaking from those wagons, leaving bright spots in the dirt of a street that I knew, where a small white dog ran after a ball that I threw, a long time ago, and trembling bumping and booming down past the street, flocks of birds flapping up, coming full-circle back, wood splintering, glass shattering, feet pounding, a dog surely barking, closer, past the tree arching over me, an irresistible voice in pursuit, and it snatched me fiercely, fully awake.

"Wags! No! Come back here this instant!"

But Wags wouldn't mind, and the girl couldn't get out of the way of the iron ball bouncing toward them, mashing the dirt as it bounced, bouncing over the leaping dog's eager jaws, bouncing and bounding straight at—

"Betsee—" and I ran out of breath.

The black man hovering nearby hurled himself as a shield. It slapped out a sound louder than splintering wood and shattering glass. Then, for one frozen moment, silence filled up our space where a shade tree blocked out the sun.

Chapter 20

A breath of air drifted through the half-open window. It found the lace of the curtain and died. My head sunk down on the hot damp pillow, I waited, watching for movement. The curtain lay slack, lifeless. The whole room was lifeless and stuffed with the fetor of fever and heat, of medicine and bandages—of me.

I flung off the blanket but not too far. It would never do to allow Mrs. Hiram Crockett—or worse, her granddaughter Betsy—to see me practically naked, sweltering one minute, shivering the next. And Betsy would see.

Even after forcing her tiny top stairs room on me, she had insisted on staying. Whenever I opened my eyes, day or night, there she would be, at the side of the bed, except times like now. She, too, had calls of nature. But unlike hers, mine were shameful and clumsy.

I kept telling myself that I should climb out of the oven-like bed and get back on my feet. Especially since the doctor had said that my fever had broken. The same doctor who, it seemed to me, had sewed up my cheek as if stitching a boot. Which wasn't fair! I tested the bandage he'd stuck on my face, then flopped my head back on the pillow. Not really caring who might hear me groan, I tried to shut out the world.

My first night there (or maybe the second, it was hard to keep track) there had been a downpour and, mixed with the rain, the sound of rumbling wheels and tramping feet in front of the house. By morning, the Rebel army had gone. Now, Betsy told me Yankees were tramping through the puddles out front.

All that killing! And for what? Yankees and Rebels, still fighting. Folks like Jeremiah, still slaves. And now, there were people who couldn't even care anymore, because they were dead. It wasn't fair!

I had a continuous craving for water, no use for food. I kept turning my face when they cheerily brought in plates heaped with the stuff, as if nothing were wrong. And that wasn't fair!

Most things I could do for myself. I told them so. No need to hold me up or shift me around when my body was urgent. Betsy kept insisting that she was my nurse. I made her leave a few times. She kept coming back. She seemed always to be there when (in a dream?) I groped for horsehair when my boot slipped from a stirrup, or when I struggled to remember whose note I was hiding inside my boot.

I shouldn't have worried about Betsy's hovering, because nothing made any difference now, because the man who had saved my life, and my grandfather's life, and Betsy's life too, in the end—the man who, more than anyone else, knew what the war was about—that man was gone, never to taste the one thing he'd carried with him more faithfully than he'd carried his hoe: his right to be free. And that bloody well wasn't fair!

Betsy tried to make small talk and tried to convince me how proud they all were, the note from Stonewall and all. Turning my face from her, I stared at flies on the wall, pleading for the ache to go away. Not the ache in my cheek—the ache that had snuck back into that secret space next to my heart.

Afternoon sun was finding its way through the curtain and with it a breath of fresh air. G'Pa came in with yet another tray of food. He walked sort of stooped over; he, too, must be hurting. He placed a hand on my forehead, nodded, and attempted a smile. "We are going to hold services for Jeremiah," he said. "Tomorrow morning," he added, looking at me pointedly. He put down the tray, moved the medicine from the bedside table, and, firming his back, left the room.

Betsy jumped up. At once, she speared some meat and brought the fork to my mouth. Grabbing the fork from her, I finished the job myself.

*****

A funeral? This? Nearly an hour of just standing around? In my case, standing meant slumping against the giant oak shading Judge Crockett and Betsy. Strangely, the crows weren't complaining at our intrusion. There were no crows. No birds at all. Like the Rebel army itself, they seemed to have fled from all the tumult and death. The cicadas remained, their mournful throbbing the only living sound in the graveyard next to Saint Paul's.

I shifted my feet. Why was this taking so long? Scuffing the soles of my boots on the fresh-cut grass, I filled my lungs; the perfume was spicy and sweet. For a fleeting moment, it fended off other smells that kept coming and coming. Too bad this was taking so long.

Three days abed in Betsy's cheerless little room, nearly as long without food.

Hard to stand still, to stand at all. If only my brain would quit reeling away on waves of stench that deviled my nostrils and watered my eyes, then surely I would have control of my legs, could step away from the tree, and stand up like a man.

But I couldn't control my eyes. They kept going back to the misshapen blanket, steamy in the hot morning sun. No coffin. Nobody to make a coffin for a black man killed by the war.

G'Pa had required a deep hole to be dug; deeper than normal, deeper than required by Sharpsburg law. He didn't explain. But I thought I knew: the deeper the hole, the less likely that anyone would come, after we'd gone, and—

Again, my eyes went to the blanket. Beside the hole, a sodden heap of earth sent up a thin vapor; it leaked a rich earthy smell like you might find in a just-weeded vegetable patch.

At my grandfather's urging, I had remained in the oak tree's deep shadow with the Judge and Betsy. Now I moved away from the tree. If G'Pa could stay on his feet, so could I! He had been standing alone in the blazing sun, holding a prayer book. Every so often he drew a hand to his chest. Strips of tightly bound linen made it hard for him to stand and to breathe at the same time. So why was he taking so long?

I touched my cheek; the stitches beneath the bandage were driving me crazy. I recalled the doctor's firm warning and took my fingers away. Dropping a hand to my belt, I found the smooth handle of my father's revolver. G'Pa had held it out to me, his gray eyes smoky and moist as he placed my fingers around it. I found no real pleasure in the feel of the thing and couldn't feature what to do with it now.

Except for a squirrel, an acorn in its mouth, there was no movement here. And still no sound but insects humming. 01' Poke (I'd given in and ridden the short distance) was nearly asleep, ignoring the flies flitting in and out of the hair by his eyes.

I took a long look at myself: I was the only one not dressed in black. G'Pa had borrowed ill-fitting, somber clothes from the Judge, the sleeves stopping well short of his wrists, the front of the coat hanging baggy and loose. Me, I had borrowed clothes too: what I'd slid into back in Autie's tent, the night Rob Pescud had shoved a note in my face. Our belongings, gone up with the cottage. A few precious items, locked in our trunk, were all we had left. Good thing Betsy had scared up some black cloth to tie around my arm. Too bad it had been one of her best dresses, though she'd stuck out her chin and declared that black didn't go with the color of her eyes or her hair, and that I'd just better listen to reason for once!

My eyes went back to the blanket. With a start, I discovered that our mule wasn't alone in attracting buzzing things. I hurried out of the shadows, went straight for the small whirring cloud, and windmilled my arms. And there were ants. I stomped, scuffed my boots, got down on my knees, and attacked with my hands. Finally, I got to my feet and locked my knees, to stand guard. Jeremiah would not be plagued by bugs!

I roamed my eyes past a long row of headstones to an open church window. Now, a spirited mutter came through it. How long before my grandfather got going? Why was he taking so long?

When we'd arrived, I'd heard rasping and with it muffled screams, from inside the church. Someone must have seen us filing past the stone columns and marble slabs, because all at once there was nothing but silence, at least for a while. Still, you could see and smell, almost taste, the reason for the turmoil in there: a dripping, lopsided pile right below that wide-open window.

I closed my eyes and attempted to make a game of it, to sort out the smells: unburied Rebs (the Yanks had been shoveled over already, Judge Crockett told me), a bloated pileup of horses, greasy black smoke roiling up, just two blocks away, the grotesque collection of shapes by that window.

Moving out of the dirt, scuffing my boots on the grass again, I followed G'Pa's eyes back to the church. The babble inside was louder now. Surely, it had nothing to do with what surgeons in there did to bodies still warm, or what other men did to bodies already cold, which was another smell I could sort.

Some things, though, I just couldn't figure. I had learned why that giant had come gunning after Jeremiah. But why after G'Pa? Why after me? All of us Shipleys? Could it have something to do with the official-looking brown envelope G'Pa had brought back when he'd salvaged the trunk? Maybe that had something to do with what I'd overheard him say to the Judge: "Didn't I tell you, Hiram, that the evidence, such as it is, would become crucial someday?"

I knew that the envelope was tucked in a pocket of G'Pa's ill-fitting coat.

Somehow, I suspected, whatever was inside that envelope could go off like gunpowder. And the sputter going on inside that church, it might be the match.

A side door to the church swung open. Three men came out, all squinty as the light found their eyes. G'Pa's chin came up; his prayer book came up; he thumbed it open. And now I knew. He had been waiting for these men and had known they would come.

They came with chins high. The two men in back, wearing gray suits that seemed to need pressing, hustled along as if eager to reach us. Yet they appeared to give way to the man in front, who came even more briskly, his arms and legs swinging with purpose, his cream-colored suit coat bellying out as he moved his vast bulk right over any marble slabs that stood in his way; his straw hat cast a shadow all the way down to a heavylipped mouth that must have sucked something tart.

G'Pa began to speak: "I am the resurrection and the life, saith the Lord. He that believeth in me, though he were dead—"

"A moment, if you please, Mr. Shipley," the cream-colored man cut in, "but earlier on, when we saw no casket, we lifted that blanket and... and there appears to be a bit of misunderstanding here, because—"

A small figure in black darted out of the shadows. "Oh, yes, there really and truly has been a mistake!" Betsy called out. "We're about to bury a very dear friend, and it's so awfully nice of you to come too, but you're not wearing black, and—"

"No, no, Miss, that is not why we—"

"But it's all right," she went on brightly, "because Johnny doesn't have any black clothes either, so I made him something from a dress I have, and I don't have it here, but I do have this skirt, so if you'll just—"

"Mr. Shipley! As deputy mayor of this town, I must get right to the point!" The man gave his straw hat a tug, then, lowering his chin a bit, tried to establish eye contact with my grandfather. G'Pa kept his eyes on the prayer book.

Betsy tugged at the cream-colored trousers. "Please don't get upset!" she practically sobbed. "It's truly all right, because I have another skirt at home every bit as good, so I'll just tear this one, and then you and your friends will have something black." And at once she began ripping, even using her teeth, till she clutched a ragged black streamer that would have made a fine tail on a kite. The man balled his fists.

Betsy looked up pleadingly. "Would you help me, please?" Her blue eyes were beginning to glisten. "With tearing this longish thing into three separate pieces, I mean, so I can tie them around your sleeves."

"Really, Mr. Shipley, our purpose here is to—"

"Your purpose, gentlemen, is abundantly clear." My grandfather's words were slivers of ice. "Before we proceed," he continued, looking up now, "I suggest that you accommodate the young lady. She is quite correct. You are not wearing black."

Betsy herself divided the streamer. On her tiptoes, she tied on the armbands, double-knotting them, as the three men blinked at the sky.

Another of the men stepped forward; he was still squinting some as he fisted a long hawkish nose. "Now, now, this simply won't do, Mr. Shipley!" He fumbled a handkerchief to his forehead, then to his nose. "You and I, we are both attorneys, and we both know the terms and conditions of the agreement under which you purchased this plot. It is to be, unequivocally, a family plot!"

"Yes. I read the agreement, with the utmost care."

"Of course, when the transaction took place the other day, we assumed it was for, uh, well, perhaps, for your late son's remains. In any case, the contract provides that the right of sepulcher in this cemetery is conditioned upon the decedent being, uh, of the actual family of the party in whose name the title stands."

"As I called to your attention but a moment ago, I understand the terms of the agreement."

"And yet you deliberately choose to disregard the—"

"Are you quite certain that your real concern is breach of contract? Could it be that your disingenuous insistence is due to the fact that there are—as yet—no black persons buried here?"

"Well, now that you touch upon the point..." G'Pa stood like a statue, staring, unmoving.

The hawk-nosed man again put his handkerchief to work. "It is true," he said, "that only white folks are buried here. But then no application has ever been put forward by, uh, by persons of, uh, color. I assure you, however, it is the restrictive nature of the contract itself that dictates our official position in this matter."

My grandfather withdrew a paper from inside his coat. Expectantly, I looked to see if it was the large brown envelope. It wasn't. "As it happens," he said, "I have a copy of the contract right here. And you are correct, for the most part. The right of burial is, as you say, confined to...let me read it 'the immediate family of the plot purchaser.'" G'Pa looked up; his gray eyes shot sparks. Composing his face, he said, "Is it then true that no other conditions exist which would prevent our finishing," he swung his eyes to the blanket and back, "what we have already begun?"

"Why, uh—"

"And that any failure on your part to honor the contract would constitute breach? And that a court of competent jurisdiction, by Writ of Mandamus, would be bound to enforce your compliance?"

The handkerchief fluttered busily; the man cleared his throat but didn't speak; he ran a finger under his stiff white collar.

The last of the men strolled forward, thumbs hooked on a watch chain that drooped across the front of his vest. He spent a few silent seconds shaping a pointed gray beard before reaching for the black cigar he had clenched in his teeth. "My dear fellow," the man said at last through a cloud of smoke, "I myself am a justice of the peace of this competent jurisdiction. Quite obviously, this buryin's gotta cease and desist. Instanter! What's more, your further pert'nacity is gonna nullify the agreement in its entire, and your title, ipso facto as it were, will revert to the church. Whereupon you—yeah, all of you here— will be subject to prosecution for trespass! Now then, why don't y'all just cut your losses and—"

G'Pa's hand had gone back into his coat, and this time, I was not disappointed.

Without speaking a word, he shoved the large brown envelope at the lackadaisical fingers that held the cigar.

The man lazily puffed another cloud, lifted the flap, and removed the contents. As he read, he blinked several times; frowned; opened his mouth, nearly lost his cigar; and finally, thrust the papers back at G'Pa.

"I find nothing in the agreement," G'Pa said, looking at each man in turn, "requiring the decedent to be a blood relative, only a member of the immediate family. Not of the actual family, as you erroneously stated."

I'd had enough: "I can't make heads or tails of this hocus-pocus! I aim to bury Jeremiah! Here and now!" I took a step toward the blanket or tried to. I'd been too long in the sun and was too stiff in the knees. Nausea grabbed at my guts; dizziness rolled through my head. Relaxing my knees but firming my jaw, I made fists of my hands. "What do those official-type papers mean?" I had to lock my knees again.

"What they mean," bellowed the bearded man through his cigar, "is that Mr. Shipley, in his patent ignorance of the law, is allowing himself to appear foolish! As with any contract, it is the intention of the agreement that controls its effect. And that, young man, is abundantly clear!"

"None of this is abundantly clear!" I tried to calm myself, but sometimes it's easier to stand like a man than to keep your mouth shut. "What do those blasted papers mean?"

G'Pa drew in his breath a few times; it looked like it pained him. Very softly, he said, "These, Sonny, are papers of adoption, approved last spring, just before your arrival. Legally, Jeremiah is my adopted son."

As I stood dizzy and dumbfounded, G'Pa turned to the three dumbfounded faces. "Jeremiah, gentlemen, is a member of my immediate family. As such, he is entitled to burial in these grounds."

The sun pounding down seemed to be making me giddy. Trying to shake the cobwebs away, I said, "But if all this makes Jeremiah your son, then that makes him my… my—"

G'Pa's attention was elsewhere. Fixing the three men with a stare as cold as any headstone, he said, "You raise the issue of intention. Yet when we negotiated my purchase, nothing was discernible from your questions, your statements, your actions, nor the looks on your faces, suggesting—ipso facto as it were—that the agreement should not stand on its merits. Any court would—"

"Oh no, not a bit of it!" sneered the hawk-nosed man. "What about the Dred Scott decision? Everyone hereabout knows that the decedent was a runaway slave! Therefore, he ain't entitled to any dispensation of the court!" He stuffed his handkerchief back in his pocket. In a rising, jubilant tone, he added, "If he was a slave, he was somebody's prop'ty! Can't be adopted! Uh-uh!"

As the three men exchanged gratified glances, my grandfather caressed the prayer book, his fingers moving deliberately over its worn black cover. I knew that he was holding back, biding his time. Yet I also knew what to expect. Cool and unruffled as well water most times, he could bring his blood to a boil pretty fast.

For a moment, his eyes looked into mine. I think he wanted to count me in, a man, two Shipleys standing together, defending one of their own. But what had I done to prove myself worthy? To prove anything? Instead of being warmed by my grandfather's regard, I felt hollow inside.

Still steady as glass, G'Pa removed one more envelope from inside his coat; he held it out. This time, no one would take it.

"This is an Order," he went on in a voice you had to strain to hear, "which is duly signed by the Presiding Judge of Washington County, Maryland. It was signed pursuant to my personal affidavit, which declares that the subject of our discussion here was indeed a slave." He paused. From the rising and falling of his chest, I knew that his fury, slow-burning till now, had run out of fuse. "Yes, a slave. Owned by my late son!"

The three heads jerked up, eyes bugging out like barnyard chickens sensing a danger.

G'Pa held up the paper. "This Order contains Articles of Manumission." Speaking slowly, levelly, he added, "After passing to my son's legal heir—Johnny Shipley, who stands before you—the slave in question became, by virtue of my authority as my grandson's legal guardian, a free man!"

"That-there Order can't be genuine!" The cream-colored man struggled to rid himself of the double-knotted armband, finally tugged it down the length of his arm and flung it off. "No court would sanction a nigra's adoption by a white person!" he declared while brushing the sleeve as if it had been defiled. "No precedent for it! No basis in law! Socially reprehensible! No judge would—"

The man cut himself short. G'Pa had turned away, turned to face the big shady tree. As I followed his eyes, Betsy scampered across the grass, the sunlight flashing off her knees, her hair. She darted into the shadows and in seconds was back, golden, composed, her fingers entwined in the large pink hand of her grandfather as she tugged him behind her.

"Why… why, Judge—" The man snatched off his straw hat; beside him a handkerchief went mopping again; cigar smoke, hurriedly batted, was filming away.

"Didn't, uh, see you back in those shadows, Judge Crockett, them black clothes and all," muttered the man as his fingers tapped the brim of his straw.

Despite the fact he had been standing out of the sun, the Judge's face was redder than usual. "The Order on which you have cast aspersions," he spoke up, "it bears my signature, does it not?"

"Well, it appears somebody has subscribed your name, Your Honor. But after all the discussions I've had with you about nigras and Dred Scott and such, surely you would not sign such an Order. Or if you did, it might have been the result of... of false information, perhaps?"

The Judge's features appeared to get even redder. For a moment, a look of sorrow, maybe of regret, crept across his face. He stroked his snowy chin whiskers thoughtfully, shifted his eyes to the blanket, and brought them back to rest on the small hand nearly lost in his own.

"The Order, I assure you, is genuine," he said finally. "Do you have a legal basis for challenging the Court's handling of the matter?" He looked pointedly at each man before his eyes softened as they came to rest on his granddaughter's yellow profusion of curls.

For long seconds, the humming of insects was the only sound to be heard. Judge Crockett's voice cut through the stillness: "It would seem appropriate, sirs, that we proceed with the service!"

The three wouldn't look at him and wouldn't even look at each other as they turned away.

I glanced at the blanket. It resembled a sack of meal, mostly empty, cast aside.

I took a hard look at the three rigid retreating backs, then took a sharp breath. One last chance. Stand for something!

Unlocking my knees, I went on the heels of the departing three figures, scrambling past a marble shaft on their flank; my legs were trembling, but I'd cut them off. "The funeral ain't over!" I hurled at them. "The Judge said *we* should proceed with the service. That includes you!"

Something sparked in my mind. In anticipation of what I intended to do, my innards twinged. "There's another reason you gotta stay here," I said to them.

My grandfather and the Judge exchanged quizzical looks. Betsy seized the moment to whisk up the cast-off armband. Smiling brightly, she held it up to the strawhatted man; when he ignored her, she forced it back up his sleeve.

G'Pa began to read from the prayer book again. Betsy and the Judge, hand in hand, lowered their heads. I stole a peek: two men were staring at clouds; the third had his straw back on, his eyes fixed on the door to the church. Behind it, rasping and moaning once more. And the stench—I'd rather be locked in a privy.

G'Pa closed the prayer book. I knew by the look of him that he wasn't done. But then neither was I.

"Sometimes, when earthly souls are faced with crisis, God lifts the curtain of obscurity to reveal the consummate man." G'Pa's voice wasn't soft now; it had the bite of a lash. "Jeremiah was such a man! His sacrifice was as large as this land, as enduring as time. For a man can have no greater love than laying down his life for a friend!"

A thrill raced through me. My grandfather's words were not for a slave; they were for a man! And I had a feeling that his words were for me, too, a grandson who surely was man enough now to make his own way, to arrive at a truth of what was important in life, and maybe in death.

"But how long, O Lord," G'Pa continued, the beat of his words as measured and mournful as a funeral drum, "how long must some men's birthright—their freedom—be purchased with their last drop of blood? How soon before they may find honor, even in death?"

The three men were moving again, toward the church door they'd left open, for the putridness from which they had come.

"Not yet!" I fired the command hoping that I sounded something like a Parrott gun going off. When the men clumped to a halt, my innards started thrumming again.

I went to the grave and kneeled by the blanket. Lowering my head, I looked over at Betsy before slipping her tiny gold cross up over my ears. "Jeremiah should have this!" I announced. "He didn't even know Betsy. But he gave up his life to save her. He heard me call out her name. That's all he knew, that she was my friend!"

I turned to G'Pa. "His headstone should read 'Jeremiah Shipley'!" My voice cracked; it didn't sound like a Parrott gun at all.

"I was going to suggest it myself," offered G'Pa, brushing at his eyes before leveling them on the backsides of the three suits, retreating again.

"Turn around!" I hollered. "You're gonna watch this!"

As I brought my hand to the blanket, I had to fight back a painfully tight clutch of air that wanted to explode in my throat. That blanket, it was the same one Jeremiah had placed around me, just before an iron ball had come bouncing… bounding… mashing the dirt. The blanket felt moist and warm. Sliding my fingers beneath it (they were trembling, thank God no one could see), I brushed flimsy material, then a shoulder, a sleeve, the arch of a wrist, the fine-boned back of a hand, the cold curved fingers, two of them stubbed and gnarled at the tips, one hand resting atop the other. I brought the cross to lay between them.

I looked over my shoulder to make sure I had everyone's eyes, because I still had a mission. And I'd only begun.

I swung my legs and painfully lowered myself out of the sun, into the bowels of the burial pit. When I dropped, puddles of rainwater squished under my boots. I felt clammy and queasy. My elbows bumped the shovel-cut sides of the grave.

"I gotta have some dry dirt down here!" I called up. "We can't be laying Jeremiah in the mud!"

Almost at once, Betsy's blue eyes were looking down. She must have gone deep into the sodden mound with her hands. In seconds, small gobs of undampened earth came raining down around me. I stamped my boots till a carpet of dry earth lay beneath me.

I'd held back long enough: "If those mealy mouths are still here, could somebody get 'em over here, please!"

After some stirring and mumbling, three wary faces appeared. Brushing dirt from my eyes, I told them, "My grandfather has busted ribs, so you'll have to do it!"

"Uh, beg pardon?"

"You'll have to lower him down to me."

My head being a good two feet below the level of their shoes, I couldn't see much—but enough. The straw-hatted man made a move to unbutton his coat before his hand fell away; he jerked his head this way and that.

"Perhaps you would have the girl and me do it!" I tried to picture the Judge's face, getting redder behind snowy chin whiskers, bristling, I'd bet.

"Oh, of course not, Your Honor, certainly not. But... all this mud..."

"To make sure you don't slip up," I called out, "it'll take all three of you!"

"Do... do you mean to say that we—"

"I mean to say that all three of you are gonna have to lean down. That means get on you knees!"

The only face I could see, incredulous before, had become a mask of horror. I stared up, waiting.

Girding themselves with little expulsions of breath, they creaked to a kneeling position. Right off, their hands were slathered with ooze, their suits scummy with muck. At last, leaning and lifting like some damaged machine, they hefted the bundle of blanket and held it shakily above me.

I didn't reach up. Folding my arms, I said, "Do you get it yet? Do you know what this war is really about?"

Nobody answered. I craned my neck, trying to get a better look, but the blanket obscured their faces. I told them, "The answer's right there in your hands!"

Looking like they wanted to immediately rid themselves of their burden, they leaned down farther. A heavy watch must have skated out of its vest: it bumped the blanket as it swung erratically on its chain; a straw hat must have lost its hold: it came down next to my boots, which was bad luck, as I crunched it underfoot, the space being pretty small.

When still I didn't reach up, the three tried to reach down. I reached down myself, snagged what was left of the straw, took careful aim, and sailed it back out. Undaunted, they again tried to reach down.

"Not yet!" I told them, pausing a few heart-throbby seconds before adding, "You need to hold onto the thought!"

*****

When at last we'd finished—while Betsy and I were wiping our hands with a handkerchief the Judge had brought out, and three other pairs of hands were scrubbing the grass—I stole a glance at G'Pa. He was brushing his eyes. But his face looked more radiant, I think, than I had ever seen it.

Then the Judge truly amazed me. We had not really finished; he announced to everyone there that he and I would come back later, and, working together, take turns with a shovel.

The three men finally made good their escape. There was something about their faces, though, as they hurried away: eyes that glittered hatred, hatred as chilling as a giant's had been, seconds before the hiss of a hoe.

*****

Poke refused to hurry. It was all right. I had scads of things to do, but for the moment, I was in no hurry myself. Not now, my belly stuffed with countless morsels from Mrs. Hiram Crockett's big oaken dining room table.

I'd made short work of the midday meal following the service—competing with flies that had returned in force—and though letting my appetite loose, chewing and swallowing pretty much nonstop, had managed to keep talking as well, also pretty much nonstop.

My legs still had a wobbly mind of their own, and the bandage, freshly white on my cheek, itched like blazes. Still, I felt more prime than I had in months. And, G'Pa had beamed, we would rebuild the cottage, bigger and better! No need to sleep in the shed anymore! He might even practice some law. Not in Baltimore—he'd shaken his head, muttering something about Copperhead agitators—but right here in Sharpsburg. He had stressed the "might," because the town still needed a schoolteacher. Course, up Keedysville way, there was a man I knew who had a hankering to teach school and who maybe had salvaged my jacket from atop a creaking wicker basket, surely empty by now.

Neighbors had dropped by to share in the meal, to offer their sympathy and their congratulations. It was amazing how quickly the graveyard news had captured the town. Betsy's Uncle Josh Newcomer had laughed long and hard about his missing foxtail hat, though I insisted that I still owed him for the use of his Sharps.

And yet a few questions still hadn't been answered or asked. Waiting till the guests had gone, I cornered G'Pa. "That man with the big boots, Jeremiah really was his property, wasn't he?"

G'Pa glanced at the Judge before answering. "Yes, legally. And he probably had papers to prove it. If so, he could demand that we turn his property over to him.

"Nevertheless, when I presented my petition and affidavit, the Honorable Judge, without batting an eye, ruled in my favor." G'Pa again looked at the Judge, who was stroking his whiskers.

"Did it strictly out of friendship for you, Charles. As well you know, I would be summarily removed from the bench, if that truth ever surfaced. And yet, I would do it again. When the law catches flies but lets hornets go free—when clearly and morally the end justifies the means—that law, somehow, must be kept inside the statute books!" Turning to me, he said, "Notwithstanding all that, I regret one thing, Johnny-me-lad."

"You do?"

"I, uh, have a propensity, sad to say, for rattling on ad nauseam, ad infinitum. Indeed, after ruling in your grandfather's favor, I told him—in confidence, I presumed—that I would keep the proceedings off-record, hush-hush, so to speak, inasmuch as the basis for my ruling was without legal foundation. And indisputably, upon submission of applicable evidence, that ruling would be overturned at a stroke."

"Unfortunately, Sonny, that oversized man had oversized ears. He heard the remark. And when he took to cussing and kicking, his Honor here held the lout in contempt, had him thrown in jail overnight, then escorted by the sheriff down to the Potomac at the point of a gun, with the admonition to never show his face north of the river again!"

"But you always figured he'd come back?"

"I always feared that he would, given the opportunity, to lash out his hatred. And Jeremiah *knew* he would come and took it upon himself to be here when that happened. His duty, he called it. But beyond his own survival, and mine, he felt a profound need to reach out and touch the lives of those who touched his life. Especially you, for he knew how much you mean to me."

What G'Pa didn't know was that Jeremiah in his need to lift up a life had also reached out to a four-footed brother, a brother just trying—like himself—to survive.

"Perhaps," he went on, "perhaps Jeremiah went too far when he put an end to that giant's fiendish brother for the repeated ravaging of his precious little girl and for the heartbreak that drove her to put an end to herself. But perhaps Jeremiah, too, knew when to cold-shoulder the law, knowing full well what kind of justice he would find in a white man's court." He looked at the Judge. "But at least he found justice in *this* white man's court!" G'Pa turned his eyes back on me. "And, of course, there was always that flimsy evidence locked away in our trunk. He probably came for that as well, to attack it hammer and tong, to get his property back, a fate worse than death! But all that went out the window, I think, when rage consumed him. When he saw you! Then and there he resorted to the threat he had made."

I leaned forward in anticipation.

"He swore he would get even with every Shipley on the face of the earth!"

Still stroking his whiskers, Hiram Crockett said, "Swore he would get even with a certain judge as well. Which your... our black friend made sure would never happen. And doesn't that put an entirely new light on words that I repeatedly hear?" He blinked a few times before breathing a sigh. "Yes, I will be more attentive henceforth when the bailiff declares, 'May God preserve this Honorable Court.'"

*****

I dug my heels into the mule. Poke wanted to call it quits sometimes, but I had business to take care of. Serious business. David Reel's farmhouse lay just ahead.

I raised myself in the stirrups and looked toward the spot I'd last seen a pair of metal-tipped boots. Good. Nothing but a huge, unsightly mound of earth. I dismounted and looked long and hard at the door. Scratching my head, I turned and contemplated the way back to the road. I struggled with a notion: get back on 01' Poke; let him take me away.

My hand went to my belt. Couldn't give it up. Not Pa's revolver! Especially since it was far fancier than the one I had borrowed and lost. Besides, Mr. Reel's pistol might just as well have gone up in flames, like everything else in his barn. No one would know the difference. I would have to fess up about Ty, of course, which might be enough, and I'd practiced the words. But the revolver—

I sucked in my breath, firmed my fingers on the smooth walnut grip, pulled the weapon free, and with another huge sigh, moved my fingers down onto the barrel. Yes. Hold it out by the barrel, handle first, when delivering it into farmer Reel's own hands. Barbara took a long time answering my knock. Then I remembered: a cellar full of shotup Rebs. No, her father wasn't home, she told me before giving me a whopping big hug, which I nearly shrugged off before assuring her that I would come back, because her father and I had grim, important things to discuss, face-to-face and man-to-man. Yet even after she'd closed the door, uneasiness nagged me. Something else I needed to do?

My mule had wandered. I stumped over to where he stood nosing the grass, where it came up past my knees, still bemoaning my cruel fate—having to give up my precious revolver. But then and there, thoughts of the pistol flew clean out of my head. Because my eyes had fastened on something. It sent a shiver straight through me. That something else I needed to do—now I knew what it was.

I reached down and lifted the hoe. My hands were shaking. As I stroked the worn wooden handle—every bit as smooth as the grip of the pistol—a hard-to-figure notion danced into my head, as if Jeremiah himself had taken my hand and given it a tug. Time to go back? Uh-uh. Time to go onward. I was sure I knew where. But I wasn't sure why.

Poke shied at the wreckage still littering the slope. But I'd seen it before. Besides, there would always be wreckage: at Kernstown, at Harpers Ferry, and at Sharpsburg—and at hundreds of places I'd never heard of before—wherever soldiers went, hell-bent on killing. And wouldn't they keep on killing, until political winds blew themselves out, or until there were no more soldiers to fight?

Allowing Poke to find his own way, I fiddled with the revolver. It was unloaded, so I took aim and snapped off a few imaginary shots. Not at Yanks or Rebs, just makebelieve shots, at things laying on the ground, things the Yanks and Rebs had needed once but not anymore. The weapon my father had marched off to war with, I would have to give it up, a trade-off for the pistol I'd taken, and never returned. My father's pistol: a few days ago, I'd craved the thing, to uphold Shipley honor and to have my revenge. Now, Shipley honor meant giving it up, without having used it in a meaningful way.

Revenge? Hadn't I seen enough blood?

As the mule plodded past some scrubby trees at the base of the slope, then through a gap in the fence, I spied a collection of Yanks, off to my left. They appeared to be charged up about something, jabbing each other, grinning, pointing.

Surely, that pale lumpish pile on the ground beneath the side window of the Dunker Church hadn't set those people to grinning like cats. Not the stink, neither. Lots riper down here than up in town.

"What's going on?" I called out to a man giggling and slapping his sides. Now, I noticed that some of the soldiers had their rifles up, aiming.

"A varmint!" The man stopped slapping himself and wagged a finger at the tiny white building. "We were moseying by this-here schoolhouse when—"

"It's not a schoolhouse, it's a church!" As I announced the fact, something twitched in my belly. That varmint—I knew I had to act fast!

"Well, whatever," the soldier continued. "Like I say, we were moseying on by this place when we up and hear, 'Tallyho, there he goes!' I tell you, we took after that critter lickety-cut! Lots better than chasing down Rebels, I tell you! Lucky thing some of us brought our rifles along!"

Something like a sob seemed stuck in my throat. It was because of me—because I'd left a little latticework door cracked open—that the critter had found a place to hide for a time, where I'd hidden myself, when bagging a varmint had seemed a fine thing.

"I said it's a church!" I raised my voice to be sure I could be heard above all the laughter and mutter. "There was a bounty on that varmint once," I rushed on, "but then he holed up under this church, and... and now there's a curse on anybody that tries to harm him!"

Some of the soldiers laughed; others elbowed one another; a few shook their heads.

"I even tried to shoot him myself," I threw at them. "Because of the bounty. And look what happened to me!" I jabbed a finger at the bandage on the side of my face. "And I ain't even a soldier!"

The laughter died in an instant; the rifles came down. After a few seconds of sidelong glances and throat clearing, the blue soldiers began to drift away.

As my fingers caressed the shaft of the hoe, my memory reached back to the man whose hands had worn it smooth, who, even now, seemed to have tugged me back to this place. That critter under the church wasn't Jeremiah's brother any longer; he was my brother now. And wasn't there another farmer I should search out? Mr. Henry Piper still must have a few chickens that needed tending, and must have a box to haul around a cackling hen, after the sun went down—after all the soldiers had gone.

Another gap in another fence. Poke went through it, into the pasture grass: chewed up, beaten down. Surely, there would be no grazing here for a very long time. I aimed him to cut the pasture in half, flanked on our left by the Hagerstown Pike, on our right by the Smoketown Road. Across the sweep of field, a little hummock of earth bumped up, a litter of limestone, some young leafy trees. A special place, special for Jeremiah, for Ty, for a critter that warily carried scat in his mouth, which made it a special place for me, too, their brother.

As the sun came out from behind a cloud, a blare came from the sky, pretty far off, getting close fast. I searched for it, found what it was, and watched it glide down.

Before, it had been a whole flock of geese, and they had kept going, screeching, intent on going someplace to the south. Now, only one, and it came down easy, its shrill nearly muted.

I was too far away to see exactly where the bird came to earth. Somewhere in David Miller's cornfield, though—what was left of his cornfield. Still, I couldn't help my mouth turning up. There might be just enough corn left for a bird that knew its necessentials!

Then I saw something else, something not right. I squinted through the glare, and my heart shrank. I gave Poke a quick taste of my heels.

We lumbered by a row of bodies, bloated and stinking, laid side-by-side. Almost at once, I forgot them, fixing my eyes on a familiar earthen mound, two hundred yards in our front. A pair of bedraggled bluebellies stood on the mound. One of them, bare to the waist, held a shovel, the other a pick. But now they were dropping their tools, inspecting the rocks that lay scattered about the mound. Poke wheezed his protest as we closed the distance.

I craned my neck and ranged my eyes: everything so terribly changed. Yes, clumps of blue, begrimed, soldiers no longer, sprawled as they'd fallen. The pick-and-shovel men still eyed the rocks. Poke brayed his annoyance when I flailed my heels.

"Hold on there! You just hold on!" Thank God for my lung power, but the Yankees ignored me. They stooped and began lifting rocks. I screamed at them, "No!" When that didn't work, I tried flailing the hoe. Looking sideways at me, they stretched lazily, yawning, finally bending their eyes at me, grinning their smugness, as Poke and I came charging on.

"Looks like this puppy's tiltin' at windmills!" one of them cracked, cradling a large chunk of limestone in his arms. I stopped waving the hoe but could not stop a great apprehension that was building inside my chest. Those Yank hawbucks were within inches of Ty, his last resting place. My breath coming in gasps, I slid off the mule.

"You… you can't be burying people that way!" I managed. "Not with nothing but rocks piled on!" Now I noticed one more form on the ground, off to the side, faded in color, like washed-out dirt. The Yanks must have followed my eyes.

"We aim to bury our own boys nice and proper," said the bare-waisted soldier. "But that one over there, that's just a Reb." The other man leaned over and grabbed hold of a rock. "Rebs are nothing but scum," he said, as he straightened himself.

"But you have to bury him decent! Every man deserves that much, every man-jack of us! Here, I'll help you do it!"

"Gonna use that-there hoe to dig you a hole?"

Bile had got in my throat. This place was special! I raised my hand to cool the flame on my face but found only bandage. These soldiers—whatever they fought for—thought that some folks were scum!

The bare-waisted man took a step toward me. His eyes gone wide, he cradled his rock and reached out a hand. But he wasn't looking at my face any longer; his eyes were fastened on the jim-dandiest revolver he was likely to see this side of the Potomac River. When he took another step forward, a silent little bomb went off inside me.

"Need me a look-see at that shootin' iron!" the man said, his eyes wider still.

I dropped my hand, let it come down easy. Sliding the revolver from my belt, I said, "Tell me first why you're fighting this war. Tell me why you want to kill Rebs."

"Hey, we're Union men! That's what this war's all about!"

The response didn't surprise me. But it was one that I wouldn't accept anymore. "Wrong answer," I said evenly, as I raised the pistol and pointed it straight at the bluebelly's head. For a moment, the man looked as if he'd swallowed his rock. He took a step backward, another, shrugged his shoulders, then tossed his rock to the ground. "Well… well, we might just forget about them rocks," he mumbled. He turned to go.

"Not yet!" My exclamation caught him mid-stride. "You haven't buried him!" I pointed the pistol at the ragged Confederate sprawled in the weeds.

"Now just you wait a minute! You can't be ordering us to—"

I thumbed the hammer back, dead-certain they both heard the *click*. I pointed again, this time with the hoe. "Over there. In the grass. Not in the weeds."

The Yanks fetched up their tools and jumped to their task. I guessed they'd just better. Already the sun had slid far down the sky. And I still had scads of things to do.

*****

After the bluebellies had shouldered their tools, walking quickly away with disgust on their faces, I let my eyes take in what they had done. Fresh mounds of earth: blue and gray covered over alike. Heaving a sigh, I nudged Poke toward the rocky mound. I reined him in just short of the rocks. There, a whisper of wind found its way to my face—nearly a breath, almost a sigh...

We're all of us brothers, Young John

The End

About the Author

A lifelong student of the Civil War, Brooke Albertson is a graduate of Lakeside School and received his BA in history from the University of Washington. At a very young age, he dove into his father's library and discovered first-edition volumes of *Battles and Leaders of the Civil War*. The "Civil War" was fairly meaningless to him, but the numerous drawings of soldiers on horses, waving swords and shooting guns, captured his interest, then grabbed his passion. He took special pride in wearing the cap his great grandfather wore at the Battles Vicksburg, Missionary Ridge, and Sherman's March to the Sea. His debut novel *Johnny Comes Marching* is the culmination of his attraction to the who, what, and where of that conflict, heightened by the numerous letters of his ancestors who fought on both sides—all of which triggered a drumbeat in him to take aim at telling this story.

Albertson resides on Bainbridge Island, Washington, with his life partner Janet and their beloved cat Cassie, where he draws inspiration from the eagles and deer and from taking long walks alongside saltwater beaches.